# AMERICAN
# APOCALYPSE

# AMERICAN APOCALYPSE

## THE COLLAPSE BEGINS

BY

**Nova**

Ulysses
Press

Published in the United States by
Ulysses Press
P.O. Box 3440
Berkeley, CA 94703
www.ulyssespress.com

An earlier version of this book, entitled *American Apocalypse: The Beginning* (Volume 1), was published by Flying Turtles of Doom Press.

ISBN: 978-1-56975-903-5
Library of Congress Catalog Number 2011921430

Acquisitions Editor: Keith Riegert
Managing Editor: Claire Chun
Editor: Rick Clogher
Proofreader: Elyce Petker
Production: Judith Metzener
Cover design: what!design @ whatweb.com
Cover photo: fire © Rui Gouveia/istockphoto.com; U.S. Capitol Building
    © Daniel Stein Photography/istockphoto.com; crow © grybaz/
    istockphoto.com; wire © Ross Images/istockphoto.com

Printed in Canada by Webcom

10 9 8 7 6 5 4 3 2 1

Distributed by Publishers Group West

*For Marilyn and Elizabeth*

# ACKNOWLEDGMENTS

This book began as a series of posts on *Calculated Risk*, the economics blog. They began growing in length, and it was suggested I move them to another site and link back to them. This book was written and posted to the *After the Crash* blog site, and then moved to the *American Apocalypse* blog.

I wrote this "live." I would write a section, proof it, and post it. I usually had no idea of what I was going to write until I started. The news of the current financial crisis influenced the direction, as did comments from the readers, and the comments in general at *Calculated Risk*.

When I say "comments from the readers" it does not convey the amount of inspiration and story ideas they provided. I could not have written this without their help and encouragement. I would like to thank, in no particular order:

Max, reticentlurker, FSHB, zapoteca, rsj, tj and the bear, bobn, LA Confederate, D^2, pdxr13, Lergnom, Mike in Long Island, unhappyCakeEater, Kevin John, Jim in Mo, Hoopajoops LTD, kidbuck, Joanna, CounterPointer,

The Notorious AIG, Jerry, TampaSteve, WWIRUgger, bohica, and everyone else. Thank you.

I would also like to thank Bill at *Calculated Risk* for allowing me to post my stories and the link backs without complaining. I would also like to thank him for providing the blog that opened my eyes to the world of economics, and all the people who comment there. You cannot mention *Calculated Risk* without mentioning Tanta, who is no longer with us, for writing posts that made my head hurt. Tanta vive!

Most of all I would like to thank Jon Dansie. Not only for his comments from the very start, but for the outstanding job he did in pulling it all together. Without his help, this book probably would never have happened.

## CHAPTER ONE

# EARTH PEOPLE

Looking back now, it's clear when I began to lose it—*it* being my grip on the American lifestyle. Previously, I would have said *life* but now I see we all have one. Even the six-year-old kid picking through the refuse dump outside some smoldering, intermittently powered Asian city has a life. Lifestyle—now that is different. *Lifestyle*, it rolls off the tongue, all cocky and aerobic; say it to yourself and smell the fine women, taste the magazine food, and imagine life under a roof that does not leak. Take away the money and you take away the lifestyle. What is still amazing, to me at least, was how much of my life then was really lifestyle and how totally blind I was to it.

Please, don't get me wrong: I was never rich by the prevailing standards of the time. I had a job, a car, some cool toys, a girlfriend, and a condo—what I thought of as the basics of life. Nowadays . . . well, we all know; the standards changed—and changed so very fast. The "good old days" seem like a dream to me, as I am sure they do to so many of us. Some of us, especially politicians, seem to believe they will be coming back—or maybe they just *want us* to believe that. Maybe they will come back, but not in my lifetime.

Have you ever been standing still, yet still you feel as if you're falling? It is a terrifying and helpless feeling, especially when it is your life. You know it's slipping away, but there's nothing to grab on to. Being helpless makes you feel so small. That feeling of being helpless—it steals part of your soul. Partly because it leaves you feeling like less of a man; you end up wanting to embrace the tawdry, self-pitying idea that you were a victim, just another of Fate's bitches. I told myself I could have done *something* if I could have only gotten a physical handle on it. There was no handle, there never is: a bitter truth—one that I found out the hard way.

I had this job—not a great job, but it paid the bills most of the time. Nowadays you find people who either do not want to talk about what they did or want to brag about from what heights they have fallen. Me, I dropped from the first step to the ground, and it still broke something inside me.

I was working for a financial company—never mind the name—doing tech support. Like everything in life, it had its food chain, and I was somewhere above the mail room and cafeteria help. Above, but not by much. The good thing was, I went everywhere. You called, and if they could not fix it over the phone, then I was summoned to take a look. Most of the time it was an easy fix, and I got to meet some very attractive coworkers. Not that my willingness to be affectionate was ever returned. Their attentions were bestowed on the guys pulling in those fat commissions. I used to envy those people.

Money raining down on them . . . nice cars . . . good drugs . . . beautiful women—it puzzled me then, and it still puzzles me.

I mean, I know I am not the sharpest knife in the drawer, but how did they do it? I know now: fraud, lying, easy money. But how did they personally end up sitting in a thousand-dollar chair, making it big, and I didn't? They were not smart. God knows, that became obvious after my fourth or fifth call to go see someone on the broker floors. They were basically freaking idiots.

But I digress, which means I am also not watching my perimeter. Nowadays you have to have eyes in the back of your head, especially when you are out and about in the areas I frequent. Everybody carries maps in their heads of the areas they spend a lot of time traveling in. I never really moved away so I have my old map and my new map. My old map had where the nearest Starbucks was, where traffic backlogged, and where I could get decent Chinese. My new map has bike paths, bad areas divided into different types of bad, food—preferably free—and shelters.

Traffic is not something I worry about a lot anymore. Eating at least one meal a day and avoiding getting any open wounds—or getting dead—pretty much occupies my time. Sometimes I talk and hang out with a few of the guys I can trust. Today I am hoping to run in to Carlos. Word is he has a throwaway cell that he is bartering time for; it would be nice to call my mom and listen to the disconnected message again.

I am sitting on a milk crate. Milk crates are not comfortable to sit on. My ass probably looks like a waffle but I don't have any cardboard handy to pad it with. My back is to the wall of a closed gas station and my bike is laid down flat next to me. A guy I hung with for a month or two taught me to do that, back in the beginning, when I was a rookie.

He taught me a few other things: *Keep a low profile. . . Don't advertise the fact that luck favored you with something extra that day. . . Always watch your perimeter. . . Trust your gut.* Those were his rules, and they have become mine. Too bad he didn't follow them. That's all it takes: Screw up once, and you go down for good. No medkits, restarts, or extra lives in this game.

His name was Shaun. He was a pretty cool white kid who had it together, especially for so early on in "the Crash." Back in the first days of the Crash, people were more likely to help each other out. That lasted, oh, about eight months or so. When the hope around here ran out, so did the caring and sharing. Kind of a bitch. It was the only thing that made my life almost tolerable on some days, especially since I don't drink or do drugs. Shaun liked getting high and he liked women. So when the girl suggested that she knew a safe place where they could go and get high, well, he was all in. The rest you can guess— although I think cutting his head off was a bit excessive.

I'm waiting here to check the free clothing room at the shelter, hoping to score a pair of shoes. I'm not going for food. Maybe tonight I'll come back for that. The shelter is county run so I won't have to dance for Jeebus to get them to give me a pair. Plus, I have a friend there; that always helps. At the Salvation Army, well, Sally makes you listen to a prayer and a short sermon. That is as far as I am willing go—at least so far. Lately, the fundy-run shelters and food stops have been getting a little weird. They really push hard for you to come to Jeebus.

Actually, everything is getting a little weird. Some days I am not sure if I am crazy or the world just slipped yet another gear. I guess it will help if I explain what my little part of America is like today—with an emphasis on *today*, because who knows what it will be like in six months. One thing I am sure of: It won't be better. So, what is the most important thing in my world? Water. It's also my number one pain in the ass. Water is bulky and heavy, and it can't be just 95 percent okay. Plus, you always need it, especially when you are using a bike for transportation. Come summertime, I need a gallon of water a day, and that's just for drinking. I am long past pre-Crash cleanliness standards, although I try more than most people in my condition, I think. The only time you need to get really cleaned up is when you visit the "Earth People" in their natural habitat. That's what we call those lucky clueless who still have a house and a job. They still live on the planet. We just kind of exist in limbo.

Water is important because you need it to live. That simple fact came as quite a surprise to a lot of people. There are still idiots and noobs who drink from the streams—them and people who came from countries where the water quality is even worse than here. The rest of us, well, who wants to spend a year with the shits when you're homeless and your bathroom is the closest clump of trees? So yeah, water is a big deal for us.

We are not one mass of happy homogeneous poor; there are clans and groups—our own special hierarchy of poverty. The younger ones gravitate to the clans, especially the males; it is their old gamer world made real. The media calls them "gangs," but when has the mainstream media ever gotten anything right? They probably wanted to avoid the word *clan*, as that still has a lot of baggage associated with it, especially among their viewing demographic. A lot of the younger ones are not wrapped too tightly. Once they lost high-speed Internet access, iPods, and texting—well, I think their brains crashed. When they rebooted them—and not all managed to do that—they did not come back quite . . . right. Sometimes, I watch them talk: Their lips move but so do their thumbs.

Also there are the "Tree People." They are generally okay. The ones who aren't, well, you hear about them soon enough. The Tree People live in the woods, mostly in shanties they built themselves. They love plastic: Showing up with a blue tarp for trade sets off group orgasms. They generally survive off of government paychecks, theft, and charging tolls for the use of bike trails that run through "their" woods. Lately, they've started asking for water for the toll; one eight-ounce plastic bottle will get you through.

I go around them. Like I said, water is a pain in the ass.

We also have "Squats"—the squatters. Some of them like abandoned housing developments; others go for the commercial real estate, especially the bigger office buildings. They are a lot like the Tree People except that their roofs don't leak as much. When I first started out I would always hear stories about them blowing themselves up or being found dead from carbon monoxide poisoning. Some people have to learn the hard way not to build a wood fire in a gas fireplace without making sure the gas is really off. The rest of the denizens of my magic kingdom are either insane, stone-cold druggies, or alkies. A few are all of the above.

Then you have the random predators—random only in the sense that they show up in your life especially when it will make a bad day worse or when you have something they want.

Some of them want whatever you have; others, all they want is your youth. They are vampires preying on the poor, the defenseless, and the drug addled. They want to drain their quarry of any innocence they still have after descending this far down. The kids—the prized prey— usually have some of that special quality left, which is surprising, as they have followed mom as she bounced from one bad decision to another. Usually, they never make it as far down as the Tree People. Most often they stop somewhere around the Car People level. That's not so bad; at least the Car People try to look after their own— especially at night. Plus, "Baby Moms" will get something from the county and maybe a little from the state. The problem for them is getting into the system. For that, you have to have remnants of an earlier and luckier life. The system wants a checking or savings account to deposit the benefits to and an address so it can come and check on the kids—kind of hard to do when the drop to the bottom has been so fast and ugly. Some of the shared addresses have twenty or more moms listed.

Then you have "Drug Mom." She blends in because this is where Drug Mom was destined to end up. Some of her kind were already here before us. Sometimes, I think Drug Moms just have the kids so they can make money off of them both ways: government money and predator money. Lucky Drug Mom kids end up in the clans that will protect them; unlucky Drug Mom kids disappear. Some clans actively recruit the kids, partly because a lot of them understand from experience what a bitch life can be when you have a Drug Mom, partly because the little ones can be more vicious than you would ever want to believe.

I may have come across so far as a person who is somewhat decent. I agree, although others may not. You see, I hate these predators. When I find one—sometimes him, sometimes her, less often him and her—I kill them. Usually painfully. They have always been with us; they never go away. It gives a purpose to my life. . . I like purpose.

## CHAPTER TWO

# WHO CAN KNOW THE MIND OF A WOMAN?

I sat there on my milk crate watching what passed for traffic nowadays go by, waiting, for The Woman. That's how I thought of her in my head—always in capital letters, each letter edged with a faint glow of white light. At other times it was her name: Carol. She was one of the few people from before the Crash that I knew and liked. She knew me by, and actually used, my birth name rather than my street name. She was the only person left in my life that I allowed to do that. As far as I was concerned, the person who had worn that name died a long time ago, except to her.

We had gone to high school together. It really didn't seem all that long ago, yet it was. Time may have passed but she was still the same beauty I had seen standing in the door by the cafeteria so long ago. I had loved her from afar ever since I was a freshman—afar, because we did not travel in the same circles. She was smart and funny and actually attended classes; I was one of those guys on the edge. We were there one day, gone the next, our absence passing unnoticed except to the handful of others who were just like us.

Occasionally we would run into each other. Sometimes we talked, usually at parties, where she would be inside and I would spend most of my time outside—unless I knew she was there. Then I had to go inside, just to see her. We would go outside and get high and drink a few beers. Well, she would drink a few and I would drink a lot. Then she would leave the party and I would let her go. Given a choice then, I always went for getting numb. To be honest, I knew I wasn't what she needed or deserved. My life was about one thing: getting high.

I had loved her. It didn't amount to anything then, and it wouldn't amount to anything now. Yet she was a memory I clung to during the dark days that followed. I knew she had liked me. The idea that someone that good, that beautiful, had once liked me gave me hope that perhaps someday it might happen again.

I had moved to a lot of places after that brief year that I had known her. I asked about her when I was able to make my way back to the area, but the chaos that was my life kept dragging me down streets that I did not want her to know about. I did find out that she had stayed here, gone to college, and had gotten married. Her current life was as alien to me as mine would be to her. Sometimes, I thought, the only thing we had in common was the same language and a few faded memories—memories that I clung to. I had not been making any good ones lately that I could replace them with. That was for sure.

While I waited for her arrival I kept an eye on a group hanging around and occasionally slipping into an abandoned 7-11 about a half block away. They would have been there whether or not there had been a Crash. If there hadn't been a 7-11 to stand in front of, one would have magically appeared. A 7-11 and these guys went together like a born-again and intolerance.

This group in particular always made me feel better about life, because one of them was a mortgage broker from my old company—one of the clueless idiots who had everything until he woke up one day and no longer did. He didn't recognize me then, and he doesn't recognize me now, but I had happily watched him from the first day of his arrival. I asked around about him after I spotted him standing there. He didn't go directly to the corner. Very few did. He had been one of the Car People for a while until he had pissed off the wrong person, probably from boring everyone about how he once been somebody. Maybe he couldn't let go of the fact he was no one now and still expected to be treated like he was someone important. That has a tendency to grate on people, especially as most of the Car People had also once been someone, somewhere else. One day he found that he had no car, just some metal and broken glass. He was lucky they hadn't torched it with him in it. After that he showed up wheeling a grocery cart, the poor man's Cadillac of the streets, and wearing a suit—a nice suit at that.

His cart was loaded up enough; that was for sure. He must have had other clothes to wear, but he never changed. Instead, the suit just got dirtier. Then the metamorphosis began, only in reverse: from butterfly to chrysalis. He started to mend his suit with silver duct tape. That was when he made his move to his current location. The duct tape was beginning to take over now, and I gave him another six months before it was more duct tape than cloth. He had always been an asshole: Now he was a crazy asshole. It was also a bitter reminder of what awaited me should I give up. I might not weave myself a chrysalis, but I knew I would at least end up in a burial shroud.

Carol didn't show up. She probably was not going to either. Punctuality was not as important anymore for a lot of people—too many things to go wrong. For her, it could have been a roadblock or car trouble. For me, well, I didn't own a watch, but I was pretty sure it was a Tuesday.

One of the hardest changes to adjust to is the sudden amount of extra time you have, once you fall out of society. You have huge blocks of time to spend doing nothing, or you now spend huge blocks of time doing the simplest things. Some people had real problems with it. I had grown to like it. Getting to where I am now in life was only difficult emotionally. The actual sequence of events was like an effortless bad dream. Even now, when I look back on it, it retains a sense of unreality. One month, all was well. Then three months and a week or so later, I'm wheeling my bike into the woods to spend the night. You may laugh, but the only weapon I had to take into those woods was a used garden trowel. It had a nice point and the handle fit my hand nicely. Defense against what I was not sure; I just knew that there had to be something bad waiting in the woods. Back then the woods were not my friend.

Getting fired had been a shock: *Not me!* Why *me*? I am a good worker bee. Well, they told me, it was *not personal*. They would *love* to have me stay . . . *blah, blah*. They called us into the office one at a time. Our manager and some fat lady from Human Resources broke the news to me. It was not hard to figure out what was happening.

We all sat around in our cubes and pretended that it was no big deal if it was to happen to us. I think most of us actually believed that, too. I know I figured that I would take a week off, sleep late, and then go find a job: no big deal. My girlfriend, Tiffany, did not seem to think it was a big deal either. Fast forward two months, and we are sitting at her place having dinner. That was her idea of how she could "show her support." She *hated* to cook, and as I chewed on what she called "dinner," I remembered why we never did this. "I don't see why you're having a problem finding a job," she said. But what I heard was: *You are not even trying! Get off your ass!* It ended up in a nasty fight, and I ended up sleeping alone.

The next day I sold my big-screen TV and my stereo. I called Tiffany and told her we were going to dinner. Of course she had to ask if I had gotten a job. "Never mind that," I said. "We're going to Legal Seafood, and then to Old Towne for drinks." It was nice hearing the chill leave her voice—a chill I was hearing more and more often. I didn't understand the tone then; I just knew it made me sick to my stomach.

She came by around 7:30 that night—late, which was unusual. I was going to drive. With my temporary windfall I could afford to put gas in the car. The car note was three months past due, but I had talked to them. I told them I would electronically transfer the money the next day for a month's worth of payments. The women assured me that it would save the car from repo. So there we were sitting in my almost empty condo, and I am desperately trying to get a smile from her . . .

She had been stunned when she had seen that almost everything was gone. I didn't get it. It was just stuff to me. I told her, "We are what's important." Her mumbled response and failure to meet my eyes were not reassuring.

After a rather long and—for me—painful silence, we got up to go eat. We had already missed the time I had made for the reservation, but I didn't think it would be a big deal. It was not like they were going to be crowded nowadays. I knew, because I had applied to work there as a waiter. There was only one problem: My car was gone.

"Lying bastards!" came out as a strangled shout. They had come and snatched it. I stood there and started to shake. Not just from knowing that my car had been towed. No, it was a symbol for everything that was going wrong in my life. Everything was being towed away, and I think then I realized it wasn't going to come back, either. I looked at Tiffany. I suppose I was waiting for her to say something supportive. Instead, all I got was a look of scorn and a "Well, maybe you should have made the freaking payment!" She stomped off to her car, which she had insisted on driving separately—me following her. . .

We went back and forth during the next week, but it was over: "I'm sorry, I don't think we have a future," she told me. My translation: *You're a loser and I don't do losers.* It definitely didn't help me in my struggle to keep my act together.

## CHAPTER THREE

# SURPRISES IN THE WOODS AT NIGHT

The first time I killed a man was almost by accident. Almost. I did not go looking for him, nor had I really even thought about it. If anything, I was thinking about killing myself. The idea of living in the woods, vacant homes, or wherever I ended up did not resonate well with me as a long-term lifestyle choice. This was in the beginning, when I still was not comfortable at night in the woods by myself. It turned out to be a good thing—good, because that is when I found a purpose for living.

Because the woods made me uncomfortable, I slept in the woods near one of the lots where the Car People parked. I settled in about three hundred yards away. Originally, I had tried sleeping about a hundred yards away, but that did not work out: Too many people walked out about that distance at night to take a piss. Plus, it put me close enough that the lights and hum from the parking lot lampposts bothered me. Moving back that extra two hundred yards got me out of physical range, of both the weak bladders and the resulting smell. Eventually, the county would drop a couple of Porta-Potties there. As far as I know they never came back to empty them. The Car People just hooked a rope to them before a rain and dragged them into the woods.

One night late in that first summer I was lying there, unable to sleep, pondering exactly what the hell I was going to do when it got colder. It was probably past midnight since the Car People usually went to sleep early. Back then, they had to move their cars out of the lot before the employees began coming in. And, it was hard on the battery to run anything other than the "house" lights after dark. Later on, they could park there forever, as no employees were going to be coming to work anytime in the foreseeable future. Eventually, the bolder ones found a way in and began living in the empty building itself. The joke was, they had gone "from granite countertops to marble floors."

I noticed, but did not really register, the headlights of a car entering the lot. It was no big deal, even that late. What I did register about thirty minutes later was the sound of footsteps coming toward me—especially when they did not stop at the outer ring of urination. Instead, they kept coming, and I was able to hear voices.

Male voice: "C'mon, quit whining; your mom said it was okay."

Kid voice: "I don't have to go potty."

Male voice: "Sure you do, kid, sure you do."

Silence for about ten seconds, then the kid voice: "Ow! Stop it. You're hurting my hand."

Now they were almost on top of me. I had picked out a nice patch of small boxwoods and pine trees to make my home for the night. I recommend pine trees: They smell clean, and the pine needles make the ground much more comfortable to sleep on. Another advantage is if you have to move around, you can do it quietly. You don't get all that *snap*, *crackle*, *pop* that you get from walking on dead oak leaves.

Whoever was leading the kid had zeroed in on my little copse, which made sense. I had selected it because I needed enough room to roll out my sleeping bag, without being seen. If you were looking for a place to take a private dump, well it would do nicely for that also. I didn't understand what was going on. I was getting a strange vibe from the voices, but I hadn't learned yet to completely trust my gut. I figured that Dad, or whoever, had been told to take Junior someplace so he could move his bowels. I didn't want them to do it in my new bedroom, but I was too embarrassed to jump up and say, "Hey, find someplace else to shit!" Yes, I know: What the heck was I embarrassed about? I mean, these people were sleeping in their cars for God's sake! I don't know. I do know that I rolled out of my sleeping bag, quietly picked up my trowel, and crouched next to a boxwood.

The man, with kid in hand, had detoured around me. *Strange*, I thought, *his breathing sounded so labored*. The kid was whining and sniffling. He looked maybe seven or eight, his pale face glowing in the darkness. His brown hair needed cutting, and the bangs were hanging in his face. The kid did not look happy. Actually, he looked scared to death. He had a plastic Transformer—it looked like Optimus Prime—held tightly against his chest. Seeing his expression triggered something in my brain. Something was not right here, yet I had no clue exactly what. I still didn't fully understand that monsters weren't just creatures that lived in the deepest, darkest woods and attacked for food. There was another species of monsters that used the woods for far worse things.

They came to a halt about eight feet from me and I was able to get a good look at the mouth breather. He was probably six foot two, around two hundred forty pounds, of which at least forty looked to be pure Grade A fast-food lard. Most of it was hanging over the waistband of his khaki shorts. He wore a blue Polo shirt and had a Red Sox ball cap pulled down low. His face was covered with black and white stubble. I did not have to meet him to know I didn't like him. Events began to pick up speed here. Memories of what happened next flicker in succession through my head with a strobe light rapidity and brightness: the fat man dropping to his knees . . . the kid squirming in his grip . . . the sound of clothing being undone . . .

The kid's voice: "Stop it!"

The fat man's reply: "Ssshhhh, hold still, damn it!"

The kid again, but louder: "Stop it!"

And then: "Don't hurt *me*—"

The pleading rising in fright at the end. *Flash*—I am out of the bushes—*Flash*—the forged-steel trowel smooth and weightless in my hand—*Flash*—the kid's face frozen in fear mixed with anger—*Flash*—the grotesque fat man and his busy hands; his khaki shorts undone—*Flash*—a burning hot, red anger filling me up with an intense, overwhelming need to—*Flash*—a pudgy face turned to me, reflecting surprise, the fat man, coming to his feet . . .

"I was just . . ." he tries to explain, his eyes widening. *Flash!*

I bury my trowel deep into his fat gut. Time slows down and then stops. I hear a wheezing sound, followed by a sucking sound as I pull out the trowel—and bury it again. This time I go a little higher: I don't want fat; I want *vital* organs.

I drive my trowel deep into his solar plexus and twist it with a strong wrenching.

*Flash!* The wheeze turns into a groan. Out of the corner of my eye I see movement: The boy pulls his pants back up. I put more muscle into shoving the trowel out of Fat Man's back. Blood trickles, then pours out of his mouth.

His eyes roll up . . . one chubby hand feebly paws at the trowel. I feel alive, so intense, like I've never felt anything before. The anger is gone now, replaced by a light. I feel whole in a way that getting high never could give me, watching his life fade away . . .

Flash . . . He is down. The blood is black; it is everywhere, still warm and sticky on my hands. I look over at the kid: He is staring at the body. He looks up at me; I have no clue what he saw, but he kicks the Fat Man in the side of his head. Fat Man's head goes side to side as if he is saying, "Oh, no."

For some reason this sets me off. I start laughing and can't stop. The kid looks at me; he smiles and kicks Fat Man in the head again. We are both laughing. The kid kicks him over and over in the head, growling something under his breath. If he had been wearing anything other than cheap Chinese sneakers, the Fat Man's head would be caved in by now.

Strobe light.

I am whispering to the kid, "Hey. Hey! Little man."

He stops kicking. No one is laughing. I have no idea how much time has gone by. I tell him, "It's okay, stop." I lean over and wipe what I can off on the fat man's shorts; being such a fat ass means there's plenty of cloth to work with. I roll him over to use the back of his shorts also.

I have a lot of blood on my hands; I see the shape of a wallet and help myself to it. The kid is watching me. I tell him, "He was an asshole." He replies quietly, "I know."

"You okay?" He nods his head gravely.

Damn—I feel tired. The Transformer has fallen in the grass. "Optimus Prime?"

He nods.

"Cool. Can you find your way back?"

"I don't want to go back."

This throws me for a bit of a loop. What am I supposed do? It irritates me; I try to keep it out of my voice because I know what it's like to be a kid the world is dumping on—just not like this.

"Look, little man, I got to roll out of here." I indicate Fat Man with my chin. "Somebody is going to come looking for him, and they aren't going to be happy when they find him." I look at him, "You know what I mean, right?"

He nods his head solemnly, pauses, then says, "You didn't do anything wrong."

I look away and then look back at him. "I know and you know, but will they?"

He ponders this, running who knows what through his head. He nods, and then startles me by throwing his skinny little arms around me and giving me a hug. He backs away, adjusts Optimus Prime in his arm, turns, and begins walking back to the car lot. He walks about ten feet and begins to run. I figure I have less than five minutes to be gone.

Actually, it turned out that I could have gone back to bed. The kid went back to his mom, and she wasted no time in getting the hell out of there—no surprise there. The money Fat Man had paid her was probably burning a hole in her pocket; plus, even a stone junkie could figure out that the questioning that would arise from this might not be to her advantage.

I went back to where my sleeping bag was and bundled up everything as fast as I could. I strapped my stuff to the bike and started riding hard in the opposite direction of where the Car People were parked. I came out on the other side of the office building that the parking lot had been built for and really started putting my legs into it. Only one problem: I had no idea where to go. Also, it was not the brightest idea to be out there on the road zipping along like a man possessed in the dark—not with a fair amount of blood still on me. I cut off on to a jogger path and slowed down. I needed to find a stream to wash off and a place secure enough to think.

I headed for the big drainage pipes. They went under the road near a half-completed office building, and they were big, too—big enough that I could stand up in them without bumping my head. I expected a helicopter to be hovering over the area soon, and I hoped being in the pipe would make me invisible, even to infrared. Then I realized that I had left my trowel behind! My stomach knotted up even more, as if that was possible. I had to stop the bike and throw up; I leaned over the handlebars and gave it all up—not that there was a lot. Then it was dry heaves until I made it to the pipes. There was enough water flowing through them for my purposes. I stepped back into the woods where it was flat and changed, rolling the clothes I had worn into a ball and bagging them.

After that I sat on the slope at the entrance to the pipes and waited: waited for the sirens and the sound and light of the county police chopper circling; waited until dawn and nothing came—an occasional siren in the distance, but nothing headed in my direction and nothing in the air—nothing. I rolled down a foot path and turned into the woods. I found a downed tree big enough to serve as a wall on one side of my sleeping bag when I lay down; I was asleep within minutes.

## CHAPTER FOUR

# GARDENER

Three days later I came out of the woods. I had to; I was starving. I rode out tentatively, feeling as if I had a big neon sign blinking MURDERER over my head. A federal Humvee rolled past me, Homeland Security stenciled in white along the side. The soldier in the turret did not even look at me as they rolled on by. A few cars passed me. The drivers casually glanced at me and continued on.

I knew Carol would know what was going on. Running a shelter meant she was plugged into my world, and the real world. Plus, if I was wanted, well, I was pretty sure she wouldn't snitch me out—at least I hoped so. I got lucky; she was sitting in a folding chair, catching some sun, and smoking a cigarette. One of the guys who helped out with security at the shelter was standing about ten feet away from her, watching the world go by.

The people at the shelter tried to give her space and a few minutes alone when she was having a cigarette; it was the only break she allowed herself. Tito was out there just in case some idiot thought she had another one for him— or wanted to discuss why he had gotten thrown out. She would have given you the cigarette she was smoking if you asked; it was just that her staff didn't want her bothered. I had not counted on Tito. We were not tight, Tito and I, but I figured Carol would keep him heeled if word was out about me, at least until I was down the road, if it did come to that.

The conversation with Carol left me amazed: Nobody seemed to give a damn. The guy I had killed was an unemployed real-estate agent and a Cub Scout leader who was forced to resign, even though the charges against him had been dropped. Until a few days ago he was just another Car Person who called a parking lot home. No one, when interviewed, had anything good to say about him. The kid never did come up in the conversation. Carol did say that whoever had removed the guy from the population had done a lot of people a favor. Hearing that from her made me feel a lot better inside, especially when she added that they should have dragged him behind his car for a couple miles before killing him.

I think she knew, but she wasn't going to ask me straight out. What was really interesting was that when the body was found, so was my trowel. The crowd that had gathered around the body had noticed it before the cops showed up. When the cops bagged the trowel, some wit in the crowd had yelled out, "The gardener did it!" I liked that; I liked thinking of myself as "The Gardener." What does a gardener do? He weeds the plants and flowers of invasive species. I think child molesters qualify as invasive.

I have to admit to an unhealthy liking of the Batman movies when I was growing up. After my conversation with Carol I actually spent time thinking about possible costumes, or as I preferred to call them "uniforms." *Uni-*

*forms* sounded much more dignified, even when it was only me that I was holding the conversation with. But I could not get past the image of me on the Batbike: cape fluttering in my slipstream, as I pedaled furiously somewhere "on a mission." That was a little too insane, even for me. So I gave up on the uniform idea, although from then on I mentally referred to my wheels as the Batbike. Too bad it was green. But if I squinted, and it was the right time of day, it did look black.

I wanted to do something with my life other than just scrounge a living from the crumbs of a society that never had much use for me anyway. I had grown up a throwaway. I had never mattered enough to anyone to protect. Hell, it was a big deal for Mom to remember to feed me. I knew firsthand what it felt like to be prey, in my case, prey for Mom's latest boyfriend to beat on after he got drunk. I would stay quiet and out of sight until he'd eventually turn on her. Mom had a talent for picking out a certain kind of asshole and then slowly driving him insane until he snapped. Sometimes they would come find me to beat on. Other times I would try to distract him from beating on her and take the blows instead. I had been helpless in a world where everyone was bigger, stronger, and knew more than me. I may have gotten older and bigger, but not much else had changed. Except now I had a secret, a powerful secret that made everything feel so much better. But at the same time it felt wrong, too. I went back and forth in my head arguing the different sides. In one corner I had "Why care?" with "Fuck them all" pacing in the opposite corner and "Never again" off in a third.

I didn't really like *Why care?* He was a whiner who just wanted to find someplace safe to hide away and eventually die in. *Fuck them all* was angry—very, *very* angry—a burning red violence that alternated between intense flaring heat and smoldering. He wanted to hurt people, any and all people; I knew once he started it wouldn't stop until he was killed. *Never again* was the hardest to see and promised nothing immediately. The only promise he offered was that I could get myself to a place where I no longer had to be a victim. The price was I had to do my best to protect those around me with what I learned. It turned out to be a simple choice: good wolf or bad wolf. Carol made the decision for me: When the memory of her face floated up into the three-way conversation, *Fuck them all* lashed out, and I couldn't live with that. I really did love her. I squeezed him out, a growing intense pressure that was trying to take me over from the inside, and I boxed him up and never opened that box again.

Three months went by and the Gardener killing was old news. The level of violence had increased exponentially. It was like one day a switch had flipped and people began not to give a damn. People were just angry. Angry at what they had lost; angry that no one was coming to help them; angry that it had not gone away—that every morning when they got up, nothing had changed. When it had changed overnight, it was almost always for the worse.

What really bothered people was that it was unequal: It was as if a bomb had dropped, but had only blown up some people. It made some folks crazy that their old friends and neighbors could still go to the mall, eat in restaurants, and watch the game on their digital HDTVs. *It just wasn't fair, goddamn it!* If they had to suffer, well, then other people should also. So they began making people suffer—sometimes by stealing something, other times by using sharp objects, even sometimes through the most bizarre forms of torture. But most of the time, people just sat around and hated and envied.

I spent the next three months adjusting. I also bought a new garden trowel and a sharpening stone from a hardware store. They did not have them in black—they were all green or stainless. I was beginning to resign myself to the fact that the black color scheme was not going to work out. *Then again*, I thought with a touch of humor, *if I'm going to call myself The Gardener, having everything in black sends a mixed message.* I decided *green* was good.

The weapons issue was something I wasted a lot of time thinking about. I was handicapped by two things: I knew nothing about weapons and I had no money—at least not big money. That's what you need to buy a gun. I also had no idea how I was going to become a good wolf. Right now, if I was honest with myself, all I had was a bark; my bite was not anything to scare a lot of these people with. Some of them were better armed than the police. I had stumbled onto my first encounter by accident—or fate, if you believe in that. I couldn't really expect to stumble into another situation where I'd get a chance to trowel another molester. I figured the only thing I had working in my favor was that I didn't care if they had to die to get my point across.

The local police presence had noticeably declined, at least where I was. A lot of the wooded areas came under the domain of the county park police. By now, due to budget cuts, there were probably not more than six officers. Three of those were management, which meant there really were no more patrols.

Hired security patrolled some of the business parks and their lots, making themselves the bane of the Car People's existence. But as buildings emptied out, so did the money to pay security. The local county police had also been decimated by budget cuts. That and having their pension plans evaporate did not exactly inspire aggressive policing, especially when health benefits became a joke. The state police never were around and the federal alphabet agencies could care less. You couldn't justify their budgets rousting homeless people. So what began to happen was a pulling back of the basic services we all had taken for granted: Fire, police, road maintenance— all that became concentrated where the core of surviving taxpayers were. There were no walls or signs; no one made an announcement—it just happened.

Money was the liquid that kept so much of this urban area alive. I had hit the street about two years into the money drought and the tips of suburbs were starting to die. I think the hardest thing for me to adjust to, other than a lack of hot showers, was loss of the Internet. The Internet had been such a huge part of my life that it wasn't until it was gone that I realized what a gaping hole had been left behind, worse than losing Tiffany— much worse. I realized now: I was addicted to the entire high-definition, make-believe world that I could step into and where I could lose myself—or become someone else. Hell, it had taken me forever to make first lieutenant playing *Battlefield 2142*. Now it was gone.

It was hard enough to get Verizon to come out and install DSL, more so when the only address you could give was the third group of trees behind parking lot B. You know, the one where Fidelity had its offices. Not that

Verizon could be counted on to show up anyway, even during the best of times. Word was that one of the clans had someone good enough to splice fiber. They were planning to open an underground Internet café inside an empty four-story office building and entrance was going to be restricted to people they knew or needed.

There was also the FedEx/Kinko's option, but that was expensive. They were also gone not long after I found my way to the street. I did find that free wireless was available at McDonald's for a while; there were a few other places like that and I rotated among them. I had hung on to my laptop. Well, actually, I had liberated it from the job when I heard that there was going to be a department meeting one Friday.

A lot of stuff flowed out of the departments when a Friday meeting was scheduled; I wondered why management didn't catch on. It took me a while to figure out that they probably didn't care. They were too busy looting on a scale we couldn't imagine. So I had not lost complete connection with the outside world, but wireless was limited, and I could not sit and surf for hours like I used to, let alone play *Battlefield*. It balanced out since I needed the time to keep myself fed and semi-clean. When I wasn't doing that, I was scouting out new safe places to sleep. It was becoming more and more difficult as the number of people being pushed into the streets increased. Even still having a roof over your head didn't mean you could afford to put food on the table. At the same time the various resources that had fed us were getting more sporadic; they could no longer get regular funding.

## CHAPTER FIVE

# SKIZZER

Curiosity had me searching on my laptop for news about my encounter with the Fat Man. I had done my best to gut that fat bastard in the short amount of time I had. I'd already promised myself that next time I would make sure I would not be so rushed.

More and more my laptop felt like an anchor. I couldn't let it out of my sight because it was the only thing I owned that was worth anything. Yet, for the life I was leading now it was practically useless.

I had a wireless card so I was usually able to find a hot spot. I could get e-mail, but I found that I didn't really have anyone to e-mail. That was a bit of a depressing realization. For a while, I kept in touch with some of the people I had worked with—none of them were getting hired. I would apply for tech jobs online and get the standard automatic response. I tried retail, wait staff, and I applied for a CFO position—I didn't even get an auto response for that one.

The only place that was hiring was the armed forces recruiting center. I admit it was somewhat tempting, but

I hated getting sunburned. Also, I was not too thrilled about coming home missing a body part. Word was also that the government was planning a huge troop reduction; so gradually, I quit looking.

I had a list of blogs that I kept up with for information. Some were local, and others were economic. My favorite was *Calculated Risk*, a blog I liked because it gave me a glimpse at the shitstorm that was beginning to rain down upon the rich and poor alike. The stories posted on CR described the decline of industry after industry, but the comments section with its variety of regulars and trolls told the human side of how it was changing everything. Looking back, I read it for the comments. The entertainment and insights they gave included dry, black humor with a sort of "all in it together" feeling. Other days I would read it and feel like they were all living in a world that was farther away from me than Mars.

As I lost the enthusiasm for the job search I found other ways to make money; I had to. I could get a free meal, but when I got food poisoning from one, I needed money to pay for aspirin and something to stop the runs. The money from Fat Man's wallet went faster than I had hoped. I had my unemployment checks, which were automatically deposited. That sucked at first, since I was overdrawn, and the bank simply ate my initial check and part of the second.

One of my former coworkers, Dustin, hooked me up with a loose collection of people who specialized in relieving failing businesses of inventory. My laptop made its hassle worthwhile just by my getting that one e-mail. Employees would let us know when the end was near for their employer. We would arrange a time to bring a truck or trucks to the loading dock, where someone would meet us. Depending on what the company did to make its money, they would decide who and what was needed. Sometimes it was just strong backs and hand trucks. Other times they wanted people with a clue about computers. Even a company that didn't do anything productive, at least from what I could see, would still have goodies for us.

After a while it dawned on me that we were filling orders for someone. Before we'd go in we would be told what was on the shopping list. The first few jobs were Aeron chairs and laptops. I remember one time the guy that was there, waiting to let us into a small, maybe ten-suite business, well, he had a bit of a grudge. We were getting ready to leave and he hadn't returned, so I was asked to go find him while they finished wrapping the chairs in skins. I found him in what had to be the boss's office squatting on the desk. He was finishing taking a really rank dump and was wiping himself with photos he'd taken from their frames.

"Hey! We're leaving! You coming?"

He didn't bother to stop what he was doing. "Yeah, give me two minutes. I haven't gotten to his wife's photos yet." I just shrugged and went back to the guys. He rode in the back with Dustin, who, after we had dropped off the dumper, complained to us about how he had to smell shit the entire ride back.

I found a chance one night to ask the guy running the latest job about something that had me puzzled. He called himself Skizzer, and as far as I could tell he was still living the lucky life of an Earth Person. We had recently worked a couple jobs where all they wanted was servers—not just any servers but specific ones, where we had to verify the IPs and domains before shutting them down and hauling them.

So I asked, "What was up with that?"

He looked at me coolly for a couple of heartbeats before replying: "Look, why are you doing this?"

I said, "For the money." Thinking, *Duh, like why else?*

"Yeah, you said you worked IT, right?"

"Yeah"

"What's on a server?"

I was beginning to get a glimmer of where he was going with this. "Data," I said.

"Yep. Look, dude, I don't really know for sure, but this isn't our first job. Either someone wants the data or someone wants to make sure that data is no longer available. Either way we get paid, right?" He gave me a lame "we're comrades here" punch on the arm.

I gave him back what he wanted: "Right."

"So let's do this and get out of here."

I grinned and went back to downing the server. This was going to be a profitable night for us and I got extra for my IT skills. I was already thinking about how I could increase my personal profit on the side. I had noticed a Cisco CRS-1 router over in the corner. After tonight I was going to have to talk to the clan that was putting together the Internet cafe. They would love to have something like this. Money was nice, but what I really wanted was a secure living space and access to fiber. I missed online gaming a lot. In that alternate reality I wasn't a loser. I was a sought-after squad leader who never had to worry about how old his food was.

The Cisco deal worked out nicely, and part of my payoff was a roof over my head. After the Asian clan guys verified that the router worked and that I knew how to do IT configuration, they welcomed me enthusiastically to the clan and gave me directions to my place to live. I headed for my new home fairly happy with my life. My new home was a room all to myself in an old motel. I knew where it was; I just had never actually been there before. In another life I had driven past it a thousand times: The Anchorage Motel. It was old and the entrance was built to resemble a ship's bridge—at least that's how it looked to me. Funny, it took me a while to connect the name *Anchorage* to the whole ship design scheme; I kept thinking of Alaska. At least when I figured it out, it wasn't the result of asking someone in front of a group of people.

Pedaling over to the clan motel I had to keep an eye on oncoming traffic. Some people got a kick out of seeing how close they could come to you. They probably scored themselves extra points if you went into a ditch trying to get out of their way. They would pass a regular biker dressed in spandex and shiny helmet and then, out of nowhere, swerve to get you. We were juicy targets because of the amount of baggage we had attached to our bikes— all that baggage said *expendable*. They treated you as if you had a sign reading *Go ahead and hit me! No one will give a shit*—which was pretty much true. It was like they figured good riddance, eliminating another tax burden and a potential threat to their person and their society.

While pedaling I thought about things—amazing how much idle time the brain has for processing when there isn't an iPod pumping noise into it. Clueless people who thought they could wander around the streets with an iPod cranking lost, at a minimum, the iPod.

It's like I was told when I traded mine for cash to a guy on corner:

"So, you decided to smarten up."

I must have looked at him puzzled. He looked at me pityingly, "You ever spend any time downtown in the hood?"

I nodded, of course, although I never had. I still had no clue where he was going with this. "Yeah, you don't see any brothers walking around with these jammed in their ears. You got to be able to hear who is coming up on you. In the jungle you don't see any deaf animals that live." He had it turned on and was checking the playlist. "Not bad, but I am still going to have to wipe it." I winced a bit inside when he paused at my Paris Hilton single. He didn't say anything. What could I tell him? I thought she was hot once upon a time.

Afterward, I thought about how much my vocabulary had changed since I'd become "self-employed." I thought about the Tower of Babel; Americans pretty much spoke the same language. Yeah, there were the various slangs of different subcultures. The difference was that the new subcultures, embryonic as they were then, were beginning to become full-on cultures—in some areas, the dominant ones. It was still years off, but I could see it happening in front of me. The clans spoke a language with a lot of loan words from online. They were usually the tech-literate ones without too much emotional damage. The Tree People had their own slang that reflected their living conditions. The rest of the homeless had their own language. It was generally spoken only by them, and most of their conversations were held with themselves.

Clans were still rather new. They had existed in the gaming world for years. I was a member of one myself. Yet I had never met anyone from my clan and had only listened to them through my headset or talked on a webcam. There wasn't a real sense of camaraderie. But the need for community, combined with the need for stability, brought people together. Since people, no matter their age, seek out like-minded people, and the only commonality they shared was online gaming, that became the basis for a lot of groups or clans.

Plus, parents looked to them for help with their kids. When the foreclosure rate skyrocketed, parents found that keeping a family together in a tent in the woods was not always a good idea. It wasn't that Social Services made a big deal out of the poor conditions; SS were almost nonexistent due to budget cutbacks. It was that parents wanted better conditions, including protection: the Fat Man wasn't the only one of his kind out there.

So the kids got farmed out to those who had a roof, or they just left if they were old enough. They would find an abandoned house or business and find a way to get power to it. The older members of clans would hustle food and whatever else was needed for the group. They were just beginning to branch out into cash-generating sidelines when I hit the street. Sometimes, especially in tight-knit ethnic groups, a family that had the space and enough extra to feed more mouths would take kids in. In the online world you never used your real name. You usually created a name that reflected the game you played the most. This transferred to the IRL (in real life) clans, where these kids would often recognize you only if you used your online name.

I had no idea exactly who would be living at the motel. It wasn't like there were a lot of tourists anymore. The Washington, D.C., area still got tourists, but they could find nicer motels much closer in now. I hoped they were the younger clan kids, who were not as aggressive yet, especially since I would be an outsider. The only thing I knew for sure was that it was primarily an Asian clan.

## CHAPTER SIX

# ROOM, BOARD, AND A QUICK EDUCATION

The Anchorage Motel had survived for years on county money. The county paid the owners to rent rooms to the homeless, which meant the motel avoided having to do any costly upgrades to stay competitive. That worked fine, until it didn't. When the county went bankrupt, so did the money for the homeless. The social safety net, already savaged by the Bush administration, collapsed from a lack of taxpayer money. Some money still came from Washington to the county in the form of emergency grants. The politicians weren't insane; they knew the situation was becoming unstable. Just enough federal money came to the county and state that they could continue to provide the minimum of services. But minimum services no longer included free rooms for the homeless at the Anchorage Motel.

The owners of the Anchorage were Asian. Six members of the Golden Dragon Clan lived there, all of them teens. They were a splinter of the main group that I had done some work for. Their leader was a girl who used her online clan name when she was introduced to me. The short version, which I was glad she used, was "Night." Her full online name was "YellowNightMare4U," which was a little unwieldy during an online battle. Clanmates were allowed to call her Night. I was clan now. It meant she accepted me as a part of the clan for now, until she could make her own judgment of me. She was perhaps eighteen, looked sixteen, and was seriously one of the smartest people I ever met. She was also very good at hiding this. When I met her, she had self-appointed bodyguards at her side: a pair of Asian boys, maybe fourteen years old, who thought they were ninjas. I didn't care: I was tired. I wanted a shower. A long shower with hot water and soap that smelled good. Then, best of all, to stretch out and go to sleep on a real bed.

They showed me to my room. I liked the sound of that, *my room*. It was nice: a bed, a light, a dresser, and a nightstand in contrasting wood stains. Plus, a mold-free shower and a jack for the Internet. It had been cleaned recently and the smell of institutional strength cleaner lingered in the air. I took a deep breath. It smelled good. Being in the clan suddenly seemed like the best decision I'd made in a long time.

I was so tired all a sudden that I that ended up falling asleep with my clothes on, barely managing to wait until they left. I'd shower tomorrow. I slept eighteen hours straight that first day.

The next time I tried to be a hero, I got my ass kicked and was left for dead. The ass-kicking really was probably the best thing that could have happened to me, but I didn't figure that out on my own. It was pointed out to me much later. I had gone to the shelter hoping for a winter coat. Much to my surprise I was told that Carol had left word she wanted to talk to me. I was surprised at how good that made me feel. It was still late summer, and I didn't really need a winter coat yet. I just liked dropping by the shelter.

Carol was waiting for me in her office, which she shared with her assistant. And a very unimpressive office it was: metal cabinets, metal desks, old computers. I made a note of that. The computer fairy was going to have to leave a package on the doorstep here one morning. Kid scribblings were taped to the file cabinets, and a couple of framed photos were on her desk. The assistant left after saying "Hi" to me, pulling the door behind her as she went.

We passed a few minutes with the usual "Hey, how you doing?" but Carol wasn't big into bullshit. Unusual in a woman, I had always thought. She quickly got to the point: "I want you to find a kid for me."

"Okay."

She just looked at me.

I guess I was supposed to be asking questions.

"Here's a picture," she said. It had been scanned and then printed on a HP color printer that needed new cartridges. I took it. It was of a white girl about twelve, brown hair, a crooked smile. She was going to need braces, and that was probably not going to happen. She did not look happy despite the smile.

"So where is she and why me?"

I was rewarded with a smile. I guess I was finally acting like I had a modicum of intelligence. Carol gave me the background on the kid. I felt like I was back on the job, trying hard to look like I was paying attention. I looked at the picture trying to imagine what the girl would look like if I added a year or so to her age.

"You're not paying attention are you?"

"Ah, no."

"Look, Mike, here is the short version. Her mother sold her to some asshole who probably lives with her in the woods behind the old Kmart. Her mom has sobered up, is living here, and wants her kid back. I said I would do what I could. Can you look into this for me? Please."

*Damn*, I thought, *she would have to whip a* please *on me*. "Sure, so who is the guy she was sold to?"

"The mother really doesn't remember a lot, but she is sure she saw him in line the last time the army was through here handing out MREs. She remembers the name Jackson, so I asked around. I'm pretty sure it's the guy who is living in the woods. I was also told he has been seen with a girl who somewhat matches the description."

"Somewhat?" I asked.

"Well, her hair is blue now. At least check for me, okay?"

"Sure." I really didn't want to get out of the chair, but Carol's body language was telling me my time was up. She really had this manager stuff down pat. "Okay, I'll start on it right away. I'll be in touch to let you know."

Just as I had my hand on the doorknob and was turning it, I heard, "Mike,"—a pause—"be careful."

"Not a problem," I tossed over my shoulder without looking back. I didn't look back because I was afraid what my face would have told her.

I knew where she was talking about. Sometimes a group of homeless people used the Kmart for parties that stopped only when a majority of them fell asleep or passed out. It happened only sometimes because the neighbors would get tired of the noise, drinking, and shopping cart races, and would call the police and keep calling until a couple cars got sent out to evict the partiers. That would last a few days, maybe a week or two if the police pushed a patrol past every day. Then the police would find something else to do, and the homeless would be back. The neighborhood HOA had boarded up the back entrance that was being used. It was to no avail. These people would gnaw through cinder block walls if they felt like it. There was a church nearby that was good for clothes, food, and a few bucks, so they were always guaranteed to return. This meant that there was always a hard-core group living in the woods next to it.

I didn't know anyone in this bunch, but I knew someone who did. I had done a guy named Rooster a few minor favors, like letting him use my laptop to send e-mail. He wanted to take it in the bathroom at McDonald's, but no way was I going to let that happen. He could find another way to check out porn sites. But he owed me, so I went looking. I found him sitting on a milk crate, just hanging out with a couple other guys, and passing a bottle. They were observing proper protocol this close to the shelter— the bottle was disguised by a paper bag.

Rooster had found some cardboard to cushion his ass on the milk cartoon. A drunk he was, but stupid he wasn't. He was happy enough to see me. The other two had a decent buzz on; they were discussing the riots in the UK. I listened for a bit and was impressed. I asked one of them how he knew so much about England. In return I got a condescending look, along with the reply that he had been an analyst specializing in the UK for an investment fund. I suppose he was disappointed because I did not look impressed by that tidbit. Lately, half the people I talked to had been millionaires six months ago—or so they claimed.

I took advantage of the lull in the conversation to ask Rooster what he knew about the Tree People near the Kmart. He had nothing new to add since he was the one who told me about the water. The other two, from their reactions, hadn't known there was a working faucet there. They weren't the only ones. I hadn't known about it either.

One of them asked me, "Why you wanna know?"

I told him the truth. Someone wanted me to look for someone.

"Who?"

So I told him. He laughed. "That little bitch. I know her. She will steal you blind in a heartbeat." Then he belched. The fumes from that knocked me back about a foot and probably killed any flying insects within ten feet. He wound up dead of stomach cancer six months or so later.

It also discouraged me from asking any more questions, which would prove to be a mistake. I figured I would just ride on over there, lock the bike down far enough away that no one would mess it up trying to steal it, and see what I could see. If she was there, we would talk, she would see the light, and we then would head back to the shelter. Upon our return, I would be greeted by Carol and her staff as a hero. I would, of course, act modest and do my *aw, shucks* routine.

I was already basking in the future adoration I knew awaited me as I rode over there. One of the reasons the authorities considered the Tree People to be less than, well, model citizens was that they refused to live in the official tent cities the government was setting up. Others—usually those who had a streak of romanticism or still had a roof over their head—thought of the Tree People as outlaws, like Jesse James or Robin Hood. I was still, at least partly, one of those idiots.

Tent cities were never an option for me. In the beginning there were West Coast tent cities, and East Coast tent cities. The West Coast ones were usually wild ones—unplanned, unofficial. They just sprang up like mushrooms after a spring rain. Big tents, little tents, colorful tents, and plastic tarps all mixed together. Trash pickup was nonexistent, ice chests and lawn furniture were haphazardly arranged. Dogs ran around taking doggy dumps whenever the desire struck them. Sometimes a local church, or a coalition of churches, would arrange to have a couple of Porta-Potties dropped off. The churches usually never did any follow-up on the actual cleaning or emptying of them, so the smell, when the wind was right, added to the ambience. At any given time, half the population over the age of seven was stoned, drunk, or both. The local police knew everyone by first name.

The East Coast encampments came later—mostly in reaction to the idea that the West Coast-type tent cities might actually bloom in people's backyards like poison ivy crossed with kudzu. For my area, outside of Washington, D.C., that meant Homeland Security got involved. They were just finishing up the first one in the D.C. area. It was to be the model for the new federally funded initiative to provide housing for our less fortunate citizens.

The new model, "Camp Forward," was getting a lot of media attention. It was laid out like a military encampment. Camp Forward didn't even have tents. The authorities brought in recycled prefab housing units left over from the military's deployment to the Middle East. Later they would find that amazing things came with these prefabs: scorpions, yellow lizards, camel spiders, and Kurdistan vipers. That came as an unpleasant surprise to the occupants.

The media and the public called them East Coast tent cities, despite their having, at most, three tents. They were fenced in, complete with a gate, ID check, and uniformed security. The fence was explained as necessary to protect them. If pushed, the administrators would say, "It's for the children's safety." It was tough to argue against that. You needed an ID card to enter the facility, which meant a background check, which in turn meant that some people found themselves taken to a different facility. There were organized activities for the kids, workshops, and staff who were willing to work with you if you had the "right attitude." Some people, usually ones who had homes in the area, loved them. How did I feel about them? They gave me the creeps.

I shook thoughts of tent cities out of my head, pulled off the path, locked the bike, and dropped it into some bushes. I knew I was getting closer when I started spotting trash. I could hear voices before I could see anyone. Virginia woods can be thick with undergrowth; a lot of it had thorns, and some of it was toxic with poison ivy. I had heard a story the other day about someone who had taken a dump in the woods and then wiped his ass with poison ivy. I fervently hoped it was a former mortgage broker—preferably one I had worked with.

I stepped into the middle of the encampment. A couple of guys were sitting around a Weber kettle grill-ing something that looked like squirrels; either that or someone was missing a litter of kittens. I nodded at them, "Hey, what's up." I got civil nods back. Both guys were white and looked to be in their fifties. They reminded me of hippies who been left out in the sun to marinate in a BBQ sauce made of beer. Their clothes had that nice sheen of grime that only dedicated slovenliness can produce. One had a beard—God only knows what was living in there. The other had probably stood close to a razor in the last week. Upon closer look I decided he was younger. He came equipped with a decent beer belly and a Buck knife in a sheath.

The older one said, "If the smell of the cooking brought you up here, well, we don't have enough to share."

The younger one cackled, "Unless you got something to share."

I was a bit taken aback. I had never heard anyone actually cackle before. It was rather creepy. The camp itself wasn't creepy, just trashy. The tents were constructed out of plastic tarps and stray boards. Female laughter came from the "nicest" tent, and a man's voice roared from inside, "Who the hell is out there now?"

"Just some guy," replied the older one. "I think he's leaving."

*Jeebus*, I thought, *where was the love?* I cleared my throat and asked, "Has anyone seen a young girl named Regina?"

"Goddamn it!" roared the voice from the palace in the woods. "I can never get any peace around here."

The younger one slyly whispered, "Well, he's the only one getting a piece that I know of."

They were both busy guffawing as the owner of the voice rose out of the depths of the plastic. He was about six foot two and maybe two hundred pounds. Tattoos were obviously a passion of his. So were body piercings. Personal hygiene, not so much. I thought the Harley T-shirt really set off the piercings and tats very nicely. I still wasn't worried about my personal safety. I was amazingly naïve back then about some things.

"Who the fuck are you?"

"Hey, man. My name is Gardener. I am looking for a girl named Regina. She is short, white, and maybe has blue hair." I smiled at him.

He looked at me. I could tell he was busy processing all this information. That's when the little demon bitch popped her head out. "Jackson! I bet my bitch of a mom sent him!"

Jackson got all frowny-faced at this. "That so?" he asked.

He was moving toward me, as was his little honey bunch. She had on a man's T-shirt with a Grateful Dead logo. I was surprised. I didn't see her as a Deadhead. She was rather young to have such good taste in music. He was in my face now. One of the side effects of the Crash was poor dental hygiene. He was an excellent example of that. His breath smelled like old fish.

"Is that true?" The tone of his voice had changed. *What the hell was he getting so pissed off about?*

"I told you, Jackson! It's my mom. She hired him to take me back! I know it."

"That so?"

Later, I thought a lot about how I might have answered this question differently.

I replied, "Yeah, actually it is. If she wants to come—"

Getting hit upside the head, right in the jaw, doesn't hurt as much as you would think. As my head rocked to the side, I remember going from surprised to pissed in an instant. Unfortunately, he landed two more blows in that time: Those hurt. I was trying to get my balance back when he hit me hard in the ribs with a one-two combo. Then he landed an uppercut to my solar plexus, and I went down to one knee. That's when they put their boots to me. I don't remember a lot of what happened next. I do remember a kick to my kidney, which hurt more than I thought was possible.

Somewhere in all of this I remember looking up at Regina. Maybe I thought she would help me. One look at her face dissuaded me of that. She was enjoying watching them kick the crap out of me. I do remember grabbing a leg, giving it a nice tug, and hearing someone fall into the grill. I may have imagined it, or it may have been wishful thinking, but I am sure I heard a scream. Then again, it might have been me. Somewhere in there I blacked out. I came to for a few seconds as I was being dragged feet-first down a path. I think I heard the older guy bitching about how heavy I was. I remember my feet dropping to ground when they let go of me—that hurt. Then someone gave me a good-bye kick and I was alone.

Later—how long was later? I think I was there for about six hours—I tried standing up. That hurt way too much. I tried crawling. That hurt way too much, too. I waited for rescue and slept some more. It was dark when I awoke. I could hear people off in the distance. I tried calling to them but my throat was too dry to make more than a whisper; plus, my jaw hurt. I lay there a while longer. *Shit!* I recognized those voices—at least the female one. It was that little bitch, Regina. Jeebus, I had to get out of there before she decided to come looking for me.

The look in her eyes that I had seen earlier promised that if she wanted, what I had experienced so far would just be the warm-up.

I made it to my knees. I paused, then dropped forward, supporting my weight on all fours as I spit the blood and skin tissue out of my mouth. I was so dry that what I spit out just hung there, like a rubber band. I had to actually pinch it and pull to get rid of it. I struggled to get up on one knee, and then I pushed up. My head, ribs, lower back all exploded into one brilliant red-tinged explosion behind my eyes. *Oh, damn.* Breathing really hurt now. It had been hurting for a while; I had simply gotten used to it. This was a new hurt. I thought I knew what a bad beating felt like. I had been beaten pretty badly by some of my mom's old boyfriends. The difference was they were not really trying to kill me. These guys seem to have been more motivated.

I struggled to my feet. Holy hell, that hurt. *Just one step,* I told myself. *Okay, I did it. One more step.* Thinking as I did, *I am going to come back and kill every one of them.* And then, *step.* I know I went down to my knees a few times. I was brought down from clutching my ribs when a really sharp stab of pain flashed through my nervous system.

My balance was not very good.

I didn't even bother with the Batbike. I had one goal. Make it to the shelter one painful, freaking step at a time. I didn't make it—somewhere in the darkness, I lost it.

From what I was told later, I think I made it halfway by sun up. Some good Samaritan had come across me and gone for help. I came to for a while—the pain of someone pulling me to a sitting position set off a whole new set of agonies that brought me back. I could hear a woman's voice; whose, I had no clue. I opened my eyes and saw a man in his midthirties staring intently at me.

"Okay, I am going to wrap your ribs. This is gonna hurt."

I nodded—he was right; it hurt. The woman, a Latina I had seen around, was swabbing various scrapes. She was being pretty gentle about it. Once I would have made a big deal about how bad it hurt; now I laughed because it felt so good. Then I was back down and out.

## CHAPTER SEVEN

# WHEN THE PUPIL IS READY . . .

I had a lot of time on my hands while my body healed. I found that sitting around in my motel room with my laptop, a television, and a bathroom, was very nice. Just thinking about what it would have been like trying to recover while living under a pine tree made me shudder. As it was, the first few weeks were tough. Night or someone else from the clan would come by with food each day. One unlucky ninja got to help me to the bathroom and back for a few days. I revised my opinion of him upward as a warrior when he entered the bathroom after a really toxic dump, and he lifted me up off the seat without flinching or gagging.

Carol came by and was really apologetic about me getting my ass kicked. I just waved it off. "It was no big deal." What else was I going to say? Inside, I berated myself for screwing up. I had gotten cocky. Just because you can stick a trowel in a fat man's belly doesn't mean you are a warrior. I wallowed in self-pity for a few days.

Two things pulled me out of it. The first was the news. It had not been good for a while, and it was getting worse. I had long ago given up on the mainstream media outlets as a source of real news. I did not care about what some overpaid, entertainment drug-slut had been caught doing or had just died trying to do. The local news—the few times I watched it—might as well have been taking place in a parallel universe.

Over at the shelter they had a couple of flat screens bolted to the walls in the public area for the inhabitants. They used to love it when the local news would come by and do a story on "their struggle." They would laugh at whoever got interviewed, and they'd be delighted to see themselves shown for a second in a crowd. But the news crews no longer came around.

They would still do the occasional story, but they just recycled the old clips. Eventually, people would turn away when they came on; it was no longer funny when they showed the clip of Janie talking about how she wanted to work, how she wanted to provide a future for her kids. The same Janie who two months later hung herself in the shelter shower room late one night after Child Protective Services came and took her two beautiful blonde girls.

I lay there in my bed and surfed the econ blogs and Web sites on my laptop. I had been a business major in college. Ironically, I had wanted to major in sociology but I decided not to. I didn't think there would be any money in it. I was reading *Calculated Risk* when I realized that things were not going to get better. Despite what the media said, it was becoming obvious that we had started a slow descent into third-world squalor. The news, no matter how they tried to spin it, only confirmed it. Europe was not any better off: The UK was going crazy. Some "chav" had discovered that he looked good on video and had a message people wanted to hear. YouTube had banned him a few days ago, but it was too late; he was already launched.

His main pitch was "Britain for Britains!" He was smart. When asked about Jews, he said, "I have no problem with the Jews. They have been members of the community for centuries." They weren't going to tar him with the "Nazi" label—he just hated foreigners. He didn't even say "Muslims" or "Indians" specifically, well, at least very often. Nevertheless he had found that his words were attracting an audience that was willing to listen. Britain had an "official" unemployment rate of 15 percent last month, and it was still climbing.

The terrorist attack in Liverpool during a football match, where bombs killed 173 people, definitely pumped his ratings, especially as the group claiming credit was British Muslim. That went over really well with a lot of people. In the bloody rioting that followed, at least that number of Indians and Muslims died. And it wasn't confined to the UK. The rioting swept through Europe. Even Germany, that bastion of tolerance, was having problems.

What was happening in America was what really got my attention. Not only what was being said but what was being left *unsaid*. Unemployment—at least by official count—was at 14 percent. The reality was a lot uglier. Despite what was being done and spent by the government, nothing was getting better. A couple of times things stopped plummeting so quickly, and people got hopeful, only to have their hopes and investments crushed when the downturn started again. Perhaps the Crash would have been more severe without the government intervening. We would never know. It was difficult to believe that it helped when they let the bankers walk away with hundred-million-dollar bonuses. To say that cynicism was spreading about whom the government really cared for would be, at best, an understatement.

The bank bailout provided a glimmer of hope for some in the very beginning. The problem was, those who thought it was a good idea usually still had a job and money, and they expected those conditions to continue. What had been reported as the end of the world for the great mass of Americans turned out to be a massive windfall for a few.

This was quickly followed by Chrysler departing the industrial universe and General Motors filing for bankruptcy after the government stopped propping them up by shoveling money into them. Actually, it never did stop; it just became less obvious. The Cash for Clunkers program was one of the ideas the government came up with. It was spun as "green" and "good for America." Like a lot of the ideas the government came up with, it turned out to be a short-term fix.

What most people did not understand was that Toyota and Nissan employed almost as many workers as the Big Three in the union-free South. They were not doing any better, and it created a ripple effect that began moving down the parts manufacturing chain. The third-largest consumer of computer chips made in the United States had been GM up to this point.

Nightmare—or Night, which she insisted I call her— came by during my second week of recovery. She was flanked by the ninjas and had a look on her face more serious than usual. Not that she ever looked really happy to see me. "What's up?" I asked, pushing the laptop away so she would know I was going to attempt to pay attention.

"We are glad to have you in the clan," she started off.

I waved my hand dismissively and said, "Thank you. I am glad to be in the clan. But really, what's up?" I knew something had to be. Whenever someone told me that they were happy or glad because of me, well, I knew they wanted something.

"You are part of the clan, and you got your ass kicked." This kind of pissed me off, and it also gave me a shot of anxiety. Was I no longer welcome because I had lost? *Damn*, I really was getting used to my bed and private bathroom.

"The clan leaders sent word that as soon as you had recovered, the guys that did this to you would have to get payback—if only to send the message that our clan cannot be disrespected in this way." She continued, "We would have already gone on our own to take care of it, but you were the target, and you are new in the clan, so we waited for you to recover. We were sure that you would want to be there for the payback." She grinned. She had a scary grin for someone so skinny and short.

"Hey, I appreciate that and all, but it's my mess. I screwed up. I was doing a favor for Carol at the shelter like I told you. I got sloppy. My fault—my job to fix it."

Night stared at me, grinned, and said, "If you change your mind, let us know and we will be ready." I didn't know if they were really ready or not. I did know that she impressed the hell out of me, and it changed the way I looked at the clan.

I woke up late a few mornings later to find I had company. He was sitting in my only chair, not doing anything. He was just sitting. I recognized him: He was the guy who had taped my ribs after my night in the woods.

"Ah . . . good morning."

He just looked at me, his face totally expressionless. We did the manly man staring contest for a few minutes. I won; it was my freaking room. He spoke first: "You going to rise and shine, sleepyhead?"

"Sure." I sat up, winced, and swung my legs over the side of the bed. And winced again. I was really, really going to hurt that asshole and his buddies. "Do me a favor. Throw me those pants." I had a pair of cargo pants hung over the side of the chair. I loved cargo pants because they had more pockets than I had stuff. He threw them to me and I began the painful process of pulling them on.

"So what brings you here?" I asked.

"It is time to begin your training."

"Ah, my training? That would be in . . . ?"

I was going to add something smart, but it was still early, and I couldn't think of anything. Plus, there was an aura about him that made me hold my tongue. He reminded me of a cop or some of the retired army officers I had crossed paths with in my previous life. Then again, there was that crazed Indian Amway seller who was always hanging around the break room at work. They both had that same glint in the eyes that comes from seeing a different reality. I realized that saying the word *work* in my head sounded weird. It was as if it had become a word from another language, one I had known very well once. But then I had left that country and no longer spoke the language.

"Your training in self-defense—unless you think you've got a handle on it?"

*Ouch. That was a little uncalled for*, I thought.

"So why me? How much? Why you?"

A faint smile. He replied, "You have been blessed."

"Blessed? Blessed! What the hell kind of answer is that! Man, get the hell out of my room! Are you from the clan? I said I'd handle it!" I was getting pissed.

He didn't move. He just raised his hand, palm forward. "Sit down, settle down, and all will be revealed." I grumbled a bit and sat back down.

"Okay, I am settled."

"I'm not from your clan. You have a friend who thinks you can benefit from some training."

"Who—"

"Try listening for a little bit," he said, cutting me off.

"Jeebus," I muttered.

"You can call me Max. Carol asked me to do this. I owe her. You do not owe me. When we are done, we are done. I spent three tours in the 'Stan and Iraq with the 2/7 of the First Marine Division. After my discharge, I worked for LAPD as patrol officer in Rampart Division for a year. Since the budget cuts I have worked as a consultant."

I mentally snorted at the "consultant" part. I knew that his bit about being sent from Carol would be easy enough to check. "Okay, when do we start?"

He got up from the chair. "Two weeks. I will come looking for you." Then he let himself out the door.

That was another thing—I knew I had turned the dead bolt on that door the previous night. From now on, I was going to start wedging a chair under the doorknob.

A few days later, I was starting to feel better; plus, I was getting bored. I went looking for Night or one of the ninja boys. Hell, anybody would do. There is only so much time you can spend alone, even with a computer, before the need for human contact asserts itself. I wandered out of my room, walked down the sidewalk to the clan room, which was really just another room. The difference was, Night and her brood of ninjas kept a lot of their toys in there.

It served as their clubhouse, dining room, and computer room. It had a pretty decent server, a Cisco switch, and a UPS in the corner. There were four flat screens cabled to four boxes next to the server. Night and one of the ninjas were sitting together at the small table, which took up the space the bed once had. They were both staring at the same screen and laughing at whatever was on. I could hear Chinese coming from the speakers so I didn't even bother to walk the extra few feet to look. I just eased down into one of the chairs. I watched them for a bit while they ignored me.

Night looked over the top of the screen eventually. "How you feeling?"

"Oh, I am all right. What are you watching?"

"Beheadings in China."

"Okay, sounds exciting. So, you ever heard of a blond soldier-looking guy named Max?"

That got both of their attention. The ninja asked me, "You've seen him and lived?" I laughed and nodded.

"Don't laugh, Gardener." Night had gotten all serious on me; she went on. "He was famous before the Crash. He worked as a contract killer for the triads in California and here. He is an enforcer."

Ninja boy nodded his head. "And a good one, too."

"Triad killer my ass," I told him. "If he's a triad killer, then I'm Batman."

I got up and immediately felt dizzy. Maybe coming here wasn't such a good idea. I mumbled a good-bye and to the answering silence I left muttering, "Fuck 'em."

When I got back to my room I grabbed the aspirin bottle off the nightstand, poured three into my hand, grimaced, and dry swallowed them. They went down rough, and I had to scramble for something to wash them down. The open can of soda that I grabbed to chase them with must have been three days old. That was really tasty.

I settled back on my bed, kicked off my shoes, and fell asleep imagining myself slipping through the woods, silent as a Siberian tiger, my camouflage ninja killer suit rendering me invisible to the human eye. Slashing through the woods, movements like liquid mercury, I hunted my prey in their blue plastic tents.

## CHAPTER EIGHT

# SHEEP AND WOLVES

Two weeks later to the day I woke up to find Max in my room again. I glanced over and saw that my only chair was still wedged under the doorknob. *Hmmm, interesting*, I thought. *Maybe, just maybe, there's something to this triad story*. I looked at him; he had followed my glance to the door and met my look with a faint smile. He tossed me a pair of pants from off the floor. I grabbed them out of the air, slid off the bed and into them, and stood up.

"So, Sensei, what is the plan?"

"Your first lesson is this: Don't be more of an asshole than the situation calls for. My name is Max, not Sensei."

*Okay*, I thought.

Max jerked a thumb toward my door, "Let's go for a drive."

I grabbed my jacket and we left. I didn't say anything. He had a long stride, and I had to stretch my legs to keep up. Eventually, I asked him, "So, are we going to your dojo?"

"We're there."

"Ah, we're in the parking lot."

"Very observant." He clicked his remote to unlock his car. It was a Toyota Camry Hybrid, maybe a 2009. It was hard to tell as they all looked alike to me. It was silver and could have used a wash. This was not what I was expecting.

"This is your car?" He heard the disbelief in my voice.

"What? You have a problem with it? What the hell were you expecting, a tank?"

"No, no. No problem."

I buckled myself in and adjusted the seat back. He started the car and we pulled out on to Route 50 headed east. Traffic wasn't heavy even though it was still rush hour. The D.C. metro area was considered recession-proof once upon a time. Now, like the rest of the country, it was proving that nowhere was safe from a global depression. The last recessions had been bad in the D.C. area, I was told, but not as bad as everywhere else. That had always been true, until it wasn't. Everyone had totally missed the structural change in the local economy. The metro area had once been a company town, with the company being the U.S. government. That was still big, but real estate in 2005 had become just as big.

There were also the parasites that hung off the body of the government. They had gorged themselves on tax-payer money since the Reagan administration. With that first windfall they had built their towers around the perimeter of the interstate that girded the capital city. Like castles of feudal lords, they housed tens of thousands of foot soldiers, all dedicated to reaping the harvest from the government money trees. It was a good time—until autumn came.

The government no longer had the money to support the programs that fed the money trees. It had turned out to be a perfect storm. The federal government hit the same brick wall that the state, county, and local governments did. The Fed just hit it later, and the aftereffect was larger. You can't run a lot of expensive programs if the money is not coming in from taxes. There was another problem too; the world financial system turned to out to be insolvent and that created a whole bunch of expensive problems. In between the death of real estate, the financial system and the tax base crumbling, there just wasn't enough juice left to power the local system, let alone keep an empire running.

The change was obvious to me as we drove toward D.C. Traffic was light. Light in this area meant rush hour just about anywhere else. I had driven this route before and knew the difference. We pulled off Route 50 and headed toward Clarendon. I tried making a bit of small talk, but all I got in return were grunts, so I decided to shut up, watch the scenery, and see how it played out. Max pulled off by the metro and parked next to a dumpster behind a Chinese restaurant.

"C'mon, I'll buy you a cup of coffee."

We got out of the car and walked around the corner. There was a deli open that was serving breakfast. We got our coffee, went outside, and sat down in front of the place. It was cold enough that a faint wisp of steam escaped from my cup when I peeled back a section of the lid.

"So, you have any questions?"

I came close to spitting out my coffee when he asked me that.

"Yeah—what did you mean when I asked if we were going to your dojo? And when and where do we start training?"

He just stared across the street. Since we had sat down, four or five people had shown up to stand in line in front of a double door that opened onto the street.

"You see those people?"

"Yeah."

"They're lining up for the free breakfast. In ten minutes there will be fifty of them in line. I want you to imagine you're working security and tell me who's carrying a weapon. Then, I want you to tell me if they are any good with it."

I sipped my coffee and took a look at the group: It was the usual polyglot mix that represented the new American polity around here and, as far as I knew, everywhere else. A couple of young black males looked like possible candidates, but I rejected that as profiling. So far, there was nothing I could see.

Max startled me a bit when he started talking. "You want training—maybe we will get that far, maybe we won't. I can tell you one thing. You're going to have to upgrade from your garden trowel. You got away with it once, but try more than that and you will find it will cause you more problems than it is worth."

My blood went cold when I heard that. Time slowed down and I became very focused as I looked over at Max. He met my look with nothing: nothing in his eyes, nothing in his face. He was just there. "Yeah, I'll keep that in mind."

He nodded. "Listen to me. This isn't about being a master of martial arts or being able to execute a fly at thirty paces with a spitball while you sip a cold one. It's all in your head. You get your head right, and the rest will follow—you understand this?"

"Yeah, I think so."

"When you get there, half your problems will be solved. You know why?" I figured this was a rhetorical question, so I just shook my head no.

"Because you change internally: You have a bit of it. Your aura, your energy changes. Civilians will see it and shut their eyes to it. The predators—they will see it and adjust accordingly. When the world is filled with sheep, why bother with a wolf? I am going to teach you how to be a wolf. Or in your case, maybe a big shaggy dog," he laughed.

"Funny—really funny."

"Listen up," he said. "The first commandment is this: *You are not God.* You get to thinking you are and the next thing you know the real God sends around someone faster and smarter. Your job is to protect and serve—only that will justify the steps you will take.

"The second commandment is this: *Watch your perimeter.* That is, not just your personal space; sometimes it may be blocks or miles wide."

That startled me. I had heard it before. I filed it away to ask him about it some other time.

"The third commandment is this: *When you commit, commit to kill—at whatever the personal cost.* You do not think about going into an engagement with the intent to frighten or wound; you are mentally prepared to escalate immediately to killing them."

He stopped with that.

I waited, sipped the dregs, and crumpled the cup. I tossed it toward an open trash can about five feet away and actually made the shot. He finished his, crumpled it, and without looking or turning around flipped it over his shoulder. It landed in another trash can about ten feet away.

"Show-off," I said. He laughed.

"Let's go."

We were headed back in his Camry when he asked me, "So how many people in the soup line were carrying weapons?"

*Damn.* Actually, I hadn't seen any indication that anyone was, so that's what I told him.

"Very good . . . you know why?"

"Ah, no; it was really just a wild-ass guess."

He laughed. "Yeah, well, because people who have guns don't have to stand in soup lines."

That line alone led me to more realizations than everything else that had been said that morning.

## CHAPTER NINE

# VENGEANCE

Max told me before he left that he would see me in a week. No big deal. The training wasn't moving as fast as I thought it would, but I wasn't going anywhere. My body was back, well, almost back. I hadn't pissed blood in a while. The ribs still hurt, but it was a throb rather than that knifing pain. I felt good enough to go get my bike, which, to my surprise, was still there. I went to get it half-apprehensive, half-filled with cold rage. Pedaling back I knew it was time to do something about what had happened. If I let it slide, well, then I might as well quit the clan and move to Maryland. Since I would rather live in the men's room at the Greyhound bus station than live in Maryland, I was going to have to do something soon. Regardless of Max coming through with the training, I figured I might as well take care of it this week. That way Max and I could have something to talk about. Think of it as homework, I told myself.

Just as I turned into the motel it struck me how I was going to do it. I wasn't really into guns, which made me an aberration. Everyone loved guns. If you were a male in my age group, liking guns was cool, unless, of course, you were talking to some young lady. Then guns were "bad," hunting animals was "bad." Most women really did not want to know you were into online gaming, either. By my age, most of them had dated someone who was more into playing online than he was ever going to be into them. That had begun to change: not the online gaming part—the gun part.

Being knowledgeable about guns was becoming socially acceptable with your college-educated, upwardly mobile, wannabe types. I did not like guns. Online, it was cool; offline, it was not. It was primarily because I didn't trust them. They were too complicated. You had to know too many things to get them to work. Slides and safeties, since I was left-handed, were always on the wrong side. Plus, all that black plastic. If I smacked somebody upside the head with one, I was afraid it would either break or, worse, not do anything. With a blade there was no safety, and the odds were pretty good that it was not going to break or jam at the wrong moment.

The other problem with guns was some really weird government stuff was going on with them. The feds could not ban them without really stirring up trouble. You could tell they really wanted to ban assault and military-style rifles but those weren't going anywhere for the same reasons. So what they were doing, and doing very quietly, was choking off the supply of certain ammunition. Only lately had it become noticeable enough that public questions were asked. The government said the war effort was straining production for certain calibers and that it should be resolved shortly. No one really accepted that for the same reason the public no longer accepted anything the government said. Nobody believed them, especially after the bank nationalization fiasco.

The bank nationalization probably didn't even start as one. It was never even officially called that by name. We will probably never know, as the government still has not released any information on what they were doing or hoped to do. It was billed as an exercise in determining the current state of the bank's balance sheets. What no one had realized was how bad a situation the banks were in. One of the examiners was a young lady named Meredith Gonzales. Meredith, who I watched being interviewed after everything broke loose on YouTube, was a fat, unattractive Hispanic woman with a bad accent; she was also a brilliant analyst. Her bosses had never gotten past her exterior to appreciate the interior, and she resented that. Rightfully so, I thought. Meredith had access to a lot of data, and no social life. She took the data from Citigroup, ran her own analysis, and uploaded everything to the Web. *Everything* meant the bank's data, the government data, her data, and some really huge spreadsheets, which were later considered works of art by aficionados of that genre. The result was that she blew up the American banking system. Then the dominoes, which in this case meant banks, started falling all across the world—and they were still falling. Governments fell, and in a handful of countries they did not fall gracefully.

So that's why I signed onto Craigslist to find my weapon of choice. I was looking for a saber. I would go all the way back to medieval times for a blade if I had to. But a saber was my weapon of choice. I didn't want to stick my attackers; I wanted to slice. I figured less chance of the blade getting hung up that way. I guess I could have gone samurai, but I felt that was disrespectful. Why appropriate another culture's tools, when yours had created ones that worked just as well?

Craigslist was fascinating to me: the debris of a civilization being jettisoned overboard, where it could wash up on anyone's cyberbeach. Craigslist reminded me of Hemingway and his great short story *For Sale: Baby Shoes. Never used.*

The stories behind some of the flotsam that washed ashore had to be fascinating. "Wedding dress. Used twice. Size 12." Also the engagement rings—a lot of heartbreak contained in those short posts. I found what I was looking for under "Collectibles." I actually had three choices. In theory, posting ads for weapons was against Craigslist policy, but with the flood of merchandise and the ability to repost if an ad got deleted, you could get what you needed if you moved quickly. One ad was for a Marine Corps dress sword. Nice, but no. One looked to be a cheap Chinese stainless steel fantasy sword. The last one was good—very good. A copy of an 1860 U.S. Calvary saber made from carbon steel, with a leather-wrapped hilt. I sent the posters an e-mail.

My reply arrived in minutes. They were in the area and willing to meet me in a public place close by. I suggested the McDonald's down the road. The last time I had been down that way it had been open. They agreed, and I rode down there on my bicycle to meet them. *They* turned out to be a middle-aged couple. She was eager to take my money; he was reluctant to part with the saber. It came with a belt and hanger—I liked it a lot.

Back in my room, I couldn't get the sword to hang right from my waist. I kept tripping over it or catching it on something. I felt as if I had a tail growing from my side. I decided to wear it over my shoulder instead. When I wore it that way and looked in the mirror, I could almost imagine myself as a ninja. I sat there and spent some time thinking about my plan. Not a lot, maybe five minutes. It just didn't seem all that complicated to me.

I logged in, played some *Halo*, and then logged off to go find something to eat. I went down to the clan's common room and raided the refrigerator. I gave Night money every week to pay for this privilege. Night came in as I settled down at the table with my bowl of freshly nuked soup.

I ate a lot of noodle or rice soup here. Nowadays, I was just about a vegetarian, as meat prices had become so high that no one I knew could to afford to buy it. Once in a while the main clan would send a few pounds of fresh meat to us—usually burger, probably cow, but you never could be sure. I am sure that a few ponies went missing. There were very few squirrels to be seen anymore. I suspected a direct correlation between meat prices and their absence. Dogs were also not seen as much anymore.

I was sitting at the table, trying to be patient enough to wait for the soup to cool down so I would not burn my tongue again. Night had helped herself to the same soup. We were sitting there, slurping together, after having done the ritual "Hey, what's up?" She was eyeing me curiously.

"What is that on your back?"

"It's my sword."

I had worn it to eat because I wanted to get used to the weight. She nodded her head solemnly and then sprayed soup out her nose as she burst into hysterical laughter. She would begin to catch her breath, look at me, and go back to laughing. I finished my soup, rinsed the bowl out, and headed out the door. She called out something to me, but I didn't catch it, as she fell into another bout of laughter. I failed to see what was so funny. And I decided to rethink how I was wearing it. I resolved to cover it up a bit when I went out in public.

I was determined to do it that night: It was payback time. Since they hadn't given me any warning, I wasn't going to give them any. I set the alarm for 3:00 a.m., the time when men's souls are the least tethered to their bodies. I dressed in black and green and stuffed my mask into my jacket pocket. I pulled on the backpack and headed out the door. It was quiet; no traffic was moving on Route 50. The moon was two-thirds full, which was nice. I was going to need the light. There was a nice downhill slope to the road, which I only planned to be on for a handful of minutes. Then it would be paths and parking lots until I got close. It was nice being out at this time of night. Peaceful. I startled two deer that were browsing on the grass that grew next to the path. They bounded away from me in graceful leaps. Like squirrels and dogs, free-range deer were ending up on a lot of dinner tables. I left my bike in the same place I had on my first visit. Symmetry of action: I like that. I pulled the saber from its sheath, which was stuffed into an empty gym bag, leaving the sheath in the bag on the bike's basket. I walked up the path listening to the night sounds of the forest.

As I drew closer, I was able to hear sounds of the Tree People. Someone was snoring under a tarp tent across from the dead fire. The place looked the same—no reason it shouldn't. There hadn't been a storm, and it was less than a month since I was here last. I decided to start at the blue tarp tent and work my way to the mansion, where Jackson was hopefully sleeping. At this point I didn't care if he was there or not: I would find him eventually. I lifted the saber, pushed the point through the plastic, and let the weight of the blade and gravity pull it down, slicing through the tarp. I used the tip to push aside the plastic and took a look inside.

*Nice!* My two old friends from my previous visit were stretched out and asleep, sharing the same blanket and a special love, no doubt. Both slept with their mouths open—one to snore and the other to inhale the snores. The smell was decidedly ripe inside the tent as I stepped through the rip. I wondered how it would feel to me this time. I decided to take the older one first, as he wasn't snoring. I slid the point of the blade inside his open mouth with just a bit of angle to it. His eyes snapped open as the tip grazed the inside of his mouth. Then I leaned on the blade and punched it through the back of his head where it joined his neck. He gurgled and twitched as I withdrew the blade. Unfortunately, he was loud enough to disturb his soul mate, who was quick. The second guy went from snoring to trying to grab the blade with all his strength as I centered it on his face.

It's been repeatedly proven throughout history that grabbing a razor-sharp, carbon steel blade with your bare hand is a mistake. This time was no different. Four of his fingers left his hand when I thrust. I could feel the bones almost popping as they came off. One finger dropped into his open mouth, smothering an unvoiced scream. While he choked on what I believe was his index finger, my thrust cut his throat.

Well, that was two. I felt really great. There were no flashing strobes, like when I had done the Fat Man. I felt happy and peaceful—relaxed, like I was swimming in warm water. I stepped back through the hole in the side of the tent and paused, listening for any disturbance in the force. That is exactly what I thought to myself, too.

I slipped the blade into the next wall of plastic and slid it down. Once again, I flicked the tarp aside enough to view the inside: an empty sleeping bag and an equally empty bottle. I guess the boys had not been going out together long enough to move in with each other. I stepped back out and began moving toward Jackson's tent. This was going to be a little trickier. His tent, being the executive model, had plywood sides. I thought about it for a second or two and decided *What the hell*.

I stood off at an angle from what I figured was his front door.

Then I knocked. Nothing. So I did it again but louder. I was rewarded by a roar of "Who the fuck is that?" followed by the sound of a loud, ripping fart.

I didn't say anything. My guess is, the smell of that long, ripping, cheesy fart made him stick his head out the door—and he immediately lost it. I swung that saber like a bat, putting my hips into it. His head actually bounced—very cool, especially as it landed eyes up. I wished I hadn't worn the mask. I would have liked for him to have seen my face. I looked cautiously into the tent. The girl was gone—just as well. That might have been awkward.

Using the saber and my hands, I dug a shallow hole in the bushes near my bike and then wiped the hilt with my shirt to make sure no prints were on it. I had already wiped the blood off the blade on Jackson's shirt. I put the sword into its sheath in the gym bag and then buried the saber in its grave before I picked up my bicycle.

I kicked myself for not remembering to bring a plastic bag with me so I could have sealed it against moisture. I was going to have to hope for the best. With luck, I could come back and dig it up. I rode back to my room picturing an archeologist digging it up someday and getting excited because he imagined it coming from a bloody Civil War skirmish. I returned without incident, rolled the bike into my room, and took a hot shower. Afterward, I quickly fell into a deep, dreamless sleep. The next morning I woke up and stretched. No pain! That was a pleasant surprise. I reached for my laptop and to my dismay found that it was dead. It took a while before I figured out that the outlet on the power strip was bad. It had run on the battery until it had exhausted itself sometime during the night. I plugged it in another outlet and let it boot up. Since I was running Unix, it booted without all the conversation Microsoft required.

## CHAPTER TEN

# TOMORROW, THE WORLD

I was in the bathroom shaving, thinking about how my money was running low again and that I needed to figure out what I was going to do next. When my laptop finished booting, it was set to bring up my browser with CNN displayed. From where I stood, the bathroom mirror reflected the screen. Two-thirds of the CNN page was taken up by a photo of a mushroom cloud. Cold chills ran through me. There was no way this was going to be good. I sat down on the bed, my half-finished shave forgotten. The freaking Arabs had gone ahead and done it—they had nuked Tel Aviv.

I started reading the news. There wasn't a lot of information yet, or the Israeli government wasn't releasing it. Whoever had done it had timed it for just before nightfall. It made for a spectacular photo, and at least three people had filmed it. Jeebus: YouTube, Twitter, and CNN better have upgraded their servers lately, because they were going to take a pounding. This was the kind of event that you didn't want to watch and then sit around thinking about by yourself. I went in search of company. Apparently, I wasn't the only one who felt that way; the clan break room was full. Even the owners of the motel had wandered in and were sitting with Night on the sofa.

It dawned on me: This was more of an extended family than a true clan. The owners were not being nice to strangers; they were helping out their family. *Damn*, I bet Night was their daughter. My excitement over my analytical skill was quickly reduced by the cold splash of history playing out on the screen in front of us. Someone had hooked a laptop to the big screen and was using that to display the info feeds. Night was somewhat reserved in her greeting, while the two ninjas gave me polite nods and big smiles. So did the other two kids, who I hardly knew or even talked to. *What the hell?* Something was going on here under the surface. I knew I would figure it out or someone would explain it to me sooner or later. I gave the owners a polite nod. I guess I was going to have to mentally start calling them "the parents." I looked around for a place to sit. One of the ninjas hopped out of his seat next to Night and offered it to me. That was nice of him.

I asked Night, "Have the Israelis retaliated yet?"

She shook her head. "Anytime now is my guess."

The screen was showing aerial views, probably from a satellite, of Tehran, Mashhad, and Damascus. People were streaming out of them, apparently in anticipation of the Israeli payback. This was going on in cities all over the Middle East.

"They have any idea of who is responsible?" I asked her.

"No. The Americans, the Russians, and the UN are all analyzing the fallout, looking for the signature."

"I bet the Israelis already know. They are just clearing airspace and tanker support with us." I rubbed my eyes.

"Did anyone think that maybe we should be watching this from the basement?"

Mama-san surprised me by answering. "No, we are okay—this time."

*Okay*, I thought, *she seems pretty certain.*

Night, much to my surprise, reached over and patted me lightly on the arm. "You're a good guy. I am sorry for laughing at you yesterday." Everyone in the room—including Mom and Dad, to my surprise—nodded in unison.

"Okay, whatever."

We watched the death of Tel Aviv for a while—watched the first responders in their protective NBC suits; saw the images of the dead and wounded; saw people who looked okay now, but who were walking dead, because of radiation. People were wailing as the government officials of various Middle Eastern countries took turns denying any involvement.

A report from Saudi Arabia had someone on who was promising a billion dollars in aid. Then it happened: The Israelis and the Americans were reported to have landed at purported Pakistani nuclear storage facilities and begun to raid them. Predator raids and Tomahawk missiles were hammering the Pakistani border area, as were land- and carrier-based aircraft. The Israeli air force was reportedly busy in Iran. Multiple strikes were being reported in numerous areas, mostly suspected uranium enrichment or possible bomb assembly areas. There were also minor air strikes by the Israeli air force reported in Syria, Iraq, and Lebanon. The Israelis had decided to run the table while they had the opportunity.

Hours later, just as I was getting up to go back to my room, the Israelis nuked Islamabad. As Pakistani cities go, it was not huge—not like Karachi and Lahore, which had almost twenty-five million people combined. But it served to make the Israelis' point to the world's governments: *Control your borders and your people, or you pay the price.* This did not all play out in a matter of hours: It took days. I would sleep, get up, and sit next to Night while we all ate soup and watched it unfold. The Iranians at first had a very muted response. Then it was as if someone had flipped a switch or shot the current leadership, because they did a complete turnabout and came out swarming like hornets.

The Iranians had lost any chance of real surprise, and they were eventually slaughtered. One U.S. army battalion did get overrun. That was primarily from being in the wrong place at the wrong time. The Iranians took an estimated four thousand casualties taking out that battalion. The United States may have been on its way to declaring bankruptcy but there was still a lot of inventory left on the shelves. Later, I read it was old-school five-hundred-pound bombs dumped from B-52s that really wreaked havoc on the Iranians. They were being led by someone who concentrated all their forces into one area as they rolled over the hapless American infantry battalion. That did not have a history of working out real well against American air power.

Life went on. The craziness level ratcheted up a notch. There was no point in going into Washington D.C. and spending any time in the Federal Triangle or the Mall area, unless you either had a government ID or didn't mind standing in line to get a visitor's pass. Getting a visitor's pass meant having a retinal scan, getting fingerprinted, and giving up a DNA sample. Government workers were having the same done to them and then having it down-loaded to a chip on their IDs. The D.C. tourism board ran commercials and covered the metro system with print ads to promote it: It was called the Freedom Pass. European tourists really loved it, especially when they found out they had to pay for it. Not that there were that many tour-ists anymore. Europe was busy having its own version of a nervous breakdown.

On another level—the one most people lived at—the systematic failure of so many things that people took for granted was beginning to intrude on lives that were already stressed. *Calculated Risk*, my favorite blog, had called this well in advance, as it had so many other things that were happening. The supply chain was breaking down. Most people had no clue how fragile the entire mechanism was for keeping people fed and clothed. The "Just in Time" delivery system was predicated on the assumption that each part of the machine would never break down. Major cities did not keep food stockpiles. At best, they had two days of food on the shelves or in transit at any given mo-ment. The problem was, the machine was beginning to break down. Why? I am not smart enough to completely understand everything that was happening, but two of the main drivers were the lack of liquidity and the death of the dollar.

Wal-Mart was one of the first and biggest casualties. At one time it seemed invincible. It was the giant that came into small towns and crushed local merchants like the economic dwarves they were. There was only one flaw: an Achilles heel—one that was so glaringly obvious that once it was exposed, people were amazed they had not seen it. Virtually everything on Wal-Mart's shelves came

from China, and China now wasn't exporting anything
to the United States. Since Wal-Mart stores lived by the
just-in-time import model, they died by it—not a long,
lingering death either. One day the trucks just quit coming. Within a week the stores began to look like a poorly
stocked rummage sale. There was another side effect.
Wal-Mart was the largest U.S. employer. Once you had
that pointed out—and you realized the company *made*
nothing—you began to grasp how truly insane things
were and the scale of what we had let happen. Of course,
by the time people figured it out, it was far too late.

## CHAPTER ELEVEN

# PEACEKEEPER

My world, which was a tiny, insignificant piece of the big world, was rapidly changing. The government had created four zones for the metro D.C. area: Zone One was the Mall area; Zone Two was the rest of D.C., except for Georgetown and most of the NW portion of the city, which were considered Zone One; Zone Three was Maryland inside the Beltway; and Zone Four was Virginia inside the Beltway. We were outside the Beltway, barely, so we became a border town.

This had both its advantages and its drawbacks. Some days you would see the good and the bad of our location in a single day, like today. I was sitting under a big oak tree. It was two blocks south of the shelter that bordered the market parking lot. From here, my seat gave me a nice view of the shelter entrance and the market across the parking lot. Under the oak tree there were a couple of chairs, a board balanced on cinder blocks, and a La-Z-Boy recliner with a broken handle. The market was mostly folding tables set up under the overhang of an empty strip mall. Sometimes it was busy; most times it wasn't. I sat there, my back to the oak, watching a whole lot of nothing pass by.

Max and an old man named Aly, who said he'd been a department manager at the Home Depot in Seven Corners, were keeping me company. Max had me wearing a real gun. I had shot about a thousand rounds through it and had practiced dry-firing draws until my arm felt like it was going to fall off. I didn't like wearing a handgun: It was heavy, awkward to wear, and attention getting. Max told me I would get so used to it that eventually I would notice the weight only when it was gone. He turned out to be right. He had told me a couple months ago, "From here on in we are going to be seeing a lot of firearms; you carrying a bayonet to a gunfight is not really a good idea." I liked steel, but what he said made sense. Plus, I could always carry both. I was carrying a Ruger Vaquero in a nice leather holster and belt. Max had gone as close to ballistic as I had ever seen him when I came back with that.

"What the hell is that? I told you to go see Sarge, pick out a gun you felt comfortable with, and see how much ammo he would let you walk away with. I expected, oh, I don't know, something useful. Not a freaking cowboy gun from a hundred years ago!"

That last part he blasted at me at maximum volume. His face had turned red, and a vein was standing out on his neck. I was rather impressed with how riled up I had made him. "This has got to be Sarge's sick freaking idea of a joke," he continued. "Well, gimme the gun, and I will go find Sarge and exchange it." The way he came down on the word *exchange* made me pretty sure what he really meant was he was going to find Sarge, stuff the gun up his ass, and pull the trigger. He had his hand out, waiting for me to hand over my gun.

"No," I said. We both stood there, staring at each other. "I went to the NRA building in Fairfax like you asked me too. I found Sarge, dropped your name, and he took me into the armory. I must have fondled twenty handguns. This is the one I liked."

He stared at me and then said very slowly, "You do realize that weapon"—the word *weapon* was drawled with unmistakable sarcasm—"is a single action?"

"Yes! Isn't it cool?" I proceeded to show him how completely idiot-proof it was. A single-action revolver can't fire unless it is cocked. I demonstrated the cool clicking sound it made as you pulled back the trigger. "Plus, it is really easy to tell when it is loaded. Look at how well it fits in my hand, and it works for me left-handed. I shot it at the range, and Sarge said I was a natural with it. You really ought to think about getting one. After all, that Colt .45 of yours is almost as old."

He looked at me, shook his head, and said, "Okay, tomorrow we go back to the range and you can show me what a 'natural' you are."

We did, and I was. Although when he saw me wearing it I thought he was going to bite his tongue in half to avoid laughing. As if he had any room to laugh—"Mr. Marine" with his "operator" leg holster. I got a lot of stares and the occasional snicker on the street. But before long, people learned that it took a life just as easy as any black plastic, foreign-made, action-movie weapon. Plus, getting hit upside the head with what was essentially a five-inch piece of forged steel was an attention getter by itself.

It was amazing how much the pace of our lives had changed. The frenetic edge was long gone. A day would pass slowly, almost lazily, and then go into turbo overdrive in a matter of seconds. *Snap!* Five minutes later someone would be dead, and time would begin to fall back into place. Slowly, Max was becoming the sheriff of our little area and I got the role of his trusty sidekick. I say *slowly* because Fairfax County police still patrolled the area—not often, not well, but they would come through. They were not happy at seeing anyone carrying openly, but there wasn't a lot they could say. Virginia was still an open-carry state. Plus, Max had a concealed-carry permit and usually found a way to work in his Marine Corps background.

There were a lot of vets working for the county. As we got known, they got friendlier. It helped even more when we became official. Fairfax City had its own police department. We fell within their jurisdiction. The department had been losing officers pretty steadily over the last six months since it couldn't pay them, and they didn't want to work for free. Last week Max and I had gone over to the Fairfax city hall and been sworn in as officers of the law—well, as volunteer auxiliaries at least. Which meant—as far as pay, health care, and retirement benefits—exactly nothing. We did get to wear a uniform when we were active, and we had credentials.

Max had spoken to the mayor and the chief of police privately. He told me about it on the way over there. "Chief Grier and I discussed what our duties were going to be. Officially, we are equivalent to security guards working the night shift at an abandoned Wal-Mart."

"Wow, you really know how to negotiate. I am impressed."

"Oh, I forgot to mention your personal duties to the mayor."

"And that would be . . . ?" I asked cautiously.

"You get to blow him every Thursday." He thought this was pretty funny.

"Gee, I guess you needed a day off to rest those lips."

He quit laughing and changed the subject. "The official part is to cover the city's ass in case someone decides to sue us."

I thought that was pretty funny because "officially" my net worth had a negative sign in front of it the last time I had checked; still, it was probably more than the city of Fairfax was worth and I told Max so.

Max grinned like a shark, "Yeah."

The swearing in was brief. We were introduced to the remaining patrol officers—well, two of them. The third one was asleep, having worked the night shift. We were issued the official city of Fairfax police patches and told we had to buy the rest of the uniform. The good news was that the city was getting free ammo from the feds, plus other goodies that were military issue, like body armor.

The feds, state, and county people would stop and strip you of it if they saw civilians wearing body armor; they hated it. Legally, they had to tolerate civilians carrying weapons, but no way in hell were they going to be put at any more of a disadvantage in a fire fight.

They told us in no uncertain terms that we were to forget about arresting anyone. If we really felt the need to, we had to call the chief or get one of the regular patrol officers to come by and "evaluate the situation." As Chief Grier had told us, "Don't arrest them. County doesn't want them. There is no room and no money for them.

You boys keep the peace, and let us or the feds do the heavy lifting."

"Not a problem," Max had assured the chief. Max had told me before we walked into the building for the swearing in that I was to keep my mouth shut and nod a lot. That was not a problem for me. I didn't have all that much to say anyway.

## CHAPTER TWELVE

# WORKING THE BEAT

So that was how Max and I came to be under the oak tree watching a whole lot of nothing going on. It was our job now. We had worked out our beat, which we walked every day. We patrolled every day from early in the morning until the market closed at sundown. We made sure the merchants, especially the grocery cart vendors, got packed up and down the road safely. We made the rounds of a select handful of functioning businesses in our area. *Select*, because most of the businesses that remained open had made it quite clear they didn't want us. They preferred to rely on the "real police" or they had their own security. The ones we did look in on were expected to kick something back for the service. Usually, it was a meal or something from their diminishing inventories. One of our main jobs was "moving people on." We did a fair amount of that, especially in the first week or so. Most of them were people known to us as general pains in the ass.

The other part of it was dealing with people who had been turned back at the Zone checkpoints due to their IDs not being in order. Since we were on one of the main roads, and a half mile from the border, they would often bounce back into our laps. If they decided to hang around, we would move them on. We had not had a real problem yet with anyone deciding they didn't want to be moved. Max stood up, stretched, and asked me, "Feel like going for a walk?"

"Yeah, sure." I stood up and looked over at Aly. "See you later, big guy." Aly was maybe five foot four.

"Okay, you guys be careful out there," he replied, and laughed. He always said the same thing and he always got the same response from us: nothing, except maybe a grunt. It never stopped him. We started walking over to the market. The sun's heat reflected off the asphalt. The morning sun had warmed up the asphalt of the parking lot enough that it was only just noticeable, not the in-your-face heat that was only hours away from becoming another day's reality.

"You ever think Aly's head is running the same Bollywood movie in an endless loop?"

"No, he's a Muslim from Pakistan. They don't usually watch Bollywood movies," Max replied as he casually scanned the area for anything out of the ordinary.

"Paki? Damn, I always thought he was Indian."

"That's what he wants you to think."

That made perfect sense: Pakistan was about as popular now as Germany was circa 1946. It also made sense why he never went into the Zone. Not only was his ID lacking, there was a good chance he wouldn't be coming back.

The parking lot was still used as parking for cars. There were never a lot of them, but people were still driving, just not as much as they had before. Gas had not come down a lot after Tel Aviv and the Israeli retaliation. It probably never would. The government was talking about another stiff gas tax to fund "green" projects. This wasn't the first government green project. Every administration had them. They never seemed to amount to anything, at least not for anyone I knew

We split, each going to one side of a burned-out BMW whose charred body had filled a parking spot for months now. People coming out of the Zone tried not to drive their high-end automobiles too far from the Zone nowadays. They had a tendency to catch fire. I was never sure what bothered Zone people more: the realization their car was toast or that they were now on foot in the badlands. At first it would be watching their beautiful car—burning. This always drew a crowd. Once they got a look at the faces of the crowd, they usually got past their anguish about their car turning into an insurance claim in front of them rather quickly. Things had gotten ugly a few times when an owner with an inflated ego and zero sense of self-preservation decided to scream obscenities at the crowd. County tried to respond quickly to these calls now. The people who owned the cars usually paid taxes and knew how to complain—or their next-of-kin did. Because when someone from the Zone started screaming at a non-Zone crowd about their burning car, it usually ended with that person burning along with it.

We almost always started on the end of the block that the stores were on and then worked our way down. The market was built around a small, abandoned strip mall. Every store in it was gone, except for the Dollar Store. It was still run by the same Korean family, although the mall no longer had power other than what was sometimes provided with generators by the market sellers. Most of the store windows were boarded up. They had been covered with graffiti thirty minutes after the work crew had put them up and climbed back into their truck to go to their next stop. They were still covered with crap, except for a few that had been painted over in the last couple months. These now advertised the name of the seller who set up shop in front of them during the day. Instead of just using words, they painted symbols and words. The area was ethnically diverse—a little United Nations, with more than a few people having suspect paperwork.

The white couple that had a connection in the Shenandoah Valley orchards featured a nice picture of an apple. The Korean woman who repaired clothes had a sewing machine painted on her plywood. Many folks, including me, only vaguely understood what she was getting at when it first went up. Nobody used the actual storefronts; they stunk inside. All it took was one asshole peeing on the drywall to make it unusable, and the lack of electricity didn't help. Also, no one wanted to store anything in there—if it didn't get stolen that night, there was always the fear that the "owner" would come back and claim it.

Sometimes, a working girl or boy would use one of the nicer ones for quick tricks.

We discouraged that. It drew the wrong kind of people, whom we had defined without talking about it as strangers, strangers being anyone who wasn't a local and whose face we didn't see on a regular basis. It wasn't like there weren't plenty of other abandoned buildings they could use. A red-light district of sorts was springing up down the road from us in the old Northern Virginia Real Estate Association building. Yes, the inevitable jokes sprang up.

Max and I both knew there was a grain of truth in them. When the hookers were seen showing up for work in their minivans with the "I'm a Realtor" license plate frames still attached, well, that was a bit obvious. Since it was in city jurisdiction and never bothered, we figured the kickback was feeding the patrol officer's families.

We walked, stopped, and chatted with each stall owner. Usually, it was just a "Hi, everything okay?" and Max would chat them up while I did a quick walk-through of the empty store behind them. We were going to need to do a cleanup in these someday. Often I would have to remind someone not to use the back as a urinal, or at the very least to set aside some plastic buckets for it.

It didn't pass unnoticed that I was doing most of the work as we did our rounds so I asked Max, "How come I got to do this and you get to do the chitchatting?"

His reply? "Because I know what I am doing, and you don't."

That was kind of hard to argue with.

I was in the back of the store behind the Apple Couple when I heard car doors slamming and a male voice yelling something I couldn't quite hear. I drew my pistol and headed back to the store entrance. I held the gun straight up beside my head and thumbed the hammer down, listening to that beautiful clicking sound. I paused at the door, standing to one side. It was a good thing that I did. Apple Couple would have knocked me down if I had been standing in it. They came busting through it, faces frightened, the man pushing his woman, telling her, "To the back! To the back!" As they went, he struggled to dig a handgun from his pocket. The hammer spur had snagged on the fabric of his pants, and his haste and fear were not helping him.

"Stay here!" I hissed at him—the asshole had scared the crap out of me busting through the door like that. "Hey, look at me!" I put my hand on his shoulder. "Calm down. Talk to me: Where and who?"

"Three guys—they are robbing everyone!"

"Where?"

"The Dollar Store."

"Deep breaths, okay?" I looked at him.

He nodded. "I'm okay."

"Good, go look after your woman." *All right: Think and go*, I told myself.

The Dollar Store was in the center of the strip. I was two stores down. Usually, by now, Max would be at the last store, which was really just a guy with a table. He did leather repair, and I was thinking about having him make me a cartridge belt. Max liked talking to him. Leather Man was a former marine who had done his time in Vietnam. He was old.

He also liked to spit—big nasty lungers, too—which was why he was at the end.

I changed sides and eased a bit out the door. I could hear a bunch of hollering to my right; it sounded like Korean. I could see a young Asian male standing by a yellow Honda Civic in the parking lot. They had pulled directly in front of the Dollar Store. He had some kind of assault rifle, kind of cool looking, with a wooden stock. A remote part of my brain approved of his choice: no plastic crap. Another man was standing about three feet in front of the door to the Dollar Store. Both men were focused on what was happening inside. I didn't know where Max was, but I wasn't worried about it. I knew he would be in the right place at the right time. I heard a woman scream and I stepped out the door.

Stepping out that first second was like what I imagined stepping into space as a skydiver would be, or getting up to speak in front of thousands of people: a lightness that wasn't disturbing. Actually, it was pleasant. I liked it. I walked toward the door to the Dollar Store. My movement caught the eye of the man with the assault rifle, and he went into motion, shouldering his weapon. The boom of Max's Colt was unmistakable. The rifleman's eyes widened. He jerked forward and began to fall, propelled even faster by the second boom. The other man reacted to the sound of Max's gunfire, turning to his friend. For a precious second he processed that his friend had been shot and that another man was walking toward him with a pistol. He turned to me, his face contorting into a grimace as he realized that he was going to be too late. He was right: I shot him twice in the chest, then once in the head, just as I had been taught, drilling again and again on cardboard silhouettes. It sounds like overkill, but Max explained to me that we were not the only people wearing vests.

My peripheral vision caught Max's movement as he approached the man he had shot by the Honda. That is when the guy in the Dollar Store decided it was time to go. He came out the door holding as hostage the elderly Korean man who worked there.

*Damn, this is turning out to be like a bad TV show*, I thought.

Then it got worse: Max decided to be a hostage negotiator. Somehow I doubt he had learned that in the

Marines. He told the hostage taker, "Okay, man, we can work this out. Let him go, and we will let you go. Let's make this easy."

"Fuck you! Get away from my car!"

"Okay, okay. Chill." Max started backing up, away from the car.

"You! . . . You too. You back up!" This was directed at me.

I estimated the range and the probability of blowing his head off. The odds were pretty good that I could do this. Then again, if I missed or the old man twitched at the wrong time—well, it would be sloppy. But so what. I never liked him all that much anyway. I blew the side of the hostage taker's head off. Max was moving toward him as the old man fell to his knees babbling. Hostage Taker dropped like a puppet with its strings cut. *Well, that was easy.* Mama-san came rushing out the door to cradle the old man.

Max walked up to me, touching my shoulder briefly, "You okay?"

"Yeah. You?" He nodded.

"I guess we are going to have to clean up this mess." It was more like time to hide the mess, not that there were a whole lot of people who cared.

"I knew you would take the shot."

"How's that, Max?"

"Did you really care if it worked or not?"

I wasn't going to lie; why bother, I knew he already knew. "No."

I went over to collect my share. The rule was, if you killed them, you got their weapons, plus any personal belongings of value. Max was right: I didn't give a damn, never had. With Max, it was a relief not to have to pretend. He also knew I didn't care for the old man.

I had come by the Dollar Store looking for a donation from them to show their support of the local police force. The old man had given me a battery-powered nose- and ear-hair remover. At first I thought he was telling me I was missing something in my daily grooming. I went back to my room, and spent some time peering into the mirror. Nope, all clear. I decided what the hell, I would try it anyways. It worked for about two seconds, then it broke. I was not happy.

I told Max about it the next day. "He gave you what?" and then began laughing his ass off.

"What?" A dim light went off in my head. "What did you get?" He just laughed more. He never did tell me.

One of the things that some people—especially older folks who had lived well for so long—had a problem adapting to was how raw life could be. Nasty was how women usually described it; men, well, we just pretended it was nothing. Some of us actually believed that, although a lot depended on your age and how you had come up.

Life was messy now and getting messier, like this. Violence in real life was not like a video game, TV, or the movies. It was infinitely more real. It smelled, and the smell was never good. Left to ripen, a human being became incredibly fetid. It was a stink that got into your nose, into your clothes, and into your mind—and it never left.

Messy also described the way many of us were eating. Chickens were bought live, then killed, and gutted. Squirrels, dogs, cats—they all had to go from recognizable animal to dead meat. There wasn't a lot of money available to be spent on professionally chopped and wrapped meat anymore. Then what you got had to be transformed back into something that was palatable. Well, sometimes it was palatable. This, I figure, is why they made hot sauce. A little Tabasco made anything edible as far as I was concerned. Then there was the problem of disposing of all the fluids and inedible parts. It took water to clean up, and you needed to dump it all somewhere where you knew it would go away soon. Back then people didn't know about composting. Everything was still supposed to be magic. You put it in a trash can, and the trash fairy came and got it—until they quit coming because no one was paying them.

Just like these bodies: In the movies a bunch of blinking, flashing lights would show up. The bodies would be dumped onto gurneys and then—after sitting somewhere and being identified or not—they would go into the ground, usually first being run through a crematorium. If they were unclaimed or the families were too poor, well, an urn's worth of ashes would be buried in a hole at the county's potter's field off of Germantown Road. A lot of paperwork would be generated; Max and I would need lawyers—it would be a big deal.

That was the old way. Now no one in power really cared all that much, especially if the people involved were poor or, like these guys, just out-of-area losers. No ID in the pockets or wallets. Max's guy by the car had a Costco card that was expired. None of them had Zone IDs—no surprise there. Not a lot of cash either. Mama-san had brought out a wet cloth to wipe off the old man, who had been spattered a bit. He grabbed the cloth from her angrily and finished cleaning himself. He missed a few places, I noticed—not that I was going to point them out.

The old man was showing with angry body language and bursts of Korean that he was not happy that I had shot the hostage taker while he was being held. I hid a smile in a cough behind my hand.

They had a cat that lived in the Dollar Store. Sometimes I would see him sitting in the old lady's lap as she listened to her Korean radio station. The cat had come out to see what was going on. He brushed against Max's leg, sniffed at the blood, and began to lap it up with delicate little cat licks. Mama-san got all excited, picked it up, smacked it lightly, and grinned embarrassingly at us before disappearing back into the store. We had started to gather a crowd.

Leather Man was telling everyone in listening range how Max had taken them out. The Apple Couple were adding their little bits of color. I looked around. Nobody had whipped out a cell phone to make calls or take pictures. If they had tried—well, they wouldn't. We weren't looking for our fifteen minutes of fame. No money in it anymore, just trouble.

Max came over to me. "There's more here than meets the eye. They targeted the old man. I asked him how he wanted to handle it. He said he would make a call. We are going to drag the bodies into the empty store next door. The Korean Business Association is going to take care of the bodies."

I guffawed. "They aren't going to make barbecue out of them?"

"You eat Korean barbecue?"

"I did once, Max, that was enough, and kimchi is disgusting."

"So then, what's the problem?"

Max was right. The reality was they would probably end up in a hole somewhere—or as koi food. "I also called the chief. He wants the AK since I told him there was less than thirty dollars between all three of them."

"That's your weapon," I protested.

Max waved his hand dismissively. "I'm okay with it." Not much I could say to that. "You can have the one by the door's gun if you want."

"Okay."

It was over except for dragging the bodies into the store. Mama-san had come out with a bucket, a brush, and a dustpan. She was splashing the water on the blood pools. The chunky parts would be swept up. The guy had come in by front door. Now what was left of him would be going out the back door. I checked out the gun from the door guy: It was an older-looking, chrome-finish Taurus 9 mm. I'd have to ask Sarge what I could get for it.

## CHAPTER THIRTEEN

# MARKED

Max had a cell phone but I didn't. I realized a while back that I didn't need one. I had no one to call. The time I was spending online was dropping—real life was now far more interesting. Plus, I was mad at the Internet. Yeah, I know how silly that sounds but it was still true. Virtual friends I had known for years turned out to be worthless. When I needed them, they were there. The problem was where *there* was: inside a computer—nice, but essentially worthless. Even stuffed animals would have been more useful. At least they would have been huggable.

The entire Internet experience had begun to seem like nothing more than a dream. Much of the time I had spent in it was already forgotten. So much of my time had been wasted there. What I did remember were short fragments, all of little or no substance. Life wasn't always about killing people online or offline. This was probably a good thing. Eventually, you would run out of them, and then who would you have to talk to? Or kill, when the need arose? That would be pretty damn boring—not that it was going to happen anytime soon.

I guess it was my attitude that made Max decide to pull me aside a few days after the Dollar Store shooting. He was a little uncomfortable talking to me about it. I can always tell when someone is dancing around what they want to say. He was dancing.

"Look, Max, just tell me," I finally said, since it was getting kind of irritating.

"Well, look, it's like this—the killing thing. I know . . . I mean . . . well, don't get to liking it. You go down that road and you're not going to like what you find."

I just stared at him. He looked me in the eye and shook his head. "You know about me. You know where I've been." I nodded. "I saw guys like you in the Corps. You get to liking it—the power, the reaching out and snatching a life or three. I was like that; maybe I still am a bit. I never really figured it all out."

He was looking away from me now . . . far away. I don't know whether it was inside himself or out under a hot sun in a place where so many others had died.

"I had my sarge take me for a walk. Wasn't far—you couldn't go far there. All that space, and we could only use a tiny piece at a time. That's when he told me this." Max closed his eyes and recited:

"Some men are born to a love of violence; others acquire a taste for it. In wartime many consider it a tool to be put aside once victory has been achieved. Nevertheless, all of those who have experienced it will find they remain marked by it until death. For those of us born to it, only a few will realize that it is a gift that must be contained, hidden, and controlled, for otherwise it will destroy us. Like fire, all it knows is that it must burn. Who and what it consumes in the process means nothing to it."

He told me that his sarge had learned it from an old German back when he was a private and stationed there. He never said one way or the other, but my guess was the German had served in World War II. "What I am saying is, don't let it burn you out."

I sat there for a minute and then said, "Well, Max, that was some profound shit. Thank you for sharing that with me." Then I grinned at him.

"You're an asshole, Gardener. I don't know why I freaking bother." He was smiling as he said it. I knew what he was trying to do. I didn't really understand it, but it was cool. We had our little moment and then it was back to reality. "We got a job tomorrow."

"Really? Anything good?" I doubted it, but you had to ask.

"Yeah, it isn't that bad. The chief wants us to go over to the Forest Meadow development. You know which one I mean?"

I did. It was a development of brick "executive manors" that had once sold for $1.4 million apiece. They had only built out about half the development before the Crash. When the builder went bankrupt there were about ten houses built; nine of them were empty last time I biked through there on the way to somewhere else.

"Yeah, is that the teardown?"

"Yeah, we need to go through one last time. I guess they're expecting some brass to show up for the bulldozing. Supposedly, the sheriff's department went through and cleaned the last one out. We just got to make sure no one's moved back in since."

I had read about it and heard the talk. The federal government was giving out money so "excess housing" could be torn down. It would create a few jobs, and the local municipality would get the land once it was cleaned up. Supposedly, a park was going to be built, but I doubted it. There was no money. That is, unless a vacant field fit the description of a park, which it probably did. Word was, the city was going to sit on it until the economy came back, then sell it to a builder.

*Good luck with that*, I thought. We made plans to meet at 0800 hours over at Forest Meadows. A couple of the city patrol officers were going to show up to help. We parted ways, and I went back to my room to eat some soup and get some sleep.

## CHAPTER FOURTEEN

# BARBIE

I was there the next morning at 0745. Max was already there waiting. It was a beautiful morning—cool, with a nice light breeze out of the east. We sat on a pile of bricks, kicked our heels, and talked about nothing until the city patrol officers rolled in around 0815. I won the bet. Max had figured on 0830 for their arrival; I had taken 0815 or earlier. He was buying lunch next time. I heard him mutter, "What the hell? Was the coffee place out of bagels again?" I laughed.

We did our greetings, spending about ten minutes doing it until Willis—he was the sarge—said "Well, might as well get this over with. You two take this side of the road; me and Robbie will take the other. Shouldn't be nothing to it—oh, and don't get lazy on me either. Check downstairs and upstairs. We don't want anybody getting run over by a dozer in front of the suits."

"Yeah, yeah, we got it covered," Max told him over his shoulder as we walked away.

"How we going to get in, Max?" I hadn't seen any keys change hands.

"No problem—no doors." He was right: Most were missing their doors, and if it wasn't a door, it was a window.

"Hard to believe they got more than a million dollars for these." I had never been in a house that cost that much when they were actually functional.

"Yeah, well, it doesn't look like they did," Max replied.

We started checking them. Max would go in through the back and check the basement and garage. I checked the first and top floor. Usually, there was more than one staircase to the main floor, which is where we would meet. There was a lot of space in these houses. My room was about the size of a bedroom closet in these places. They must have been nice once, but not anymore. They had been hit by waves of destruction.

The first wave came with the owners' departure. Some owners, not all, had gutted them of the appliances. Others, perhaps harder up for cash, went for everything else of value. Carpet would be ripped up, wood flooring would be pried up. Craigslist was a good place to get a deal on cabinets and vanities or flooring back then. The second place we checked was missing all the light switch covers. Sometimes the owners would do malicious damage; sometimes not.

Then the second wave would come through: the scavengers. If the owners left the appliances and everything else intact, well, that was a great day in a scavenger's life. They went for copper wiring and pipes. The way they harvested it was hard on the drywall. They were like giant rats gnawing through it to rip out what they came for. The neat ones used a knife; the others just punched a hole and began ripping.

The third wave was squatters and kids. They built fires and crapped where they felt like it. After all, there were plenty of houses to move to when the stench got too bad or they were moved along. They never left anything the way they found it. Windows would be left open, and rain would soak everything—eventually the mold would take over. Animals—especially raccoons and squirrels—would come in, take a look around, and build nests. Which reminded me: I needed to keep an eye out for wasps. They loved these empty houses, too.

We were on the fourth house—this one had an intact entry—when she pulled up. Max had just gone around the back. I heard the car and quit kicking the front door in. It was a Volvo that had seen better days. I walked down the driveway toward the car when she stepped out. She was one of the "hard to tells." That's what I called them, because it was hard to tell their age. Whatever your first guess was, you usually ended up adding twenty years to it.

She was pretty from a distance—they always are— blonde, almost slim, with a nice rack of silicone. I don't know a lot about women's clothes, but hers fit nicely and looked expensive. Back when I worked for the mortgage company, a lot of the female brokers looked like her. Well, the new ones usually didn't, but after they worked there for a few months they would begin the transformation. First they did the hair, then the breasts, followed by the face, ass, stomach, wherever. The clothes would get more expensive, tighter, more revealing. Their attitude would also change. They became "broker bitches." Simple tech support guys no longer had a chance with them. We couldn't afford them. If you caught one early, well, you had until a couple months after the transformation began. Then you would get dumped. After all, a girl needs her space. Oh, occasionally they might forget, like at an office party, but the next day it was as if it never happened.

So as I watched her approach, I was not radiating awestruck appreciation of the goddess who would be soon was standing in front of me. She pushed her sunglasses up onto her head, hesitated, and then gave me the smile—she had a great smile. "Hello, officer. I thought I would come by and see my house before they blew it up or whatever it is that you people do."

"Ah, we bulldoze it . . . well, I don't. I was just checking to make sure it was empty."

"Really," she drawled this out, "I saw you knocking on my front door. Perhaps these will help?" She held up a set of house keys.

"Well, there is only one way to find out." I took them from her hand, and we walked to the front door.

"I was so hoping I would be able to look inside once more. I really loved this house."

I slid the key into the lock. It fit, as did the dead bolt key. "You had one strong door there, ma'am."

"Oh, please, call me Tiffany."

"Okay, Tiffany," I held the door open for her.

As she went through she told me, "Yes, it's not an ordinary door. It's is teak and it was handcrafted especially for—" She stopped dead "Oh . . . my . . . God." I had no idea what the house looked like before, but I am sure it didn't look the way it did now. It was nothing new or particularly shocking to me. It was to her. "Oh, my lord. What the . . . " her voice trailed off. The foyer floor had been tiled with ceramic; most of it was now shattered.

The floor in the great room had a large burnt spot where someone had built a campfire. The fireplace pit was full of trash. The walls had been tagged with profanity and a poorly done outline of a giant black penis that had been labeled Obama. Yep, nothing new or unusual here. "My floor . . . oh, my God, my Italian ceramic floor! . . . And my mahogany floor, too"—she had noticed the fire scars. "My walls . . ." Her hand was over her mouth, her eyes were large; she was slowly spinning in place as she took it all in. "It was so beautiful, it was so beautiful. . . ."

After a moment, in a quiet voice she asked me, "Is it all like this?"

"I don't know. My guess is yes."

"Oh,"—a pause—"will you show me the rest?"

"Sure. Except we're going to skip the basement. It might be dangerous." She nodded in agreement. The real reason was, I didn't feel like running into Max and having to explain—or share.

We walked the kitchen and dining area; all the appliances were gone. "They took my Vikings!" Whatever those were, their being taken had her sounding irritated for the first time, rather than stunned as she had been. She rattled on about her Natuzzi sofa and how her idiot husband had tried to mount the flat screen over the fireplace. The brackets had come loose, and the TV had ended up broken on the floor. Apparently, that had really been a big deal at the time.

She took my arm as we mounted the stairs; mounting was on my mind as I looked over at her. She gave me a little smile when she saw me looking. So what if it was past its prime? It had been a while. We made it to the top without incident and began touring the upper-level bedrooms. Once again it was endless decorating chatter—I would interject a sincere sounding "Really?" or a nod of the head if she was looking and a "That sounds really pretty." Meanwhile, I was trying to figure out where we could make it happen. Everything was dirty. That wouldn't bother me, especially as I wouldn't be on the bottom, but I was pretty sure it would matter to her. She looked like that type. We had just come out of the master suite, where she had spent what seemed like an eternity describing the master bath and the twin, cedar-lined walk-in closets.

She was looking around the room. "And that was where our king-sized bed was—Donny liked it. He told me that we would have plenty of room for playing—shit, the only thing he did in it was play possum. Even Viagra couldn't get a rise out of him."

As she finished spitting this out, the sun came out from behind the clouds and flooded the room with light. Not only did it illuminate the room, it illuminated her. I normally wouldn't have cared. I had already seen her in the sunlight.

This time, the look on her face as she spat out her disdain of her husband's sexual prowess, combined with the harshness of the sunlight on her face, was as effective as a cold bucket of water. The vicious glint of hate in her eyes, the artificiality of her body, of her soul, her mindless recitation of items purchased—it all repelled me.

An image of my last trip to a thrift store: a bin filled with old toys—on top, a naked Barbie, the dirt on it looking like bruises, the hair damaged by some kind of chemical, the body twisted. That was the woman in front of me. A cold chill ran down my back. The look of expectant pleasure replacing the glint in her eyes was frightening in its intensity. I had a vision of her reaching out, taking me in her arms, and devouring me like a fresh-baked cookie. When she was done she would leave. The only thing left behind to show I had ever been here would be my rapidly dimming shadow and a hair ball.

"Okay. Time to go." I didn't even touch her. I just headed for the stairs. I think I heard a faintly muttered "Shit" behind me, before the sound of her heels let me know she was following. We left the same way we came in. I was surprised that Max wasn't waiting there.

We were out the door and I was about six feet down the walk when she called out to me, "Wait! We have to lock the front door!"

I still had the house keys. I tossed them to her. "You can if you want. That door won't be there in four hours."

I think that's when she understood: It was over. Wherever she was going now was just another step on the way down. No more everything, no more forever. I turned away and kept walking over the remains of the grass to the next house. I didn't turn around when I heard the Volvo engine start up.

## CHAPTER FIFTEEN

# DIVISIONS

Max was sitting on the top step waiting for me. He eyed me, grinned, and said, "I guess it didn't work out—or it has been a long time since the last time."

"Fuck you, Max."

"Ah, no score; I should have known." He laughed. "Let's finish this up. I want to be out of here before the suits shows up. I don't want to end up getting stuck here doing security until they leave." We finished up a little behind the city patrol boys working the other side. They were waiting for us.

Willis, the patrol sergeant, asked, "You boys see anything?"

Max and I both shook our heads. "Same old, same old," Max told him.

"So you boys want to hang around, maybe pick up some OT?" We all laughed at that—we were volunteers, so we didn't get paid.

"Maybe next time, Sarge." We spent a few more minutes talking the usual bullshit and then parted ways.

The first cars were beginning to roll in as we walked through the tall, patchy, gone-to-seed grass of what were once manicured yards. Max and I walked and talked about nothing in particular: Some woman he had been seeing was pushing him to move in; whether or not we wanted to play softball for the city municipal team. It looked as if we were going to have to, even if we didn't want to. The only way out would be if they canceled the season, which was looking possible. We split near the market and went our separate ways for the day. I thought I would cruise the market, go down the street, get something to eat, and head back to the room—maybe see if Night wanted to watch a movie or something. I had found out from one of the ninjas that she was older than I thought, which made me feel less like a pervert about hanging out with her.

I was still shaken up a bit from my encounter with the American harpy. Maybe I would just sit under the oak tree and talk with whoever was there or wandered by. Hopefully, it would be quiet. Some of the problems that were brought to us were so fucking petty that you wanted to shoot both parties involved. We were hearing more problems lately. People seemed more quarrelsome. Either that or we were just a lot easier and faster than getting enmeshed in the county legal system. We were definitely a lot cheaper. Official justice was an option increasingly available only to those with money. The courthouse charged for everything. Even a simple complaint could be very expensive to someone who had nothing. It wasn't that the county fees had gone up; rather it was that so many people's incomes had gone down.

Some people, especially media types, pontificated about how Americans would grow closer despite our diversity. Usually, it was a white person doing the talking. Their idea of diversity was based on what they observed at work. It never occurred to them that the reason a company had such diversity in its lower ranks was because it paid the lowest salary or wage it could. They also seemed totally unaware that those same people knew to the dollar what kind of bonuses their "betters" were getting. Too many people in positions of power in this country mistook ass-kissing for actual affection.

I was walking past the shelter and heading for the oak tree when Tito, the security guard at the shelter, waved me over. "Hey, you got to go in there and see what's happening on TV." He was watching it through the window. I walked up and stood next to him so I could see. There was a group of people watching it inside. It looked like there was a riot somewhere that was getting seriously out of hand.

"Ain't that some shit! Where is it?" I was expecting him to say Los Angeles or Miami from the complexions of the rioters.

He laughed. "That's Arlington."

*Damn.* Arlington was about eight miles down the road. What made it even more surprising was that it was inside the Zone. I thought security was too tight inside to let anything more than an argument break out.

"Thanks, Tito. I got to check this shit out." I walked in and paused behind the crowd of women who were gathered in a tight knot, raptly watching the big flat screen. The few who had cell phones were off to one side getting more information from friends and family about what was happening.

The shelter only housed women and children. It had been at capacity since the day it opened. Carol was standing to one side with her staff so I went over to join them.

"Hey, Carol."

She looked up at me and smiled. "Hey."

"What's happening? Who set them off?

She whispered to me without taking her eyes off the screen. "You know the Safeway on Wilson Boulevard?" I nodded—it was the only grocery store left in that part of the Zone. All the mom-and-pop ethnic ones failed for one reason or another in the past year or so. A lot of people thought it was part of a conspiracy to make the populace dependent on one easily managed location. I thought too many people had way too much time on their hands when I heard the theory. "Well, a Latino woman—I know her sister, Rosario—she was caught by security for stealing food," Carol said. "Anyways, she made a run for the door and made it. She was running through the parking lot—store security was just yelling at her—when some guys from Homeland Security pulled up. They saw her running and heard security yelling, so they started yelling. She didn't stop, so they shot her. Then someone in the crowd started shooting at them, but one of the officers managed to shoot a couple bystanders, including a pregnant woman, before they went down."

"Jesus," I shook my head. The rules were: If you made it out the door of a grocery store and off store property, then you were home free. The security guards knew why people were stealing food. They also knew they had to go home after their shift. They never put any effort into it once people made it out the door.

That part of Arlington was packed. A lot of people were afraid to leave the Zone because they knew they wouldn't be able to get back in. It had been a hot area during the real-estate boom, but that was long past. A lot of Hispanic families lived there, two extended families to one small 1950s red-brick house. Work was hard to come by, especially for the males. Many people spent the day and night standing around outside in that area. Usually, there was a group by the Safeway parking lot. Most of them were angry about something, and if they weren't angry, they were probably high or drunk. There were also some hard-core gangs around there. Yeah, this was going to be interesting.

What made it even "better" was that the Homeland Security patrol had been white. They needed only one more thing to make this really flammable: a video of them shouting racial slurs as they shot the women. It turned out they didn't need it. Arlington County police were the first responders. They were generally good, professional officers who were not known to reach for the baton or gun without being provoked. Homeland Security also responded. The name Homeland Security was really an umbrella covering a lot of agencies. The officers who were now lying dead or wounded on the asphalt belonged to one, the Federal Protective Service. Their original job of building security had been changed to providing security in the Zones. The local police hated them. Government agencies like the FBI, DEA, and the U.S. marshals looked down on them as wannabes who couldn't get into a real agency. They liked kicking ass. They thought the Zones were war zones, not special security zones. They had managed to alienate everyone they'd come in contact with, in an amazingly short time.

They responded in force; Arlington County police almost had things under control when four FPS vehicles arrived and disgorged four officers apiece. The crowd saw them and everything amped back up. Meanwhile, the crowd of TV watchers at the shelter was growing restive. One of the Hispanic women—Maria I think—shouted at the screen, "Kill the white motherfuckers!" Since the residents in the shelter were white, black, Hispanic, and other, someone was bound to find that offensive. Somebody did.

It was a woman I mentally called "Fat Ass Annie." Annie was three hundred pounds of lard stiffened with peanut brittle, stuffed into pants that were so tight that you could see the cottage cheese ripples on her ass. She was bleach blonde and bellicose. My guess is she was born in a double wide and had ascended for a brief, shining moment to a tract home in Manassas Park before life cruelly deprived her of what was rightfully hers. Then she washed up on the shore of the shelter—another American whale brought down by the harpoon of adjustable-rate mortgages. "What the fuck do you mean 'Kill the white motherfuckers,' Maria? It's your goddamn fault that the country is so fucking messed up!" Like an oil tanker in a crowded harbor, Annie was steaming toward the diminutive Maria. The crowd moved out of her way, some with grins of anticipation at the show that was just seconds away from starting. Others, depending on their race, were nodding in agreement with Fat Ass Annie. Some were changing positions in the crowd, getting ready to come to Maria's aid.

"You goddamn lying Mexicans bought them houses with your liar loans and then walked away! That's why the economy sucks! That and you took all the good jobs from real Americans. Now you won't fucking go home!"

Normally Carol and her staff would have been on this like white on rice, defusing the situation before it got out of control. I looked at them: Like the residents, they were a mixed bunch. Carol's main enforcer was Theresa. She was obviously struggling with mixed emotions. Tito was still outside, looking in. I could feel the rage and ugliness, like an electrical current, shoot from person to person—feeding on each contact and growing in strength.

Maria and Fat Ass Annie were face-to-face now. The room, which previously had not been divided by race, was rapidly rearranging itself. *Shit*, I thought, *looks like it's me*. I pushed my way over to where the two women were screaming at each other. Annie was spraying spittle everywhere—I have always found that attractive in a woman. Maria was waving her hands, screaming back. I stepped up and put my face in the midst of them.

"Both of you, shut up—now!"

"Fuck you, Gardener!" Fat Ass Annie replied.

*Ah, thank you, God,* I thought. I had been hoping she would be the one to push it. "Annie, listen to me carefully. If you don't shut up right now, I am going to take my Ruger out of my holster and jam the muzzle so far down your mouth that I will be scraping your hemorrhoids off the barrel. Do you understand me?"

She opened her mouth. My hand, which had been resting on the butt of the holstered Ruger, moved down so I could grip it better. I began pulling it out of the holster as I whispered, "Say something, Annie . . . anything." The anger went out of her face like a candle flame extinguished by a cold breeze. I felt a hand gently brush my arm.

"Hey, it's okay. Back off, please." It was Carol, probably the only one in the world who could have done what she just did.

The screens went blank. Someone, probably Theresa, had cut the power to them. "C'mon. Let's go outside." I let her guide me out the door. I couldn't take my eyes off Fat Ass Annie. She hadn't moved. She just stood there, rooted, and then she burst out crying, and then moved on to full-out wailing. Tito had moved inside, probably when he had seen them go face-to-face. Alone outside, Carol and I stood there for a minute, looking at each other. Then she stepped closer, reached up, and hugged me. For a brief second I buried my face in her shoulder and hair. She smelled good, like fresh bread with a trace of shampoo and old cigarettes. She let go before I did and stepped back. "Thanks." She smiled, turned, and was gone. I sighed. I stood there for too long, turned around, and walked through the gathering darkness toward my empty room.

## CHAPTER SIXTEEN

# AN INVITATION

I woke up the next morning to find Max sitting in my one and only chair, just sitting there, staring out into space. "You know, one day I am going to catch you slipping in here, and I am going to squash you like a bug."

"That is as about as likely to happen as me slipping in here and finding you sleeping double."

"Asshole." I swung out of the bed, pulled a semifresh pair of pants off the floor, and slid into them. "So why am I honored with your presence this early in the morning?"

Instead of answering he reached into his backpack, which was at his feet, and pulled out a silver Thermos. "You want some coffee?"

"That sounds good." I found a cup that didn't have anything crusty in it and handed it to him. He popped the Thermos and the smell of coffee flooded into my room. It smelled real good and real strong. I poured it into the cup and knocked it back. *Damn, it was hot.* I held out the cup, and he poured me another one.

"So what's up?"

"The chief wants to see us bright and early."

"Any idea what his little brain has coughed up?" He had never done this before. We were pretty much left alone. Max tithed him from what we made. If I did anything on the side, I tithed Max, who took care of everything upstream.

"No, but I guess we are going to find out. We're leaving in five." He stood up and scratched himself. "See you in the car."

I dressed, got my gun belt on, threw a couple of bottles of water in my day pack, and followed him out the door. I was surprised: No Camry—instead he had an old Ford F-150.

"Where's the Camry, Max?"

"In the shop, where it has been sitting for the last three weeks waiting for parts. It will probably be there another three weeks too. The guy at the shop told me their whole supply chain is falling apart."

"Damn, I thought you had gotten it fixed. Where did you get the truck?"

"A friend."

I wasn't going to tell him, as he seemed kind of cranky this morning, but I liked the truck better than the Camry.

We walked into the Fairfax City Police Dept. headquarters about twenty minutes later. There was only one car in the parking lot, a silver Lexus. We let ourselves in and walked down the hallway to the chief's office. The door was open, and the chief was sitting behind his desk, staring at something on his computer's flat screen. His feet were propped up on a corner of his desk—he didn't move them.

Without looking away from the screen, he said, "Thanks for coming by, boys. Just give me one more minute." Max and I looked at each other and I rolled my eyes. "I saw that," he said. I just laughed.

The chief dropped his feet to the floor. "Sorry about that. Thanks for coming by, men."

*Uh-oh,* I thought, *we've been promoted from boys to men. This must be some serious shit.*

"Okay, let me be frank with you. I am probably going to ramble a bit, so please bear with me."

We both nodded, and I relaxed my face muscles into my "listening to management with rapt attention" mode—something I had learned in high school and had polished to perfection on all the crappy jobs I had worked since then. I scanned the chief's office while he talked. I had only been in it once. It was what you would expect: an American flag behind his chair; wooden plaques stating what a wonderful cop, man, and Elk he was; a lot of "grip and grin" photos with other white guys.

One picture caught my eye. It was him, much younger and leaner, in some kind of striped fatigues, standing with a couple of guys—one was shirtless. They had a number of AKs on the ground in front of them and a RPG. *That's right, Max had said he was a marine a long time ago.*

I tuned back into his monologue when I heard him say, ". . . and I know I can trust you two with this information." No doubt, this had to be the buildup to whatever pitch he was going to make. I was right.

"One of the advantages of this job is that I get the daily Homeland Security Threat Analysis. I have also been doing this job for a while and have made a few friends here and there." He paused, went for full eye contact and maximum gravity. "Gentlemen, the shit is about to hit the fan in this country. I don't mean cat turds either; I mean elephant-sized ones. Even worse is they are going to keep coming."

He paused here—I knew what he wanted and so did Max. We bobbed our heads in enthusiastic agreement with this strategic analysis from our "general." He liked that—they always do. Too bad it had never gotten me anywhere. He went on and he lost me again. It was the typical refried, right-wing cant: *We had a black man, and it hadn't worked out*. The one that we elected after him had not turned out all that much better. *He was a good man and all, but it was time for us to face the facts*. America as we knew it was going down and it was going to be ugly. . . .

The reasons he listed were not unknown to me. I may have even known more about it than he did. I wasn't going to mention that, especially as he had not mentioned anything about the collapse of the dollar and the Chinese efforts to replace it as the world's reserve currency.

He pulled me back into the flow of his monologue when he said, "So I and other members of the community have made the decision to bug out." I think he was taken aback by my startled expression. "Yes, I know"—here he raised his right hand—"it does not seem very noble, but we also have a duty toward our families and our country. Yes, our country!" He came down hard on this. We must be nearing the end of this grand experiment in democracy. "We will come back, when it is time, and rebuild this great land, which is why I need you two. I need you to run a shipment to where we have begun to build a 'gathering place' in West Virginia. I am also confident that after you see it and listen to the colonel that you will want to join us in this great endeavor. We would be honored to have men of your caliber."

The last part was directly addressed to Max, I noticed. Max stood up. "Sure, chief. Not a problem. Just let us know when and where." I stood up also and began edging toward the door. I was just waiting for Max to wrap it up so we could get the hell out of there.

Then the chief came around his desk, stuck out his hand, and said, "Gardener, you're a good man . . . you don't mind if I talk to Max for a few minutes alone, do you?"

I grinned. "No, not at all, chief, not at all," and I pumped his soft white hand three times, thinking, *You are a fat fucking asshole*. I looked at Max and said, "I'll be out front," and left the office.

I sat around the front office and listened to the phones ring at empty desks. There had to be a door somewhere linking these offices with dispatch, the holding cells, and the locker room somewhere. I wasn't in the mood to look for it. I tried reading one of the *American Police* magazines that were stacked on an empty desk. They were all three years old or more. They were kind of funny and also kind of sad. It seemed so long ago, the world and threats they described. I was just sitting there, reading the posters on the wall for the tenth time when Max walked by me. He didn't even break stride. "Let's go."

*Okay, that must have been an interesting meeting.* When we climbed into his truck, he was still not talking. I knew him well enough by now to know that it was for a reason.

"Did you know the outside of the station was miked?" he asked.

"No."

"I thought it might be. I just wasn't sure until now." He didn't enlighten me as to how he had figured this out. I thought there was more to come, so I just stayed silent.

"Don't be pissed about being left out. He doesn't trust you for a couple of reasons."

"Okay, and they are . . . ?" Jesus, I hope I wasn't going to have to drag everything out of him.

"Well, you're hard-core enough, that's for sure. He just doesn't like that you were never in the Corps, or at least the army."

I interrupted him. "Yeah, well, I was a Boy Scout."

He sighed. "You saw the photo of him? The one when he was in Nam?"

"Yeah?"

"Yeah. He was Force Recon. He probably killed more people in a week than you have so far in your short and pathetic life." I just shrugged. It was ancient history to me. He might have been the man once, but that was the key word, *once*. "He is also worried about your political reliability."

"My what? That has got to be a joke. I don't have any politics to be reliable about."

"Yep. That's what I told him. I also told him you would have been a hell of a marine."

I knew Max well enough to know that he had just paid me a very real compliment. Maybe the highest compliment he knew.

"Thanks, Max." I waited a beat, "And you would have made a fine Boy Scout."

He looked over at me and grinned. "Always the asshole, Gardener, always."

"So what's he want from us?"

"He wants us to deliver a truck—and its cargo—to West Virginia."

"Let me guess, the 'gathering place'?"

Max nodded. "Yep. Been to West Virginia lately?"

"No. I can't say I have been missing it either. So when do we start? What's the pay? What's the cargo and is it just us?"

"We leave in two days from city hall. We each get an ounce of gold for going up, payable upon delivery of the truck. I am not sure what the cargo is going to be, but my guess is weapons and ammo in front, food or supplies in the back by the door. I've got to look at a map and make some calls, but I figure it will be four hours up, unload, return the next day. Not a big deal—oh, and it's just you and me. That answer all your questions?"

"For now, I suppose."

"Where you want me to drop you?"

"My place for now. I'll see you later—say noon at the market?"

We made plans to meet up and do our regular foot patrol of our little section of town. It turned out to be another uneventful day except for the smell of smoke in the air. The riot in Arlington had spread. People were stoning law enforcement vehicles on sight. Spontaneous protests had broken out in D.C. but nothing violent was happening in the main downtown federal zones themselves, at least not yet. Arlington was still crazy: burning cars, burning buildings, and people with a burning desire to whack any FPS officer or vehicle they came across. Someone finally wised up and pulled all uniformed FPS personnel out of the area.

## CHAPTER SEVENTEEN

# NIGHT

I was sitting in my room, staring at my laptop and a copy of Seneca's *Letters from a Stoic*. I was trying to decide which one I wanted to pick up. The book cover was rather unappealing. Seneca looked a lot like the chief. The book itself was interesting and I had already read about twenty pages. One of the changes I had noticed was my ability to concentrate for longer periods of time, once I stopped surfing the net for hours. I wasn't sure if that was a good thing or a bad thing yet. I heard a knock on my door. I didn't recognize it, and it wasn't the pattern the ninjas and I had agreed upon.

I slipped out of bed and pulled my Ruger from the holster. As Max had taught me, I didn't stand in front of the door, instead I stood off to one side. I opened it slowly. It was Night. This was rather surprising. "Hey, Night." I stood aside to let her in.

"Hey, Gardener, I thought I would come and say good-bye."

"Huh? Where am I going?" I was genuinely confused for a minute. She cocked her head one way and her hip the other.

"West Virginia, you big doofus."

"Oh, yeah. How did you know? And if your mom or dad see you coming or going from my room, there is going to be hell to pay—for you," I added pointedly.

"I don't care. I'm over eighteen anyway."

"Fine. But I do; you need to go." And I pointed to the door.

"No, I need to talk." She reached over and dumped everything I had piled in my chair onto the floor and sat down in it.

"You, too." She waved toward the bed. "Sit down. I don't want you standing over me. It's intimidating."

That was funny. "Right, somehow, I don't see you and intimidation in the same sentence, let alone the same room."

"Whatever. Sit."

I sat and I looked at her.

She was sitting there, back perfectly straight, hair gleaming in the light, perfect skin, her hands clasped in her lap. She was also hesitant—very unusual, maybe even the first time for her. She looked away for a minute. If she wanted to study my room and my worldly possessions, then ten seconds would have been more than enough.

"Do you think you are ever going to let go of this thing you have for Carol?"

Well, that was pretty direct and to the point. "I don't have a thing for Carol." She just stared at me. "Okay, Carol is married, happily married. She isn't going anywhere . . . Yeah, I will always have a soft spot for her—"

"You mean your idea of her," Night cut in.

I looked away and sighed. "Night, I don't know what to tell you. I am not a good person. I will never be a good person. If I live past thirty, it will be a miracle . . . and you know what, Night?"

"What?"

"I have a hard time caring. I don't mean about you: I mean about everything and anyone." I shrugged.

She sat there, her eyes unreadable as usual. "Fine. Well, know this: *I* care." Then she stood up abruptly. "I better go."

I stood up and followed her to the door. She surprised me by pausing, the door half-open, turning to me, and pulling my head down to her, kissing me firmly on the lips. She held my head that way for a second, her eyes watching me, and then she turned and left. I shook my head, half-sagged against the door, and thought about how life is always too fucking complicated.

The next morning at 0400 I was outside waiting for Max. I had not slept at all the night before. This way, at least, I was spared waking up to him in my chair. Max pulled in a few minutes later, still in his borrowed truck. He was surprised to see me.

"What the hell you doing up and ready to go?"

I threw my day pack into the truck bed and stepped up into the cab. "Rough night?" He actually sounded concerned.

"No, just wanted to get an early start." He nodded and let it go—thank God.

"Well, good. We can stop and get something to eat if you want."

"I'd rather get some coffee," I told him.

He pulled in at the 29 Diner and I got out, fished my Thermos out of my day pack, and went in. I set it on the counter and asked the waitress to fill it up. The place was empty, but I could smell fresh coffee brewing. She asked me if I could wait a few minutes for it to finish up. I told her, "Sure." She was still staring at me. "Yes?"

"Oh, I'm sorry. You just look familiar."

I looked at her name tag—Courtney—and then I knew her. It had not been all that long since high school. She had been a beauty back then; she wasn't anymore.

"I don't think so. I'm in a bit of a hurry," I told her pointedly.

"Oh, I'm sorry!" She flashed me a yellowed grin. I caught a nice display of the tartar buildup before she went to fill up the Thermos. When she came back, I paid the bill in paper money and tipped her a silver dollar. She was overwhelmed. I could still hear her thanking me as the door shut behind me.

## CHAPTER EIGHTEEN

# A DRIVE THROUGH OLD AMERICA

We pulled into the parking lot of the meeting place. They had changed it: We were picking up the truck at the old Kmart off of Route 29. The parking lot was empty, as was every single store in that strip mall. The Indian food place had hung in there until about seven months ago; then it and the Muslim grocery store had disappeared within days of each other.

The chief was there, along with a guy I had never seen before. He was tall, white, with a military-style haircut, and in good shape, maybe six foot two and two hundred ten pounds. He was either a cop or someone who was not very far from his last active-duty day. He was polite, we were polite, the chief was curt and to the point: "Don't fuck around. Get the job done and come back." He tossed Max the keys and got into the passenger side of the car that was idling next to the truck.

The stranger was good: He managed to walk to the car without completely turning his back to us. I don't think he did it because he was worried about us. I think it was just habit. Max watched him until the car pulled away then swung up into the U-Haul cab. I heard him mutter "Operators" to himself and laugh.

We rolled west on Route 50. It was dark and traffic was nonexistent. Max didn't turn on the radio and I didn't ask him to. Listening to the sound of the truck and road put me to sleep before we reached Chantilly. I woke up about five miles out of Romney, West Virginia.

"You want to pull over in Romney, Max? I really need to piss."

"Yeah, I could use some breakfast and a piss myself."

We rolled through Romney in a few minutes. There was a boarded-up Dairy Queen and a closed Subway. We circled around in an empty lot at the edge of town and pulled into the only open gas station and took care of business.

Max asked if there was any place open where we could get something to eat, and the old woman behind the register gave him directions to the best place in town: Shirley's Diner. It was probably the only place in town. We pulled in and had a pretty decent breakfast there. We still had a long ways to go on Route 50. About ten miles before Parkersburg, we were to head south and the directions would start getting tricky.

"You notice anything different, Max?"

"How so?"

"Everybody is white. When's the last time you stopped in a gas station and a white person worked there?"

"Yeah, I can do you one better."

"Okay, and that would be?"

"We are being followed."

"Interesting—any idea who?"

"Well, they are both white, and I think I recognize one of them. I think the chief doesn't trust us completely."

I didn't even turn around or peer into the side mirror; I impressed myself. "So, you want to find a place to pull over so we can kill them?" I was only partially kidding about that.

"No, I think we will just do what we are being paid to do: Deliver the shipment."

We continued, and I watched a different America appear on both sides of us: an America that thought homes were modular, an America that thought trailers were good starter and finisher homes. Real houses were usually made of wood and usually old, meaning more than forty years at a minimum. Some were brick. I saw a handful of wood houses that were only partly painted, usually a faded white. I figured the lack of paint was an indicator of when the money had run out—a financial high tide that rose only to the first level of the two-story houses. Or perhaps Jethro had decided the hell with it, or it was deer season, or he ran off with the guy who changed his oil— a "Brokeback Holler" kind of love. A lot of closed businesses dotted the road. An open business was a surprise: gas stations, a few fast-food places, and bars. Sometimes the gas station would be a grocery store with gas pumps attached. I didn't see anything that looked like it provided a job paying more than minimum wage.

"What the hell do people do out here for a living?" I asked Max.

"Not much of anything."

"Yeah, I figured that part out. What did they used to do?"

"'Bout the same."

I could tell he was thinking about it. I stared out the window and waited for the rest of it. "Well, once there was some logging. Most people went to Winchester for work. There was a bit of real estate–related work, some government work. I think that all pretty much dried up and blew away. Probably some growers are doing their thing, and some half-assed farming. People around here are used to being poor. It's one of the few things West Virginians are good at."

"Well, I can see they get a lot of practice, probably one of those things that gets handed down. That reminds me of a joke: What do you get when you have twelve women from West Virginia in the same room?"

"I don't know, a bible meeting?"

"Nope, a full set of teeth."

"Very funny. You might want to keep your West Virginia jokes to yourself until we get back home."

"How about marine jokes?"

"Yeah, them too. Unless you're around a bunch of guys wearing navy ball caps. Then you can have a rollicking good time. Though, if they are navy guys, you can expect help when you go to take a piss."

"Gee, you military types really know how to have fun."

"Quit being an asshole and check the map. We should have a turn coming up soon."

We did. We veered off Route 50 and headed south. West of us, and not far, was the Ohio state line. Ohio was one of the first states to start charging border-crossing fees for nonresidents. They justified it by saying that you were using facilities, such as roads, that were maintained by the state. I thought it made sense, although it sure had pissed off a lot of people, especially when it was ruled that travelers passing through on the interstate were exempt. So, unless you had to stop, you were fine. But in West Virginia they didn't have any border-crossing fees. They were thrilled that someone wanted to come to their state, even if it was just to drive through to get to another one.

Max had begun waving at drivers going the other way. Just a few fingers lifted off the wheel. It was always returned. "You know these people?" I asked, amazed.

"No. You need to start paying attention. This is what you do in rural areas. By the way, when you address an older woman, you will say 'ma'am.' You will say 'sir' to any man older than you that you don't know. If for any reason someone should ask you if you have been 'born again' or 'washed in the blood of Jesus,' you will tell them you are 'churched,' and you will say it with a straight face. I am not fucking around."

"I know; I got it. I won't embarrass you in public."

"Look, I am not sure what we are getting into, but I have a few ideas. I made some calls, sent some e-mails. This colonel is not a guy to mess with. I know some of the people he has with him by reputation, and a few I know personally from the 'Stan. These people are professionals. I am surprised that they are here and not somewhere else, killing whoever has pissed off D.C. this month."

"They're that good, Max?"

"Yeah, some of them are. None of the names I saw were the scary good ones. But, yeah, they are good enough."

*Hmm . . . this might be an interesting trip.* I was actually looking forward to something, a feeling that had been rare in my life lately. We made a few more turns and then we were on the road that would end in the gathering place. We passed an old house with a young man sitting in a rocker. He was on my side of the road and I didn't wave; neither did he. I watched him in the rearview mirror as long as I could. He pulled out a cell phone before I lost sight of him. I looked over at Max; he nodded.

The road was well-maintained gravel now. If two cars were to meet, it would be a squeeze for both of them to pass. The shoulder looked as if it would hold if you had to use it. I noticed chicory growing undisturbed in more than a few places alongside the road. That was interesting. This was a poor area, and chicory could be used to make your coffee go a lot further. Yet here it was, blue flowers and all, untouched. We had gone a few miles, farther than I had expected, when we saw a chain across the road. Off to one side was a small house with a porch. The man standing next to the pole to which the chain was attached—now he was imposing. So was the man standing in the doorway of the house. And he was armed with one of those black plastic guns that some people loved.

## CHAPTER NINETEEN

# DELIVERY

I rolled down my window, as Max did his. From the house I could faintly hear a radio playing country music. Far off in the distance I could hear automatic weapons fire, coming in short, staccato riffs.

Max smiled at the guard. "Hey, what's up? Got a delivery here for Thermopylae Incorporated. This the right place?"

"Yes, sir, it is. I need both of you to step out of the vehicle. Please bring your personal belongings and any weapons you might have."

"Okay, buddy. Not a problem. Leave the truck here? Or move it and park it?"

"No, sir. Exit the vehicle, bring your gear, and report inside the building."

*Why do these guys always sound like robots?* I wondered. *Was it the movies? The military? Or did the movies just copy the military's strange little reality?* I swung out of the cab and dropped to the ground. I could hear the thud of Max's boots as he dropped to the ground on the other side. I grabbed the gym bag I was using as luggage and waited for Max to come around the front of the truck. We filed into the house—someone had turned the music off.

We entered what would have been the living room. It had a long counter built across it, about two-thirds of the way back. Behind that and taking up one-third of the wall space were a number of steel lockers. An American flag was hung on another wall, and a couple folding chairs were on our side of the counter. Everything was spotlessly clean. I liked that. I had to take a dump and had been putting it off. I liked a clean bathroom, and I had not seen any indications that there were any in West Virginia.

We walked up to the counter. I was watching Max out of the corner of my eye. He swung his bag up onto the counter, and I followed a heartbeat behind him, not that it was all that heavy. A box of ammo, my cleaning kit, a set of clothes, shave kit, and volume one of Gibbon's *Fall of Rome* series. The ammo and the book were the only things giving it any weight.

"I need all your weapons on the counter, gentlemen."

The counterman was somebody different. He was a black male, past middle age, yet he still had the bearing of a soldier. I was a bit taken aback by him being black. After the chief's comments, I had expected an all-white crew here. The guard who had stopped us at the chain had come in with us, but he was now standing in a corner of the room watching us. I took off my gun belt and put on the counter. Max followed by pulling his Colt from its holster in the small of his back and setting it next to my gun belt. You could feel much of the tension leave the room.

"One more time: I want all your weapons, including knives; anything found on your person outside this room will be confiscated, and I know you don't want that."

*All right* . . . I waited to see if Max was going to pull out his backup. When I saw him bend over to pull off his ankle holster, I sighed and joined him. *Damn*, I did hate giving up the sheath knife I had on my belt. Strange how naked I felt when all my hardware was stacked in front of me.

Counterman said, "Let's see what we got here. He had pulled out a clipboard from under the counter. "This is how it works. I will sign your weapons in, and then I will store them in one of those lockers behind me. I will give you each a key. When you return, you give whoever is on duty your key; they will then give you back your weapons. Now, I need a name, starting with you."

"Max."

"And you?"

"Gardener."

"All right, let's see what we have here. One Colt 1911, series 80, with custom Pachmayr grips, very nice, and a Colt Detective Special—I see you like Mr. Colt's products." Max didn't even reply. He just stared at him. I don't think he was too thrilled about giving up his weapons, either.

"And one Buck knife. Okay, what do we have here?" He slid my Ruger out of the leather holster and held it up to the light to read the serial number better. "My God, you men do like the old-school iron. I haven't held a single action in years. You sure aren't going to throw a lot of lead downstream with this."

"You don't need to if you can hit what you're aiming at," I said. "Spray and pray only works online." I regretted it as soon as I said it—especially the online part. I heard the guy behind us laugh. When I heard the laugh I felt the cold rage sweep through me. I really hated being laughed at.

I looked at my holster, did the trigonometry in my head, knew it was not going to work, and felt that old *Fuck it* feeling picking up speed. I could feel Max shift his weight, and the counterman opened his mouth. This was it. "They are beautiful weapons, aren't they? They certainly killed enough men in their day. Perhaps we are returning to the day of the gunfighter." He slid it back into the holster. I relaxed. Counterman was oblivious.

He added the Charter Arms Off-Duty model .38 I carried to the sheet. "One more thing, gentlemen, and you will be free to go. He dumped the contents of our bags one at a time on the counter. He went through them quickly and attempted to put everything back neatly. "Thank you very much. If I don't see you on the way out, have a wonderful stay." He handed us our keys and began packing our weapons into the lockers.

"All right, guys, back to the truck." This was said by the guard who was standing in the corner.

We lifted our bags off the counter and followed him back out to the truck.

"Just head up the road, make a left, and pull in at the second house," he said, talking to Max. "People will be waiting for you there." We mounted up, he dropped the chain, and we rolled over it and headed up the road.

Max looked over at me, shook his head. "Remember what I told you that day about the Fairfax City police, you know, outside?" It took me a few seconds, and then I realized he meant the hidden monitoring.

"Yeah, I got it."

We headed up the road, literally climbing. After a couple of switchbacks, the engine started to strain a bit, then we saw the left turn. The second house number was less than three hundred yards down, and Max turned the truck up the sharply inclined driveway. I could see other houses dotted here and there on the hill; I wouldn't call it a mountain. Some A-frames, some one-level houses with big decks—it looked like a vacation home development. All were painted some variation of brown. They blended into the landscape rather nicely, I thought.

The house we pulled up to had a two-door attached garage. There were two men in T-shirts and fatigue pants waiting on the lawn. A Hispanic female was standing with them, dressed the same way, but she still managed to look like she was not a part of them. Her T-shirt was much nicer. She was also the only person happy to see us.

"Hi, guys!" she hollered at Max. "I need you to back it up, but leave me about six feet of space between that garage door and the gate. Got it?"

Max gave her a "thumbs up" and maneuvered the truck into place, set the emergency brake, and we jumped down to say hello. After a brief exchange of names that I quickly forgot—well, I remembered hers, it was Martina—we walked back to unlock the truck so they could start unloading.

That's when I noticed the thin wire strip that had been threaded through the same opening as the lock: It had been soldered at one end. Martina broke it with ease. "I see you didn't have any problems."

Max answered her: "No, it was an easy run." He put his key into the lock, and she swung the doors open. I peered in, curious to see what we had been hauling. All I saw was furniture. *No, this couldn't be everything.* The weirdness level had been far too high for us to have been hired just to move furniture.

She told the guys who were standing behind her patiently and silently, "Move the furniture out onto the lawn." She turned to Max. "Once the furniture is out, I need you to back the truck up so it is flush with the garage door, okay?"

He nodded. "Sure."

She must have seen the puzzled look on my face, so she glanced up at the sky. "Theater for anyone up there watching."

"Oh, okay." Pieces started falling into place: The gate that didn't look like a gate, the guard dressed like a park ranger rather than a combat trooper, the houses, the entire vacation home feel to everything—whatever was going on here was being camouflaged. *Not bad*, I thought.

A couple of sofas and a chest were on the lawn in a matter of minutes, and Max was backing the truck up. I stood next to Martina, trying not to ogle her T-shirted assets while she made a cell phone call, apparently not successfully. I looked up in time to catch the eyes of one of the movers, who was also checking her out. Just a fast trace of a smile, and then he was pulling on one end of a large wooden box that looked like a coffin.

Martina snapped the phone shut. "Someone will be here in a few minutes to pick you up. The colonel has extended an invitation to dinner to you both. Plus, you're welcome to spend the night and take the truck back tomorrow. Now please excuse me. I need to start inventory-ing what you delivered."

Leaving behind the glow from her radiant smile, she disappeared into the house. We both waited until she was out of sight. I was the first: "Now that was nice."

Max laughed, "Yes, they were. I saw how overcome she was by your charm. She probably had to go change. Your laser vision probably scorched her T-shirt."

We stood there and talked about nothing while we waited to be picked up. It wasn't long. In less than five minutes a golf cart pulled up in front of us.

"You Max and Gardener?"

"Yep."

"All right, hop in."

We climbed in and took off. The cart was not fast, but we were headed toward the bottom of the hill, just on the other side. It also looked good to any surveillance satel-lites flying overhead: no Humvees, just golf carts. Our driver wasn't talkative, nor was Max. I was fine with that; I just looked around. While I did, I realized what an idiot I had been. I had just ridden in here with Max. Did I do any research? No. I could have found out where we were going and pulled it up on Google, looked at a map and a satellite view of the area. I hadn't realized how far I had sunk into not caring.

We passed a couple of joggers who gave us a nod as they passed. One of them was running with a full pack on his back, and he was not looking good, either. I thought he was in his twenties at first. Only when he passed us did I realize he was probably double that. Our driver called out to him as he went past, "Suck it up, Jimbo, you got it!" Jimbo barely got a nod off as he went past.

I suddenly remembered why I had decided that the military was not a good idea for me. As we came around one corner I saw the complex. It didn't look like a complex in the military sense, but that was undoubtedly what it was. There was a ski lift, a lodge or clubhouse, a restaurant, and a couple of buildings for supporting the lift. Farther down was a metal building the size of a Boeing 777 aircraft hangar with a corral attached. From the windsock and a few smaller hangars, it looked as if they were flying light planes in and out of here. All in all, a pretty nice place.

We were dropped at the restaurant and lodge building. I wondered if they had a gift shop. Maybe I could pick up some T-shirts for Night and the ninja twins—something in camo with a catchy logo like "Camp Death" with a skiing skeleton below it would be cool. I was standing there, working on T-shirt designs, when a guy came out the door roaring:

"Max!"

"Goddamn! Murphy!"

They went to pounding and gripping each other—it was a regular love fest. I felt like telling them to get a room, damn. When they got finished groping each other, Max beckoned me over.

"Gardner, this is Murphy. Me and him did two deployments together. Damn, dude, when did you make it back?"

"Oh, about eight months ago. I was going to give you a call. You know—shit kept getting in the way."

"Well, this is Gardner. He's my partner," he slapped me on the shoulder, "and a damn good one. We're doing a bit of law enforcement in Virginia."

He stuck out his hand; we shook. He went for the grip of death, but I just blanked out the pain. I saw a bit of uncertainty in his eyes when he let go. He may have been real good at dishing out pain, but I had gone to the University of Receiving Pain as a kid—me and pain went way back.

"Come on in. Let's get some chow and I can brief you about what's happening."

It wasn't a restaurant, it was a mess hall: stainless steel trays with indentations for food. The food itself was steam-table, buffet, and not bad. Murphy apologized for the selection. The food we saw heating was just kept to feed strays like us. The next meal, dinner, was usually very good. I didn't care. It wasn't like I ate all that good anyways. I don't know if Murphy even realized that he and everyone else here was eating better than 70 percent of America these days. I pulled a tray and so did Max. It had been a while since breakfast, plus, it was a free meal. Murphy apologized for not joining us, saying he had eaten earlier.

We sat down at an empty table. I concentrated on eating while Murphy told us what our day was going to be like. "Well, the official plan was feed you, take you to your rooms, and then go hang at the range. Then it is dinner, with you two getting to go up to the big house and eat with the colonel. Damn, Max, you must have impressed the hell out somebody important somewhere. Then, come back here and we go hit the club. What do you think?"

Max shrugged. "Sounds good to me."

"What about you, Gardener?"

"I think if you show me my room, I'll hang out there until dinner."

I didn't miss the quick narrowing of Murphy's eyes. You had to be looking at him at exactly the right second; it was gone that fast. "Sure, no problem." He laughed. "You are only about a hundred yards from it."

Max and I had rooms next door to each other in the lodge. Max asked, "How can y'all afford something like this? I mean this is a nice base you got here."

Murphy's reply did not come as a surprise to me. "Foreclosure. I don't know how much the colonel paid exactly, but I heard it was pennies on the dollar." I opened my door and I threw my bag on the bed, stretched out next to it and took a nap.

I heard the knock at the door. It startled me—for a second I thought I was back in my room. Max's voice cut through the door: "Fifteen minutes until dinner . . . be out front."

I heard his door shut and the sound of the plumbing running. I got up, ran a comb through my hair and a toothbrush over my teeth, and I was ready for show time. I went outside and stood around. Men and women were straggling in to eat, some of them with children in tow. The children were well dressed and better behaved; very few were in any kind of uniform, yet it was easy to picture them in one. These were soldiers, and looking at them, my guess was they were good ones.

Max startled me. "You missed good times at the range."

"Really? They have any rocket launchers here?"

"Nothing visible. They do have some nice toys. They have a full range inside that hanger with the horse pens attached to it. "

"Well, no rocket launchers equals no me."

"Your absence was noted—real men like to go to the range."

I laughed. "Right, I thought it was 'Real men like to carve pumpkins.'"

He was still processing that when our cart arrived—the same driver but a little bigger cart.

"What happened to the other cart?" I asked. I was picturing a rear-end collision with a cow or maybe a low-speed chase gone bad.

"Need more power to get up that hill than what I was driving."

That made sense to me. Twilight was starting to cast its net of darkness as we rode up the hill. People were out jogging. I had a feeling that you would find someone out jogging here any time of day or night. The lights at the end of the driveways began to turn on. I always liked catching a light going on at night or off in the morning—there was something magical about it. I used to believe that for every one I saw change, a wish would be granted to me.

My wish was that I not do anything really stupid tonight. This little slice of military heaven was beginning to grate on me. I knew when we approached the crest of the hill we were almost there. No way would the colonel not have his house at the top. I was right. We pulled into a circular driveway. It was well lit with soft lighting from both the ground and the gas lamps that were evenly spaced along the driveway. The house was stone and timber, an A-frame with wings. The front door was a double door. It looked old, weathered, and solid. Given the build date I estimated for this development, the door was an import.

In front of the door stood a fully outfitted male in his early twenties. By fully outfitted, I mean he looked like one of those army guys you saw in the news. The night-vision monocle, the vest, extra magazines, maybe even a PowerBar tucked away in there somewhere. I guess you never knew where those evil Muslim terrorists might pop up. It was kind of hard to imagine the Taliban blending in with the locals, though.

We thanked our driver and headed up the flagstone walk to the door. The guard snapped to attention, not that a lot of snapping was needed, and saluted. Max gave him a casual salute and told him who we were and why we were there. I watched as he murmured into his mike. He wasn't done talking before the door was opening and another male in fatigues appeared.

"Right this way, gentlemen." We followed him into the great hall where our host, two men, and Martina, the inventory checker of earlier that day, stood or sat casually around a gas fireplace. Each had a glass in hand except for Martina—hers was set to one side, on a coaster, I noticed.

Our host instantly detached himself from the group and moved forward to greet us. I have to admit that I was impressed upon meeting him. I also experienced a distinct sense of disquiet. He was the first man I had ever met who had "command presence." He also had a great tan and good teeth. For a guy his age he appeared to be in good shape—probably a jogger, I thought. He moved toward us, gliding over the polished hardwood floor; his hand was outstretched and he was grinning.

I don't hate many people—especially on sight—it takes too much energy, but I instantly hated this guy. I was careful, of course, to conceal any feeling other than my joy that such a superior human being would be so delighted to see Max and me.

He finished shaking Max's hand, all the while telling us how delighted he was that we could attend his small dinner party. I was reaching out, about to grasp his hand, when we made eye contact for real. People later described his blue eyes as penetrating—I thought they were bat-house crazy. He was ringing another alarm: I knew this guy. I mean, I had not met him before, but I knew his type all too well. What was worse was, he knew that I knew. Neither one of us acknowledged what had just happened in a way that was visible. We stood there gripping and grinning, and then he turned away and was making introductions. The other guests never really registered with me; they were nonentities. Martina was not. At this point I switched to reserved wariness and slipped on what I called my stone face. What was happening here—and ever since we arrived—was not and never had been about me. My guess was, if us delivering the truck hadn't worked, then Murphy would have called with an invite. This was all about Max. They knew something, or wanted something, that he had.

## CHAPTER TWENTY

# TOASTS

I won't bore you, or myself, with the idle chitchat that passed among us. It was current events, and those events are now history. What loomed so large then is now, at best, a footnote to what came later. I am sure that a history of our times will be written someday. I am just not sure from whose perspective it will be written. Eventually, there will be a Gibbon to write the *Decline and Fall*, but it won't be Europe or America that produces the author.

The fragmentation of information sources was accelerating. Print had failed as a business model—at least for daily news—and digital broadcast news was homogeneous for the most part. The only difference in the networks was what shade of the official color you wanted. Online news was the least regulated and most interesting. The only problem was the amount of noise one had to sift through to find a reliable source. I was still reading *Calculated Risk* then—this was before the "Information Consolidation Act" shut him down.

I watched Martina from afar. The reason it was from afar was that she had locked in on Max, attaching herself to him within minutes of our arrival. She wasn't wearing a bra, and those headlights definitely lit up when she saw him. I could have excused myself, gone in search of the men's room, and never come back, and it's highly unlikely that my prolonged absence would have been noticed until the end of the evening.

Somehow, in a way that I could not discern, the colonel was alerted that dinner was ready. "Dinner is served," he announced to us, and we all followed him into the dining room. I expected armed retainers to be lined up along the wall, but I was disappointed. It was just us and a fat, elderly white woman. She stood in a doorway, the one that led to the kitchen, I assumed, and beamed at us. When the colonel nodded to her she disappeared.

Max pulled Martina's chair out and seated her. "Oh, what a gentleman," she cooed as he did. Everyone smiled approvingly. I wondered if they would still smile if I projectile-vomited up dinner when we were done. I was beginning to feel like I had stumbled onto the set of a particularly twisted *Bachelorette* episode.

Max was seated at the colonel's right with Martina. I was on the left between his chief of staff and his logistics officer. Oh, well, at least I could watch the headlights go on and off. The colonel led us in the saying of grace, and then he stood up and proposed a toast:

"Gentlemen and lady,"—here he did a slight bow to Martina—"a toast: to Sgt. Max Whelan, USMC, the first Marine Medal of Honor winner since the Vietnam war."

*Okay, even I understood what that meant and how it was earned. He had been awarded the medal and he was still alive, plus he had all his body parts. Damn—and I never had a clue. What an asshole . . .*

We all stood and drank our toast to Max. I don't do alcohol so I was toasting with a glass of ice tea. Max had been pretty happy up to that point, but now—I was surprised to see—that was gone. A stillness settled over him, a sadness even. As we all sat down, he stood up and announced: "A toast!" We stood again. "To fallen comrades!" he said, and then he emptied his glass on the nice Persian rug that was underneath the table. I didn't hesitate—I dumped at least half a glass of ice tea including the ice cubes on the rug.

As I did it, I watched the colonel. There was a quick tightening around the eyes, and then he followed suit—so did his peckerwood flunkies, who had held off until they saw what the big man's reaction was going to be. This was going to be a really sticky floor in twenty minutes or so, which made me very happy.

The colonel sat down, beamed at all of us, and said, "Let's dig in." It was pretty good: steak, potatoes, a salad, rolls, lima beans. The chief of staff let us know that this was the same meal that was being served in the mess hall.

"The colonel always eats what his troops eat and insists that we do, too."

Logistics guy chimed in with, "Yes, thank God we are not in the field anymore." Everyone thought this was funny as hell. He then asked me the question I knew was coming. I was just surprised it had not been asked sooner. "So, Gardener, what branch did you serve in?" *The prick.* I could tell, just looking at him, that he knew the answer. Time to jerk me around, probably payback for the ice tea puddle that had formed under his chair.

"Why, I was in the GLA." I said this like I expected him to know what I was talking about; my tone implied that if he didn't, then he was a fool.

The chief of staff asked, "Hmmm, was that in Africa?"

"No, actually it was in the Galleria Mall. The Gay Liberation Army was an elite band of color coordinators who struck fear in the hearts of sales clerks wherever we appeared."

Martina was the only one of them who laughed. Max grinned, shook his head, and went back to gnawing on his steak. I looked at "Logistics," winked, and said, "Remember—don't ask, don't tell."

I might as well have ripped off a long and juicy one as far as the rest of them were concerned. I was able to finish my dinner without interruption after that. Dessert was chocolate mousse and a monologue by the colonel. The whole purpose was to let Max in on his strategic vision. As best as I could tell, the plan was that the vision would cause Max to swoon with joy that his purpose in life had been revealed. He would then sign up, become the colonel's poster child, and ride Martina off into the sunset. It sounded good to me—if I had been Max, that is, because they sure weren't going to ask me to hang around.

What the colonel said made sense. The problem, at least for me, was the logic he used to arrive at his conclusion. The solution did not sound like it would be a lot of fun, either—at least if you were one of the "little people." He started off sounding sane and reasonable; he reminded me of McCain, the guy who had run for president when I still watched television.

"We all realize that the world is changing rapidly," the colonel said. Nobody at the table had a problem with

that. "We must also accept that 'America' does not nec-
essarily mean a white America. A true American is not
determined by skin color. No, it is an adherence to a common belief system, a set of values, a sense of responsibility—for the community, for yourself, and for your family.

"We who have served our country understand the need
for leadership. We also understand the need for personal
responsibility for one's actions. All of us have seen the
results when that is not enforced: needless deaths, wasted
resources. Life is harsh. The world that our children will
inherit will be a world scarce in resources such as food
and water. Do we let them starve? Do we sit back and let
the fools who have stripped this country of everything
worthwhile continue to plunder it? Or do we secure what
we need ahead of time—by force, if necessary!"

He was on a roll now. No longer seated, he was up,
moving as he spoke, using pauses and volume swells like
an old-time TV preacher. I expected that any minute now
his staff would start in with a chorus of "Amen!" This was
actually kind of fun to watch.

"Do we let those who plundered our money, our children's money, unto our great-grandchildren wander our
streets undisturbed? Generation after generation toiling
for the good of the few! I say to you this: Those who want
to live, let them fight, and those who do not want to fight
in this world of eternal struggle do not deserve to live. We
must purify this great nation. Purify it of all that is deca-
dent! All that is wasteful! We must return to our roots."

He kept on talking long after he made his point with
me. His staff loved it, though. They sat there mesmerized.
Max was listening intently.

All I could think was: *Hasn't anyone introduced this idiot to the concept of sound bites?* If he didn't wrap this up soon, I was going to get up and leave. I'd give him ten minutes. By the seventh minute it sounded as if he was working up to the big close:

"All great movements are popular movements. They are the volcanic eruptions of human passions and emotions, stirred into activity by the ruthless violence of poverty or by the torch of the spoken word cast into the midst of the people."

Here he paused dramatically and lowered his volume:

"Max, we need you. The people need you. Your country needs you. Will you join us in our righteous crusade to resurrect America? Will you, Max?"

This was said at a whisper. Yes, indeed, it was all eyes on Max. He leaned back in his chair, looked away, and then back at the colonel, and rubbed his chin.

"Colonel, that was one hell of a speech—just one hell of a speech indeed. You have really opened my eyes. That much is for sure."

He nodded his head. "I need to think about this. Return to Virginia and make some arrangements. How does that sound, sir?"

"Why that sounds good, very good indeed," the colonel said. "We have so much to talk about, you and me. You are going to be delighted at what we have planned and what your role will be: That's just to start, mind you. Why don't you stay a bit and we can talk. Martina can drive you back, can't you, major?"

Oh, she was happy enough to do that—and she was an officer too. Not a surprise, really.

The colonel then turned to me. "Thank you for joining us, Gardener. I can't say what a pleasure it has been meeting you. John, please arrange a ride back for Gardener."

Ah, that jogged my memory. The chief of staff was John. I still can't recall the other man's name. About three minutes later I was standing outside, waiting for my ride to show up. I figured I wouldn't hear Max come back until morning—unless she was married, that is.

CHAPTER TWENTY-ONE

# TAKEN FOR A RIDE

I stood there, rocking back and forth on my heels, aware that the door guard was watching me. I was happy: The steak knives had been made by Wüsthof in Germany. They were very nice carbon steel blades that took an edge nicely and held it. I liked German steel. You had to be careful with it, as it liked to bite the hand that cleaned it. I had slipped it through my watch band and from there to my sock. I had it running parallel to my shin. Thankfully, I was wearing tight socks. It felt fine, and I had the handle protruding above the sock line. I felt a lot better about life now. Hopefully, we would have a big breakfast tomorrow and be on our way. Maybe they would have pancakes. That thought made me even happier. The golf cart was there in a matter of minutes. This time the driver wasn't alone. I saw another man sitting in the back as I walked up to the cart.

"Hey, what's up?"

"Not much, buddy, jump in."

"Who's that?" I indicated the passenger, another GI Joe clone.

"C'mon. He needs a ride. You were expecting a private limo?"

The other guy smiled at me with his mouth. "Don't worry, I don't bite."

Something wasn't right here. The feel was wrong and my stomach was tensing. I had learned this rule long before Max had taught me: *Always, always trust your intuition*.

I smiled at the driver. "Sorry, not a problem. You know how it is. It's a crazy world these days."

I settled into the seat, directly behind the driver. We pulled away from the house, the whine of the electric engine and the crickets being the only sounds to be heard.

If it was going to happen, it would be in one of the support buildings near the ski lift, away from prying eyes and night-vision scopes. I wasn't sure why they decided to kill me. Maybe the Persian rug was worth more than I thought. The man didn't know how to do a sound bite or get a rug cleaned. *Pretty piss-poor for someone who had made it to colonel*, I thought. We were approaching the lodge, but the driver turned enough that we headed north toward the support buildings.

"Hey! You going to drop me off?"

"No problem. Just let me drop Mac off, and then I will loop around and drop you off."

Well, I was not going to wait until they had a chance to crack a rib or worse. I had been there, done that, and it was not going to happen again. He was slowing down. We were going to the building that was the farthest away from everything and everyone. I reached down to scratch my ankle, keeping my right hand on my knee and in plain view. Next to me, Mac was tracking my movement, watching my left hand scratch.

"Hey Mac, you ever had athlete's foot?"

He quit watching my left hand and made eye contact with me. He opened his mouth—to say something smart I am sure—when I pulled the Wüsthof blade out of my sock.

My right arm went over the back of the seat and down tight against it to provide me with an anchor. I pivoted on my ass, the plastic surface of the seat helping, raised my left hand, and drove that carbon steel blade into his heart. He gave out with an "Oooff" and then an "Awwwhhh" as I twisted the knife to the left to pop the seal around the blade and cause more damage. Then I yanked it out and drove it in again. This time all I heard was "Sssssssshhhh."

"Hey! What's going on back there? . . . Shit!"

The driver had twisted his head around, trying to see what was going on as he dug for whatever he had in a hip holster. I was sure it was something black and plastic— probably not even made in America.

I whipped my right arm around, grabbing his forehead in my right hand and yanking his head back. Then I cut his throat. He had taken his foot off the pedal during all this. We had already been slowing down, so I just sat there until we coasted to a stop. Tonight wasn't the night to leap from a cart and twist an ankle. Plus, it was fun: We bumped right into the wall of the shed at three miles per hour. It was not a very loud thump. I sat there for a few seconds after we stopped. Then I stiff-armed GI Joe out of the cart. He was making a mess.

I hopped out my side and listened—nothing except for the cicadas. A firefly lit off five feet from me. That was kind of cool. I had a bit of blood on me—actually, more than a bit. It was cool to my skin where it had soaked through my clothes. I could feel the night breeze through it. I felt alive, more than I had felt in quite a while. Who knew killing was like vitamins and Red Bull but much faster?

I started walking back to my room. It was a nice night. The houses on the hill had their lights on, and the colonel's place glowed at the top. Gas lighting was definitely better than electric. If I ever got a place, I was going to have to keep that in mind.

At this point, most people would probably talk about how their mind coolly calculated different plans and such. What their next move would be. Myself, I didn't give a damn. If anything, it was funny in a rather bizarre way. My plan was to go to my room and take a quick shower, then grab my stuff, and see if Max was back. If he wasn't, well, I would start walking. Eventually, I would get back to Route 50. Once I got there, maybe I would call Night and see what she thought. I had at least an hour before the golf-cart hit squad was missed. I might even get lucky and have until sunup, but I doubted it. This place had to have better security than that. I would like to make it to the guardhouse and get my gun and other hardware. That way I might be able to get a few of them before they got me with their super-destructo, black, plastic-gun bullets.

I walked to the lodge. That was one of the things Max had taught me: *Never look guilty—it draws eyeballs*. I sure as hell didn't feel guilty. I opened the door. Max was stretched out on my bed with a Colt .45 in his hand.

"Took you long enough. Any of that blood yours?"

"No." My bag was packed and sitting next to his by the door. I unzipped it and pulled out my change of clothes. "You got us packed? What happened to your date? Never mind. We should probably hurry."

"Yeah," Max replied. "Don't use all the hot water."

## CHAPTER TWENTY-TWO

# IF ANYTHING
## *CAN GO WRONG . . .*

I laughed, went in the bathroom, and stripped off my clothes. I stuffed them in the empty trash can, which had a plastic bag liner. I was washed up, dressed, and back out in five minutes. He was standing by the door. The lights were off and the door was cracked. "Everything groovy?" I stuffed the tied-off bag of bloody clothes into my gym bag.

"Looks that way."

"We got a plan?"

"Other than leave quickly? No."

"Well, that's encouraging. Should we just hang out and kill people, then?"

"No, let's take a walk." We walked out the door. No hail of gunfire or sniper rounds dropped us. "Nice night," Max observed, looking up at the sky as we walked toward the handful of parked cars that were scattered around the lot. We continued past them.

"Yep. I saw a firefly earlier. Haven't seen one of those for quite a while." We were headed toward the horse barn.

"I saw an old Ford F-150 by the horse barn. I can get that running. Newer cars have way too much antitheft gear wired into them."

The Ford was being used as a work truck. There were two bales of hay and a bag of topsoil in the back. Max opened the driver's side door to pop the hood. I heard him say, "Yes!" and then the engine started. I pulled open the passenger door and jumped in. We were rolling over the field with our lights off before I had figured out how to hook the seat belt. Then we hit gravel and were rolling toward the guardhouse.

"So where did you get the .45?"

"The armory. The Gunny they have running it gave it to me. Check this out: It has a five-inch match barrel, custom trigger work, and a Dawson rail. It is sweet. Did you pick up any weapons from whoever it was you gutted?"

"No. Why did he just 'give' it to you?"

"He thought he owed me. So who did you gut? Please don't tell me it was the colonel."

"Naw, I am saving him for later. You know how the anticipation thing really works for me."

"That's nice. Give me your steak knife."

I pulled it from my sock sheath and stuck it in the bench seat cushion between us. He handed me his Colt. "Smash the house lights." I used the butt to hammer them until they crunched satisfactorily.

"Don't lose it. When I slow down I want you to jump out. Meet me around the back of the guard house. Give me five minutes after I pass it." I nodded agreement.

Two minutes later I was out the truck door and off balance.

Two awkward steps later and I was falling. I tried to break my fall with my hands. That did not work as well as I had hoped. I lay there for a minute or so while I did a systems check. I felt okay, except for my palms and left knee. As best as I could tell in the dim light, they were bleeding and had tiny pieces of gravel embedded in the skin. I got up, brushed myself off, crossed the road, and moved into the underbrush. I was a little pissed. This was the second set of clothes I had ruined on this expedition.

I tried moving deeper into the woods and quickly changed my mind. Moving in the woods at dark was not easy. In between the noise I made stepping on branches and getting caught in the brambles, which were every-where, I decided this just wasn't going to work. I moved back to where the forest bordered the road. There was a light on inside the guard house. I stood at the edge of the small clearing and tried to sense if there were a bunch of riled-up gunbots in there waiting for us. All I got back was calm and sleepy night-shift vibes. I moved around to the back of the house and then hunkered down about seven feet into the woods.

"Jesus, Gardener. Don't ever try to tell me you have Indian blood."

"Aren't you early? My superdeluxe inner clock says you have one more minute."

He ignored that. "You ready?" I nodded.

"Here is the plan: We go knock on the front door. When he opens the door I lay the Colt upside his head. We get our stuff and go."

"Sure." It sounded good to me. Besides I didn't have anything better to offer for a plan.

We walked up to the door. I stood to one side so that if the guard looked out the window, he wouldn't see two men and become more cautious. Max knocked. We listened to the faint sound of a chair being pushed back and boots clomping their way to the front door. The door opened, and I heard someone say, "Yes sir, can I help you?" Then there was a chunk and a thump. Max had him dragged over to a corner by the time I got through the door. I kept going, vaulted over the counter, and inserted my key. Everything was there.

I strapped my gun belt on and called to Max: "Key!" He tossed me his key and I dumped his stuff on the counter.

"Look around: guns, ties, and flares. Find them."

I understood two of the three requests. I figured I would find out about the flares soon enough. I went into the back of the house, where there were two rooms, besides a kitchen and a bathroom. One room was set up as an office; the other room had a closed door with a dead bolt. I started in the office. There was not much to it: a four-drawer metal filing cabinet, a desk, and in the corner a small table with a box of flares. Lined up neatly against the wall were three traffic cones and a large sign that read Slow Down: Men at Work. The PC on the desk had its screen saver on. I accidentally bumped the mouse as I was digging through the drawers, and the screen saver disappeared. Our man had been watching porn. I took another look—not just any porn. I clicked on the movie controls. He had been watching *Teen Sodomy*, and the site was dedicated to that kind of content.

I went back out into the main room and left the flare box on the counter. "You find any restraints?" Max asked.

The guard was starting to come to. He was an older man. I guess you didn't need the A-team for the night shift.

"Find any keys?" I asked back. Max nodded.

"We got a locked door back there that probably has the goodies in it. I'll watch him. You know what to look for far better than I do."

Max gave me a funny look, hesitated like he was going to say something, and went over to the counter.

As he disappeared through the doorway he said, "We got fifteen minutes, tops, before we have company."

Max still had my steak knife. I was going to have to get that back. I was growing attached to that knife despite the short time we had known each other.

I pulled my Buck knife from its sheath and snapped the blade open. I knelt down next to the guard. My hand with the knife was resting on the floor out of his line of sight. "Hey, hero. Wake up!" He moaned and I saw his eyelids flutter. Not good enough: I slapped his face.

"Awww, shit, man." He opened his eyes and I saw them focus on me.

"So, seen any good sodomy videos lately?" I asked. His eyes widened. I'm not sure if it was from the remark or from catching sight of the Buck knife on its descent into his left eye. I gave it a twist and pulled it out. I had to put my arm on his chest and shift my weight to keep his body pinned to the floor as he spasmed and kicked. Then I drove the knife into his other eye. His bowels loosened noisily. Good thing we were leaving. It was going to stink in here something awful.

I stood up, looked down on him, and kicked him in the head. "Be seeing you in hell, asshole," and I turned to go find Max. Max was busy checking an M-16 or an AR-

15—I never could tell the difference—that he had just pulled from a rack in the back room. "Do me a favor. Go look for some masking tape in the office while I load these magazines." I came back with a roll and he started taping the magazines together. He only had four—didn't seem like a lot. In the meantime I checked the selection on hand. They had a Mossberg twelve-gauge. Not my weapon of choice by any means, but you go with what you can dance with. I racked it; it was empty. "In the cabinet," Max said. I checked and found double-aught and slug rounds. "Load it all double-aught. This is going be close range." Max watched me. "Stuff your pockets with a handful and let's go."

We went through the kitchen. I grabbed a bottle of water. I pulled my shirt away from my neck and dropped it inside. Max did the same. We leaped over the counter and he grabbed a couple flares.

"Stick them in your pants. This is the plan: I want you on the roof. As soon as they pull up I want you to toss the flares: one to the road, one in the woods to their side of the house. I will be in the woods on the other side of the road. Go!" I moved.

I went around to the back of the house. I could hear vehicles coming fast. There was no way to get up on the roof. I looked around . . . no ladder! *Shit! The other side!* The guard had parked his truck next to the house. I jumped up into the truck bed and then on top of the cab. This was going to be really freaking close. I backed up as far as I could go, tossed the shotgun ahead of me and made my leap, praying at the same time that the shotgun would hold fast.

"Ow!" I was hanging halfway off the roof as I watched my shotgun slide off and into the grass at the side of the house. Cursing life, I struggled to pull myself up. I couldn't get a good grip on the roof and I felt a fingernail rip off.

I could see the glare of headlights on the gravel, so I used every bit of juice I had left to swing a leg up and over. That gave me the leverage to pull my body up. Panting, I lay on my back looking up at the sky. I hadn't realized how many stars you could see at night out in the country. I elbow-crawled up to the crest of the roof, leaving a water trail behind as I went. My water bottle had burst. I reached in and set it next to me, poor little water bottle. I was on the back side of the roof so I couldn't see anything that was happening in front.

I heard a vehicle pull up while another accelerated away from the building and down the road. I could hear gravel crunching under boots and voices in front. I knew what Max had said, but I also knew that it had turned into the wrong plan. The people below entered the building; I heard someone yell "Clear!"

Tossing the flares no longer made sense to me: It would just alert the other truck—which was still in sight although heading farther away—and the people who were already in the house. I heard a loud "Damn! Damn! When we find them I am going to kill that eye-gouging, tea-spilling, knife-wielding prick!" *Damn, that guy knew how to cuss.* Too bad it was me he was talking about. I heard "Clear!" twice more and then nothing. I guess they were putting it together based on what they had found. I wanted to move up to the peak of the roof and see if I could spot Max but I knew better. I was afraid to even shift my weight.

I heard boots move through the house and then on the porch. A voice from somewhere in front and underneath me said, "Spread out. They are around here somewhere. We are going to walk the road, two to each side. Bobin, kill the lights. I doubt they have night vision."

*Night vision!* I understood now why Max had given me the flares—not just to illuminate the area, but to blind their night-vision gear. The lights went out. I counted to ten. *Damn*, this was going to take some luck and timing. I pulled out the two flares. One was broken; the other was good, I hoped. I twisted the ignition end off and yanked it. *Yikes!* Next time I was going to have to remember to shut my eyes. I tossed it. I was aiming to drop it about ten feet in front of the porch and a little to my left. Then I started rolling like a log toward the end of the roof. I am pretty sure I heard a "What the fuck?" as I went over the edge. I don't think it was me, either.

I knew the landing was going to hurt. I just didn't expect the kind of pain I felt up in my thigh. At first I thought I had landed on the shotgun. I hadn't. I rolled over a little. My hand reached down and I felt metal. I pushed myself up enough to look at my leg. I had landed on the head of a rake. Half of the rusty metal teeth had just bitten me. Well, isn't life a bitch sometimes. This pair of pants was going to be a complete write-off for sure.

At the same time I heard gunfire. Max was engaging them, and I was too busy bleeding to help. I yanked the rake head out of my leg and threw it into the bushes. I started feeling around for the shotgun and amazingly, I found it. A little voice in my head activated itself, telling me *Pump and release the safety*—where was the freaking safety? Ah, there it was. I used the shotgun as a crutch to get to my feet. Man, this was *really* going to hurt in a few minutes.

I limped to the end of the house, holding the shotgun at waist level, almost ready to shoulder it. I figured I would come up behind them. From the sounds, I guessed they were behind the vehicle they had driven, using it for cover. My cycling the pump must have been heard, as one of them came around the corner, moving quickly. He literally ran into the barrel of my shotgun. I didn't even think. I just pulled the trigger. He was wearing a camo vest, and the blast caught him full in the chest. It launched him backward, somewhat spectacularly, I thought. At least the movies had got that part right. Being so close, the muzzle flare had set his vest on fire as he went airborne.

I stepped around the corner, jacking the shotgun as I walked. Out of the corner of my eye I watched the ejected shell as it flew away. It was red; the metal base glinted in the light just as the firefly had earlier. One person, a woman, was sitting on the ground, her back to the front wheel. She was bleeding heavily from her upper arm. The other one, who looked to be a man from the body shape, was using the rear wheel and bed of a crew cab as shelter while he returned Max's fire.

The woman had a pistol in her hand, resting in her lap. Next to it was a cell phone. Amazingly, it started ringing. Beethoven's *Für Elise* as a ring tone, how nice. The man behind the back tire heard it also. He looked at her, and his head turned to follow where she was looking. Her hand was going for the pistol. *C'mon, baby, answer the phone instead.* I took most of her head off with the buck-shot. I was jacking it again, but I knew it was going to be too late. The guy was turning. I could tell my shell would be ejecting about the time his barrel aligned on me. An unhappy ending to what had been such a fine evening up until five minutes ago.

I saw Max coming out of the bushes, running toward me. *Hi, Max!* I remember thinking. The Colt was in his hand. The guy behind the wheel had exposed enough of his upper torso for Max to take the shot. The man got off one shot as he went down. The single round whizzed past my head, missing by an inch or two—it sounded just like a turbocharged bee. The movies had gotten two things right. They must have good tech support. Then my leg gave underneath me.

"What the hell?" If I ever found who left that rake out, I was going to kick his ass. Max didn't stop running. He dived over the hood of the truck, did a roll, and came up about three feet from me in a crouch. He put a bullet in the wheezing, burning man, an act of mercy that was. He didn't bother to ask; he just pulled out his knife and cut the fabric away from where I was bleeding. Four holes were punched in the side of my thigh. They were bleeding—profusely, at that.

## CHAPTER TWENTY-THREE

# DYING

"Hang in there. I'll be back," Max said. Before I knew it, he had run into the house, grabbed the first-aid kit, and returned. "Okay, let's go." He helped me up. With me leaning on his shoulder, we headed for the farm truck. After he helped me in the passenger side he handed me the first-aid kit. "Look for the largest pads and hold them against those wounds. You up to this?"

"Yeah, just drive. I'm good." We were hauling ass down the road. Well, semi-hauling ass. The truck started shaking at fifty-five. These kinds of roads and this kind of vehicle were not designed for high speeds, anyway. The white crosses scattered along the shoulders provided ample testimony to that.

"What about the other truck?"

"Don't worry about them. They will count on us running for home. They will set up an ambush point somewhere along the route before it begins feeding into busier roads. Based on all the blood you left behind, they're going to figure you're badly wounded. So they will watch the local hospital—or have a friendly employee watch

for them. Plus, I am sure they have friends in the sheriff's department. So, we are going to see some friends of
mine in the other direction. Remember to keep that pad
pressed against that wound or you'll be doing half-price
shopping at the shoe store for the rest of your life."

"Where we going?"

"Up by the West Virginia border. I've been thinking,
Gardener: You are going to have to die."

I laughed. "That seems to be tonight's theme. Any reason why?"

"You can't come back with me. You have really pissed
off some people. I'm not sure what was behind the ride in
the golf cart. Probably they just wanted to kick your ass
and it got out of hand. What happened back there at the
house makes sense only as payback for your teeing off on
their friends. That makes it unofficial."

"Unofficial? You mean they were *unofficially* trying to
kill me as opposed to *officially*?"

"Yeah, if the colonel had wanted you dead, in all probability it would have happened. But he would not have
gone off all half-assed like that. Which is why I am going
fishing for a few days, and then I am headed back without you. Hey, look on the bright side: When I announce
you're dead to everyone, why then I'll be able to tell you
how few people care by the number of reactions."

"What if I don't want to die?"

Max had just fished out his cell phone. He stopped
and set it down. "Listen to me. When he comes for you—
and he has to now—he will kill you. And it won't be *High
Noon*, either. You won't meet them in the parking lot,
where the fastest man lives. You will be asleep. It will
be three in the morning. You will hear a loud bang as

the sledgehammer opens your door; then you will hear a *ping* and a *thunk* as the grenade hits the floor. Or, you'll be standing around somewhere, and the top of your head will come off. If those don't work, they will take Carol or Night and hold them as hostages. You will have no choice but to go to them on their ground. Then you and their hostage will die."

I didn't reply. I turned my head and watched fields and woods go by.

"Who gave us this job?" Max asked.

"The chief."

"Right, if it doesn't happen in the ways I described, then perhaps the chief calls in Homeland Security. Asks them for a SWAT team based on a tip he received. One way or another, you will die. It's up to you how many friends you want to take with you."

He was right. I shook my head. It didn't feel right, but that did not change the facts.

"So what do I do while I'm dead?"

"Nothing that would make you uncomfortable, I am sure." I laughed, as did he.

"What I need to do is get you some first-aid, the kind that doesn't show up in reports." Max picked up his cell phone again.

I rested against the door. I was tired, really tired. I think I faded out for a while. I tuned back in to hear him say, "I don't give a shit what your problems are. It's payback time. Come through or I come looking for you." He snapped the phone shut. "Don't worry. He will take care of you. His sister-in-law is a nurse. She is meeting us there. We are only twenty minutes out. Hang in there."

"So, what happened with Martina?" That already seemed a hundred years ago.

"I had her take me back to our room."

"Why?"

"She didn't want to fuck me—she wanted to fuck the medal. I got a lot of that. For a while it was okay; then it wasn't."

I shook my head. Not a whole lot you can say to that. We drove for a while. Max told me to stay in contact by e-mail, but we were going to need throwaway accounts. Using a pen on my forearm I wrote the e-mail address he gave me, maxpainmarine777@yahoo.com. Max continued, "Use that to talk to me for now. Create a new account on Yahoo or Hotmail. Don't use your old e-mail accounts or even check them for a while. Don't call anyone."

"So how long am I going to be dead?"

"Until the chief and his crew bug out is my guess."

I wasn't feeling real talkative. The pain was really beginning to talk to me. The rake tines must have buried themselves an inch and a half deep in my flesh. Max rolled down the window and tossed his phone out onto the road that was blurring by. "Just in case; we used to track our targets that way." He turned on the radio. There was nothing on worth listening to. The truck didn't have a digital receiver so we had limited, crappy options.

Out this way you didn't get all the ethnic noise. Back home the Hispanics, Koreans, and Ethiopians owned the AM band and half the FM. Most of the FM stations had been replaced by robostations. The big radio communications companies in the past couple years had either gone bankrupt or put their resources into digital pay radio.

From what was coming through the one functioning speaker in the truck, it sounded like plain old American hellfire and damnation was big here. Underground radio was beginning to pop up more and more on the free bands, especially around the cities and universities. The D.C. area didn't really have any because of the heavy Homeland Security presence. The feds could identify the location of a transmitter far too quickly to make it worthwhile.

Max switched the radio off. "No matter. We're almost there."

We were out in the country somewhere. Country in this part of the world meant a house, or cluster of houses, every half mile or so. He turned down a gravel road that quickly went to washouts and dust. We pulled up in front of an old house that had an unattached sheet-metal garage. Behind it was a single-wide mobile home with a satellite dish. A long orange extension cord ran from the house to the mobile home. There were kid's toys scattered at random and on the other side of the house, a surprisingly large garden with a chain-link fence around it. A flock of chickens were inside the fence, pecking bugs and fertilizing the crops. A truck, an old minivan, and a white Toyota—maybe a Corolla—were parked next to the house.

Max hit the horn twice. The front door opened and a white man in his late twenties stepped out onto the porch, looked at us, smiled widely, and yelled something back into the house. Max held out his hand: "Take these and tuck them away"—I looked down at two Canadian one-ounce gold coins—"Remember, you can cut these into pieces. The pieces will spend just as well."

"You sure you want to give me all this, Max?"

"We can balance it out later. For now, you need emergency funds."

He yelled out the window, "Hey Tommy! You got room in your garage for this truck?"

"Hey, Sarge. Sure! Let me open her up."

He yelled at the dogs to shut up and moved at a jog toward the garage. We pulled inside and Max turned off the truck engine. "Don't worry. Everything is going to be fine." Then he opened the door, greeting Tommy, who gave him a big hug. "Goddamn, it is good to see you again!" They pounded on each other for a minute or two.

"So, this is the man in here?" He peered through the driver side window at me. "Yep, he looks like he's seen better days. Nice leg wound, Bub."

I smiled and said, "Thanks."

"Sorry about that conversation, Max. I know what I owe you." He ran his hand across his face. "It's just the kids are sick. The wife ran off. Money is real tight, and it don't look like work is coming back anytime soon. I should have stayed in the Corps." He sighed. "Don't you worry, though. We'll take care of the boy. He'll be fine here. Shit, I don't know what got into me. You were like a brother over there to me."

"Forget about it. I already have. Here."

He slipped Tommy a gold coin. "If you need more, let me know. I want you to take good care of my brother." He stressed the *brother* enough that Tommy got the point. I was surprised how happy it made me feel.

"Right, Sarge. Let's get him into the guesthouse. Donna is in the big house looking after the kids. She will meet us there, if she isn't there already." They helped me out of the truck and across the yard into the mobile home. The steps were tough. Inside, it was obvious that the place functioned as a storage space and a craft factory. At least it had once upon a time.

It must have been the missing wife's work space. She had been into Chinese plastic doodads in a major way. Plastic packing peanuts were strewn all over the floor. They made a crunchy sound as we walked over them. My shoe was leaving bloody footprints, since my jean leg was soaked and my sneaker was filled with blood. There was just too much for even big gauze pads to deal with.

"I cleaned up the bedroom a bit. The bathroom works. Just don't use the microwave. You will blow the circuits in the house."

*Yeah,* I thought, *like I am really in a rush to make popcorn.*

"The TV works, and it's hooked up to the satellite so you can actually get channels on it." People were still pissed about the switchover to digital years later.

He put a big, black trash bag onto the covers of the bed. "All right. Get the gun off and lie down." I pulled my gun belt off and handed it to Max. Then I lowered myself onto the bed. It felt good. Real good. I heard the door open and Max pulled my Ruger out of the holster and cocked it.

A bright, cheery "Hello," the *tip-tap* of shoes, and my nurse appeared in the doorway. "I think you can put that away," she said. Max dropped the hammer and holstered it.

"Hey, Donna."

"Hey, Tommy. So this is the patient. My God! That looks like it hurts. It's okay, Tommy, no need for introductions."

"Oh, yeah. This is Donna." Donna sat on the edge of the bed and undid the tourniquet. She set a bag down

next to me that she had brought in and began taking out
bandages, dressings, and glass vials. She lined them all up
neatly. "This guy is Max. The guy on the bed is Gardener."

"Hi, Gardener. Hi, Max—Tommy get me some hot
water, really hot water, a couple towels, and scissors."
She smiled at me; it was a nice smile. "Don't worry—I've
seen worse."

Tommy's sister-in-law was Asian, or maybe Eurasian,
around five feet four and probably not much over a hundred pounds. She was also attractive, a plus in the medical professional, I always thought.

Tommy headed for the door. Max said, "I am going to
go help Tommy. I'll be back to see you before I go." As
they left I heard Max ask Tommy, "You got any coffee?"
and they were gone.

"Okay, Gardener. What bit your leg?"

I laughed. "A rake."

"Hmmm . . . you had a tetanus shot lately?"

Good question. "Yeah, about six years ago."

"Then you're okay for that." She didn't say anymore.
She took off my old compresses and disappeared. She reappeared with a towel. "Here,"—handing me the towel—
"put this under you for now." Tommy came back, carrying a steaming hot bowl, which he cradled with towels.
He set it down carefully by Donna. "Thank you, Tommy."

"You're welcome. The scissors are there, too." He
backed up a couple steps. "How are you feeling, Bub?"

"Tommy?"

"Yes?"

"Don't call me Bub; call me by my name, okay?"

"Sure," he held up his hands. "No offense, just a habit."

"None taken."

"Okay, Tommy. I think you're done here." She fished around in her bag and then stood up. "Why don't you run to the store and get some sandwich stuff for us and Mr. Gardener. The refrigerator still work in here?"

"Not the big one," Tommy replied. "The little one on top of the cabinet does."

"Good. Pick up some water and the sandwich stuff. We can put some in the refrigerator here. That way he doesn't have to come over to the house for now. Thanks." She handed him some folded paper notes. He was turning to leave when she called out, "And Tommy, pick up a six-pack of decent beer. Not that cut-rate soda water you've been drinking." He laughed and left. "Do you drink beer, Mr. Gardener?"

"No, and please, call me Gardener."

"Well, you are going to wish you had a few after I start cleaning these out. We are going to take care of the leg, then I am going to look at those hands and knees." She had me lift up enough so she could slide another towel under me. "Okay, good. Let's get these boots off. Then I need you to disrobe below the waist. Please cover yourself with this towel."

She turned around while I did what she had asked. When I was done I said, "Okay ma'am you can turn around." First she cleaned my bloody, grubby flesh with the hot water. That was quite soothing. The pain was like radio static while the hot water was the music that made it through.

"You okay?" she asked. I nodded.

It was almost, not quite, worth it to have fallen on the rake. She ignored the tent that somehow had appeared. As she worked she explained to me that she used a lot of homeopathic remedies, which I found interesting. "Okay, now this might sting. The antiseptic that she poured liberally over the puncture wounds stung enough that I arched my back and bit my tongue. "You still all right?"

"I'm fine," I told her.

"Now I need you to take these. It is hypericum. This will help prevent tetanus, stop bacteria from forming, and help any nerve damage." She opened a small vial. "This is tea tree oil. I am going to put it on the punctures to prevent infection." She then did the same thing to my knees and hands. "That gravel will fall out on its own over time." She then bandaged the puncture wounds. "I am going to leave the hands and knees open. Fresh air will help them more than bandages at this point. Do you have any clothes?"

"No, not really."

"Okay, I will talk to Tommy." She began packing up her kit. "I will be back in a few days to take a look at it. If we can avoid infection, then you should be fine. Pour some tea oil on it twice a day and change the bandages. I will leave what you need in the kitchen." Then she was gone.

I went to sleep. I woke up briefly when Tommy came and filled the refrigerator. He didn't look in on me, and I drifted back to sleep. I woke up late the next morning. The trailer was stuffy, hot, and smelled of tea oil. My thigh, where the puncture wounds were, was turning pink. I was not a doctor but I knew what that meant. Hopefully, the tea oil would get ahead of it. I hobbled out to the kitchen and slapped some baloney between a couple slices of white bread and wolfed it down. I took a bottle of water and drained it. *Damn*, I needed coffee. I was going to have to talk to Tommy about that.

I looked around and started opening windows. Little Styrofoam peanuts crunched under my feet. I wandered into the living room, found the remote, and clicked on the TV, wishing that I had a laptop. Instead, I was going to have to make do with satellite news. The feed was from DirecTV. What was left of American media news channels was and had been a joke for quite a while. CNN might have made a difference but the passing of the National Communications Act had muzzled them. Actually, it had worked against the authorities in some ways. Now, when CNN said they were going to air a hard-hitting exposé of college terrorism, you knew that Homeland Security was beginning an operation to crack down on student dissidents.

The major European and Asian countries that produced news shows in English were sometimes a good source of information. You had to filter out the home country's agenda, which was often America bashing, to get to the truth. At one time Homeland Security had tried to block their broadcasts, but it had not worked. Instead, someone had a better idea. The approved channels, especially the network alphabet ones, had sexed up the news. Now, it was soft news and porn. They knew how to keep Joe Six-Pack's eyes focused on their message.

## CHAPTER TWENTY-FOUR

# POETRY

Two weeks later I was sitting on the wooden steps outside my front door soaking up a little bit of sun. I was watching the kids play. It was my first time outside since I had arrived here. The infection had spread fast, and I had ended up on my back for over a week as Donna took care of me. I had an IV drip of antibiotics for five days, plus injections of them. The skin had rotted around each puncture, each hole combined into one long strip of rotted flesh. The smell was not unlike that of a decomposing body. For the last two days, medical maggots had been busy in the wound, cleaning it up. I gave Donna one of my gold coins to pay for the IV and medications. When she told me it was too much, I told her to buy food for everyone at the house. Gold went a long way now. Once upon a time there had been a credit price and a cash price. Now there was a cash price and a gold price.

The kids were funny. The boy was seven; the girl was six. They were both cute. They had their mom's dark hair and eyes and their father's features. One day they were running back and forth on the grass in front of me, gradually working their way closer to me despite their father shouting, "Leave him alone!" I thought it would be the boy who would make first contact. I was wrong. Somehow the ball they were playing with ended up rolling to a stop five feet away from me.

"Hey, mister! Throw it to us, please!" This was the little girl.

"I can't," I replied. They both edged closer.

"Why can't you?" asked the little girl.

"Because I can't walk that good."

"He hurt his leg," announced the boy.

"Yes, I did." Then I went on to field, oh, at least fifty questions.

They didn't notice their dad walking up to us. We made eye contact. I nodded to let him know I was okay with it.

"Daddy, can he eat dinner with us?"

The girl asked this. He nodded his assent, and I began eating dinner with them each night. I also started weeding the garden, and I learned how to find eggs and chop firewood. Tommy explained how you could never have enough firewood when you had wood heat. Sometimes Donna would come eat with us. Afterward we would sit out on the porch and talk while the kids ran around and the dogs chased each other, or their tails. It was a good time for me. Maybe the best time in my life up to that point. Sometimes Donna would teach me how to identify common weeds, and then teach me what they could be used for. I learned that, as with people, there was really no common weed.

I convinced Tommy to give me a ride into town. I needed to use the local library computers to send and check e-mail. I didn't want to send mail too often from a static IP address. Tommy had a computer, but he kept it in his office. I had used it to do some research, and there had been no news about any deaths at the colonel's. I thought hard about convincing Tommy to let me move the computer into the trailer but I decided against it. In the brief time I had used it, I had discovered that it was his sex life. He already had one woman run off. I didn't want to ask him to give up another.

I did find a couple local blogs that had posts about how the colonel's retreat was one of the bright spots in the local economy. They were buying farm tractors from anyone who would sell. They were also buying old equipment—old, as in horse-drawn antiques—and they were doing a lot of building. Nothing big or fancy: underground fuel tanks, small inexpensive houses with solar heating, windmills. They were open about it, and they were getting good publicity as a result.

I was also hoping to find a used bookstore in town. I wanted the rest of the *Decline of Rome* series. I had never read much before but the desire was now burning inside me. I read everything that Tommy had. Most of the books he had dug out of boxes in his basement. From the printing dates inside they must have been his grandfather's or grandmother's. I asked him, but he didn't have a clue.

My guess, based on the mix, was that it was both of them. Some were also from his mother's time, but not anywhere near as many. There was a fair amount of poetry, some of which I found impossible to read. Others, well, some of the verses were like flares going off inside my head. I really liked Frost. Then there was T. S. Eliot. There were a couple anthologies of poetry that were great—mainly because I got to taste a wide selection of poets. One I liked especially: It had poems written by Sassoon, Graves, Brooke, and Owen. From the anthologies I began to make a mental list of who I wanted to read more of. Shakespeare was well represented in the selection of books. I really tried but found I did not care that much for him. Some of the lines he wrote were great, but I found it to be too much work to get to them. Then I found Steinbeck. He totally enthralled me with his descriptions of his character's worlds. *The Sword in the Stone* was also an incredible book. I read that in one sitting. Sometimes after reading a passage or a great verse I would sit outside, look at the stars, and wonder about things.

I had always known I was weird—maybe even a "freak." It had bothered me a lot, once upon a time. Now, well, I found I just didn't care. I never knew how other people seemed to know certain things. It was as if the entire human race had been issued an instruction book at some point in their lives. I imagined that it was called *Handbook for Humans* and that it was bound in red leather with the title in gold lettering. It would have chapters like "How to Have a Conversation" or "How to Get a Date" or even "How to Really Care." I never found a copy, and no one ever admitted to having one. I was still looking though.

Riding into town with Tommy was interesting. Just to see new sights was a nice change. It had only been three months but the changes were startling. Maybe it was because it had been so long since I'd spent any time outside my little world. My mind held images of what a small town in Virginia looked like, but they were all a few years out of date. Reading what was happening on the blogs, seeing the news coverage, and even experiencing the changes where I had lived had not prepared me for the reality that confronted me. I knew I was in America, but whose America?

I lived and survived by sensing emotional undercurrents, in individuals and in groups. If I had any gift at all, that was it. I found that there were always multiple realities happening on every street and in every conversation. Together they would make up the one major current for that place. The currents I was feeling, especially when I got out of the car and left Tommy to go find the library, were not good ones: This was not a happy town. It was a very stressed, confused, angry town.

I did not feel comfortable and I was glad I was carrying visibly. At least 30 percent of the people I passed were also, and most of them were males. A lot of people were out on foot or bicycle. A man and a woman passed me on horseback. I was on the sidewalk; they were on the street. I thought about what it would be like to have them come at me at full speed while shooting or waving a saber, and I understood a lot more why being a peasant sucked back in the day.

The common areas were unkempt: Street signs had been hit and were either mangled or snapped off at their base. They had not been replaced. Trash was scattered on both sides of the road. The gutters had not been cleared of the past winter's sand and oak leaves. Graffiti had been spray-painted on empty buildings and had not been cleaned off. The business district looked as though it had gotten ready for the arrival of a hurricane and then decided not to take down the plywood once the storm passed. People were drinking in public and not bothering to hide it. On one corner a black man, dressed in clean clothes and otherwise normal looking, was screaming "God Bless You!" over and over. This was punctuated by fits of laughter and wide grins. He was probably the happiest guy in town.

The town had not given up entirely. Many of the cars may have been getting old and had unrepaired dents, but they had been washed. Some of the houses looked untouched by what was happening. They were well kept, with flower gardens and fences in good repair. If you switched your vision to selective, you might even be able to convince yourself all was well. But it wasn't, and to think otherwise was a very dangerous thing to do.

We had checked before leaving to make sure the library was open. The town once had had three libraries. Now it had one, and it was open only three days a week. It had not bought anything in two years and the librarians were volunteers. My plan was to check for e-mail at the library and then walk over to the used bookstore.

The library had a crowd around it, waiting for it to open. They charged for Internet access: one paper U.S. dollar for fifteen minutes and a thirty-minute maximum usage policy. I had arrived fifteen minutes before opening thinking that would be sufficient, but I was wrong. I was the tenth person in line. Everyone stared at me when I got in line and only a few responded to my cheery "Hello."

One person, a young girl, was talking on a cell phone; two other people read paperbacks; and the rest of us just stood there—all sullen but me. The librarian, an older woman with gray hair and a haggard face, opened exactly on time. We flooded in, everyone except for me having a clue about the procedure. A large sign that read Internet

Access was suspended by string over the desk. Everyone was in line to sign up, so I got in line. Most of the people not only signed up, but also had brief conversations with the librarian. Her assistant would disappear occasionally, reappearing with official-looking mail. The people would grab it eagerly, dash to the Internet access waiting line, and rip it open. Nobody seemed happy about what they received. One person cried right there, and an old man began cussing the government and went off on a short tirade before stomping out the door. That was fine with me—one less person in front of me.

It took me an hour before I was able to sit down where six Dell computers were set up. Two were broken and turned off. I got the machine that was beside them, so I didn't have anyone next to me. The county must have bought new machines right before the Crash, as these were not that bad. The keyboards had seen better days, and I felt like running some hand sanitizer over the mouse, but hey, they worked. The other machines were being used by two old people and a pretty girl of about seventeen. I'd smiled at her when I sat down and she had returned it shyly. I logged into my latest e-mail account and checked for messages. I had one from Max. It was short and I liked what it said:

"Come home now!"

I let out an exuberant "Yahoo!" It silenced the place for a second. The old farts scowled at me. Happiness was not allowed in their world.

The young girl whispered to me, "Good news?"

I nodded my head. "Yes, it sure is." I was just starting to compose an e-mail to Night. I wanted to avoid any drama upon my homecoming, and I also wanted to make sure my room was available.

That's when I heard the voices: loud, obnoxious voices with an edge that sounded like alcohol. I didn't even have to turn around to dislike them. Once I did turn around, I found I liked them even less. There were three of them, the minimum size for a gang, but they were making maximum use of the power they thought it bestowed on them. They walked up to the Internet sign-up desk. The few people in line visibly cringed at their arrival. All three were white males, in their early twenties at most, and the leader was a big kid. He had long hair and a handful of metal attachments embedded in his face. He also had all the right tattoos. His followers had been cloned at the same factory. One had a really nice Confederate flag tattoo on his biceps. Two of them had the old-school wallet chains, and they were all carrying handguns.

The leader said loudly, "Hello, auntie! We've come to use the Internet."

She told him, using a tone that had about as much steel in it as my underwear, "You know you need to sign in, Lucas."

They all laughed. He leaned over the desk and lightly patted her face. Well, he tried to; she flinched before his hand reached her.

"We'll do that, Auntie M."

He laughed and they turned to survey the table. One of the old people who was seated at a computer began gathering her stuff. She knew what was going to happen. The old guy next to her muttered something and began typing faster.

"Hi, Rachael!" the leader called out to the young girl.

His lackeys mimicked him, "Hi, Rachael!" as they swaggered over.

The leader told the two old people, "Git." The old lady was already moving before he had made it halfway across the floor.

The old man held up his hand, "Just a minute, boys! I am almost done."

He bent over the keyboard and continued typing furiously. The leader nodded at one his lackeys, who smiled. I noticed he had been neglecting his dental care. The lackey walked around, reached over, grabbed the old man by the collar, and tossed him from the chair.

He told his boss, "He's done."

The old man got slowly to his feet, rubbing the small of his back. "That was unnecessary, Lucas. I was almost done."

"Fuck you, Mr. Branson," the leader told him. "Get your skinny ass out of here before I kick it."

The old man scurried out of their way. "Leader Boy" turned to me and said, "He was my English teacher"—as if that explained everything. I nodded. I had never had any English teachers I liked either.

Whooping and hollering, the trio settled into the two now-vacant terminals. One of them came around and grabbed one of the empty chairs from the dead terminals next to me.

"Anyone using this?" he asked me deadpan.

"No."

They all thought that was pretty funny. I finished my e-mail to Night and hit Send. I started surfing the blogs, partly because I was interested in reading the news, partly because I was no longer in a hurry to get to the used bookstore.

The boys found what they had come for—porn, of course. They talked real loud and made rude comments about what they were watching. One of them got up and acted like he was going to unzip and jerk off right there.

"C'mon, Rachael, look over here."

She ignored them. Leader Boy flipped the flat screen around so she could view it.

"Hey, Rachael, that looks like you. You've been making extra money on the side? Huh, baby?"

She flipped them off and said, "Fuck you!" She was pissed and scared but she wasn't moving. I liked that. I liked the boys even less now, if that was possible.

"So, Rachael, I hear your brother and his butt buddy cousin are back from the army. How long they going to be around this time? They still got all their arms and legs?"

She looked at them, smiled sweetly, and said, "Maybe I could call him and they could come by?"

I don't know what Leader Boy's history was with Rachael and her family, but that was not what he wanted to hear. He decided to shift his attention to me.

"What are you staring at, asshole?"

I stood up slowly and looked each one in the eyes. The girl had her hands under the table. *A weapon?* Each one of them had time to assimilate the fact that I was also carrying. That familiar sensation of coldness swept through me and I welcomed it. It had been too long. Part of me registered that the library had gone silent. My field of vision narrowed to them and me. Inside—In my head? Perhaps in my soul?—I heard delighted laughter.

"So what happened to your face?" I asked. "Nail gun accident on the job?"

I saw the girl smile just a tiny bit. The boys looked confused. The boy leader processed it and realized it wasn't a compliment.

"Hey, fuck you. How about I come across this table and nail your ass? You would probably like that. Wouldn't you, you pussy." His fans approved—or at least they understood this exchange.

"You can come across the table, but I guarantee you will be dead once you reach this side." Without taking my eyes off Leader Boy, I said, "Rachael, why don't you take a walk?"

"Don't you fucking move, Rachael!" snarled Leader Boy.

I was impressed. It was a credible snarl. Leader Boy had a little more emotional range than I had expected.

"That was good," I told him.

Rachael stood up, her eyes reflecting her uncertainty. A song began playing in my head, just a fragment of it, origin unknown: *"Should I stay or should I go,"* the singer wailed over and over in a rather demented loop. It was always nice to have a soundtrack, I thought.

Then we all heard, "Yeah, why don't you go, Rachael."

By the grin on her face and the grip on her cell, it was obvious her cavalry had arrived. A texted plea for help must have summoned big brother and cousin. Big brother strode in, his cousin flanking him until they came near the table. Then the cousin arched a bit for a better angle on the twins. Brother was carrying a twelve-gauge that had probably been cut down to the shortest legal length: eighteen inches of barrel. More than likely it had begun life as a hunting shotgun. The shotgun alone changed the balance of power in the room. Cousin had a big, black, snub-nosed revolver. *Maybe we were cousins, too?* I thought when I saw the revolver.

Rachael moved toward the door, slowing long enough as she passed her brother to flip off Leader Boy and yell, "Asshole!" before she was out the door.

"Lucas, what did I tell you last time I was home?"

Leader Boy mumbled something.

Brother looked at me, "Did he touch her?"

As much as I wanted to say yes, I didn't. Brother looked as disappointed as I felt with that answer.

Lucas, being the idiot he was, had to say something to save face: "One day, you and your family ain't going to be here to save her ass and boss people around. *Then* we'll see who is tough."

Brother just laughed. "If that looks near to happening, I will come back and personally kill you and your cat and burn down that double-wide you inherited. You really think your kinfolk want to start a war over your sorry ass? I am going to tell you one more time. Any body part you touch my sister with will get cut off. Now I am going to add this: She ever tells me you looked at her the wrong way, then I am going to come and take your eyes. You got that?"

Leader Boy nodded his head. Off to the side, Cousin started laughing.

Brother stared at them for a few more seconds, nodded at Cousin, and looked at me. "Can we drop you someplace?"

"Naw, I still got some errands to run. Thanks."

He turned his back on them and walked out. Cousin followed him, walking backward. After a second's hesitation I followed Cousin, but temptation got the best me: I grinned and flipped off the trio. I got to see Leader Boy's face go from white to red before I was out of their sight.

The girl was sitting in an old Toyota Tundra. She waved when she saw me. I waved back. Brother said, "More than likely they are going to come boiling out of there in a few minutes, looking to kick your ass. You sure about what you're doing?"

I smiled. "Yeah, heck, this might even turn out to be an all-around good day."

Brother shrugged, and they got in their truck. I started walking. Fast.

The library was situated on the corner of a park. The part I was walking across had probably been a soccer field a year or two ago—hard to tell for sure since the grass had not been cut for at least a year. It was knee high and paths through it marked where people had crossed. Once I would have assumed they were from the deer that had been so abundant, but not anymore. Deer hunting was turning back into real hunting as the herds had been thinned drastically over the past few years. Maybe it would cut down on the ticks but I doubted it. Ahead of me was a wooded area. My guess was, once I reached the woods I would find a creek, some hills, and a bike path. Might even be a Tree People community or two tucked away in there.

I was halfway across the field when I heard shouting behind me. "Come here, you fucking faggot!" was pretty easy to make out. Leader Boy had rallied the troops, after waiting a few minutes for Brother to clear the area, of course.

I flipped them off again and kept walking. I heard a shot and nearly laughed. It would have taken a miracle for them to hit me. I was out of their range, which I estimated to be less than ten feet. I entered the woods, hitting a well-used trail and a weathered sign that read Edward J. Williams Park. Someone had spray-painted a skull and crossbones over the top of that. *Nice touch*, I thought. I looked over my shoulder. Leader Boy and his clones were running. I had about five seconds before the next act would begin and all the park would be a stage.

The stream was there, just as I expected. It was maybe ankle deep here, where a ford had been created using rocks. The bank on each side was two feet high or so. It was steeply pitched except at the crossing. Part of the crossing was eroding due to bike traffic. Otherwise it was no big deal, unless you were a grandma with a walker. I crossed over and stood to one side of the path waiting for them. They came bursting through—I could hear them before I could see them. The boys were blowing hard. They were just as red-faced as they had been back at the library, this time because of the exertion. They came to an abrupt stop when they saw me standing on the other side of the creek.

"Damn, boys. You need to save up your pennies and get a membership to Gold's Gym. You're blowing as hard as Lucas does on Friday night in the men's room at the truck stop."

"Fuck you," gasped Leader Boy.

"You need to catch your breath before we commence?" I asked, laughing.

It wasn't a fair fight. That was fine with me. They hadn't intended it to be. Leader Boy went for it, and a second later the clones followed. I had a couple things going for me: I was fast. Part of that was just something

I had been born with; another part was a lack of hesitation. The final parts were holster and training. I had customized my holster to match the rig Bill Jordan had made famous years ago with the Border Patrol down on the Tex-Mex border.

The training was thousands of reps in front of a mirror, practicing the draw, fire, cock, fire that was required. Jordan used a double-action revolver. Even in his day the single-action was considered a nostalgia piece. Yet it was all basically the same. His saying was "Be fast but not too fast." I had really taken that to heart and it paid off now. I was using Hydra-Shok rounds in the Ruger. Tommy, who was a bit of a gun nut, had told me about them. He swore they were the best hollow points made for revolvers, especially for use on people at close range. They had a metal post inside the bullet that somehow made the slug mushroom. That was good because it ripped a bigger hole in the target's guts. He gave me a box and we went out back, and I shot half of them. Then I switched back to the wadcutters that Tommy reloaded.

The Hydra-Shok were expensive and difficult to find, so I kept them for when I carried. You might say that Leader Boy got the "shok" of his life. The first round was an almost perfect heart shot. I doubt if I was off by more than an inch. He didn't even get his gun clear of his holster. The other two were still sucking wind, and they panicked. Only one of them cleared nylon, and that wasn't good enough.

The clones didn't die right away, but Leader Boy was gone by the time he hit the ground. The second one didn't stick around long either. The third one died hard. That was my fault. I rushed the shot and he paid for it. I kicked the gun away from his hand and knelt down beside him.

He was bleeding from the mouth and trying to talk: "Did you call 911?"

I assured him that I had and that help was on the way. He called for his momma a few times and then he died. I closed his eyelids like I had seen done in the movies—it felt very weird. I decided that the others could stare at the sun until the birds came for them. I rolled him over and pulled his wallet from his pocket. Three paper dollars. I rolled him back and patted him down. I found a soggy cloth bag that had tobacco and a pack of papers in it. That was it. I sighed. I fished his pistol out of the water and tossed it up on the bank.

A stick snapped behind me. I came out of my kneeling position, my hand slapping leather. Two black guys were standing ten feet from me on the other bank. One was in his late forties, with whiskers that were more scruff than beard. The other one was in his early twenties. The older one held up his hand in the universal gesture. Neither one was armed that I could see.

"Hey, be cool. We come in peace."

"I hope it isn't to serve mankind."

He laughed, "No, man, I avoid the long pork."

The other guy wasn't comprehending any of this—a cultural defect, or no access to crappy cable stations showing ancient reruns. I hadn't holstered my revolver.

"So, what do you want?"

The younger guy stepped forward a couple paces; the older guy's face tightened. "Whoa, is that that racist, cracker-ass bitch Lucas lying there?" the young one said. "Way to go!" His grin reflected his delight. He stepped forward a couple more steps. I holstered my revolver and stepped back a pace or two. "Nice. You got both of his buddies. Jesus, I doubt if their mothers are even going to miss them. They were freaking useless—and that was on their best day."

The older guy walked forward. Together they approached the bodies. The younger one stared at them and then kicked Lucas hard. "Just checking," he explained to me.

I was getting restless. "So, you guys live around here?"

"Yeah," the older man jerked his thumb over his shoulder, "back there. We're camping."

All right. I knew we could deal then.

"How about this: You get two of the guns and half the money. In exchange you make them disappear."

The older man didn't hesitate. "Done. Luther, start dragging those bodies into the bushes."

The young one, Luther, began with Leader Boy, chuckling each time his head bounced off a rock. Then the older guy grabbed one of the clones by his feet and followed Luther. Three minutes later they had them tucked away from any prying eyes. I kicked water over the bloodied stones and ground. The blood washed away easily—just a faint swirl rapidly dissolving in the current.

I stood there waiting for them to reappear. They weren't long.

"The one guy had no money," Luther said. "The other two had eighteen dollars in paper, and Lucas also had two silver dollars."

"I got three dollars from the one guy," I said. "I'll take eleven, you get ten and your choice of the guns. And we split the two silver dollars."

The old man spoke up, "If you don't mind, it would be better if you took dipshit's gun. Someone might recognize it." Then he asked me, "You don't plan on staying around, do you?"

"Okay, I'll take the money and the gun now. And no, I'm going to be gone before sundown. Why?"

He smiled. "Because if you needed a place to stay, you would be welcome to join us."

"Thanks, but I'm out of here."

We divided the spoils. I walked away rapidly. I was already late for my rendezvous with Tommy. This was good since I didn't want to stand around waiting for him. I wanted him ready to go.

## CHAPTER TWENTY-FIVE

# RETURN

Tommy was sitting in the car when I showed up. I got in, shut the door, and told him, "Let's roll."

He turned the key, looked over at me, and said, "We going to have a problem leaving?"

I looked at him, surprised. He laughed and pulled away from the curb.

"Gardener, I can smell the gunpowder on you. Plus, I don't see any shopping bags stuffed with books. That can mean only one thing when it comes to you."

"No, I think we are good." I stretched out a bit.

"I heard from Max. It's time for me to go home."

"All right! Must have made you feel good." He added hastily, "Not that I've minded having you around the place." A note of wistfulness tinted what he said next: "Going to be kind of quiet without you. Your nurse won't be coming around as much, that's for sure."

"She'll come around for the kids."

"Yeah," he smiled, "maybe I will get sick."

"You could do worse, brother."

He didn't say anything, and I knew he was thinking about his ex. "So, are you going to give me a ride back?"

"Sure, let me call Donna and see if she can come out tomorrow for a picnic and watch the kids while I am gone. We can do a good-bye thing for you, too."

I had him stop at the Dollar Store along the way so I could run in and pick up a couple presents for the kids. The next day I woke early. I was excited to be leaving. I stuffed the few belongings I had in my bag after taking a shower. I spent the rest of the time cleaning the bathroom and kitchen. While I did that, I left the television on CNN so I could listen to it. They were running continuous reporting on what they were calling "the collapse of a 'Narco State.'" It was not pretty, especially if you were poor, old, female, or a child. And based on the video they kept showing, one or more of those labels applied to a heck of a lot of Mexicans.

I stopped cleaning to watch it. It was fascinating in a slow-motion, car-wreck kind of way. A combination of failures was driving these people across the border in what CNN was calling the biggest migration ever in America. It was "epic"—epic in the total failure of the Mexican state; epic in the U.S. government's inability to do much of anything for any of the people involved; epic in the migration of countless people across hostile terrain, dodging angry locals and predators from both countries, ripping at them from all sides.

Mexico had watched the flow of its oil fields diminish while the price of oil dropped simultaneously to levels unseen in years. This meant no money for government programs. Combine that with a worldwide depression, returning citizens from the USA, the rise of gangs, and general incompetence on both sides of the border, and the result was the citizens of Mexico voting with their feet. They had to: To stay meant to die—either slowly, from lack of food and water, or quickly and violently. As the CNN anchor said, "It was not a drug war now; it was a civil war."

The U.S. government did not have—or at least was still searching for—a policy that worked. The white minorities in the border states, with some backing from Latino U.S. citizens, wanted the hand of God to come down upon these poor and dying people and smite them something fierce. Failing that, the whites took to patrolling the border themselves. That was generating some really nice atrocity photos and videos.

Then there was the biggest problem of all: Where could all these people go?

Los Angeles—really all of Southern California—did not have the water, the jobs, or the infrastructure to support half the population it already had. Arizona? The same. New Mexico? The same. Texas? Its aquifer was drying up quickly. The South? Repeated hurricane strikes had overwhelmed the infrastructure there. There were jobs to be found, but the exploitation of existing workers was already at third-world levels. There was nowhere for the Mexicans to go, but they still kept coming, pushing farther inland. If they had been warlike, it would have been a migration out of ancient history: the tribal movement into new lands that destroyed so many civilizations in the past. Rome was one example that came to mind. There weren't going to be enough tents, tarps, or trailers in North America to house all these people. I shrugged, turned it off, and went to the picnic.

The picnic was nice. We had chicken and rice, toma-toes and corn. Donna brought a great chocolate cake. I had forgotten how good chocolate was. I was a pig, as were the kids. Me and the kids played "Catch the kid with the ball," a game we created and whose rules were never completely agreed upon—other than that I was supposed to chase them. It was good for my thigh, which still reminded me every once in a while that burying rusty rake tines in it was not appreciated. Tommy and Donna sat on the porch and chatted.

When it was time to go I went back to the trailer, got my bag, and tossed it in the car. Then I went over and gave the kids their Dollar Store presents. The boy got a bag of green plastic American soldiers that looked like they were from World War II. The girl got a bunch of scrunchies and ponytail whatevers. They both really liked what they got, which made me happy. We exchanged hugs. The girl cried, which bothered me, and Tommy and I got in the car and drove off.

There wasn't much traffic and we made a good time. We drove silently for a while. I just watched the world flow by outside the window. I had left my cash on the bed with a note asking Tommy to use it to buy Christmas presents for the kids.

"Tommy, we never talked about Max much. How long did you know him?"

He thought about it while a couple of miles rolled by. "I knew him for a year. Then he was transferred to a Special Ops team. They were based where we were, so he would come by if we were in and shoot the shit with us. He mostly hung out with the lifers. We all figured he was going to be one himself."

"How did he get the medal?"

Tommy was surprised. "You didn't look it up on the Net? You know it is out there, right? The citation, plus some other media coverage."

"I know. I just felt like it would be prying into his business. Plus, well, I would rather think of him as Max—not super-marine."

Tommy pursed his lips, shrugged. "Yeah, I sort of see your point. You know what we called him? 'Maximum Max'—he did everything to the maximum. I'll let you go online and read the citation for yourself. It is probably better that way. I will tell you one thing, though: Max and that crew he was teamed up with were doing some off-the-wall shit. If even half of what I heard is true, then I am surprised they didn't have an accident in the air—you know, just to make sure no one talked."

"You going to tell me anything?" I was curious, really curious.

"Some of the shit the government was doing that I heard about, well, let's say I was glad I never knew the entire story, because I don't want to know. Let's just say assassinations, and some of the targets wore our uniforms. There was a lot money over there, especially in the Bush years."

We kept rolling. You could feel the pulse change, beginning to beat faster, as we approached the D.C. metro area. Traffic picked up, moved faster, and was more aggressive. The signs were for places that I knew. It was good to be back. The problem was how faceless corporate America was. There was no focus for the rage, at least no until the blog post by "Paine."

As Tommy drove I thought about the blog I had been reading earlier. It was a "Burner" blog, and the content was most certainly being stored on a server outside the U.S. It advocated "burning it down." The reasoning, which made sense to a lot of people, was to deny the pigs their profit wherever possible. There was no way the average citizen was going to make it through the security systems the really rich had in place. Plus, how could you identify the right people? So the logic was to "kill the monster"—deny the corporations their source of life: profits.

They built an empty shopping mall with your money? Burn it down! They are going to take your house? Burn it down! Burn down the banks! Burn down the office parks that don't have a job for you. They built a luxury home development . . . burn it down!

The fire department would respond and make sure there were no people in the structure. Then, unless it was a house in a neighborhood that was still partially inhabited, they let it burn. Their health care was a joke, so why risk injury? Their pensions were gone, so why give a damn. Their pay had been cut, why work? There was no money for equipment. Why use it up on a pig place? That's what they were called: "pig places."

As in: Last night someone burned down the Bank of America branch off of Gallows Road. *Ah, just another pig place—who cares?*

The other part that made it so seductive was the belief that burning it all down would force the corporations to build new buildings. They would have to hire workers to build the new places. They would need people to work in them and jobs would come back and life would return to normal. Except this time people planned on being smarter with the money they made. But it didn't work out that way. Not because not enough buildings weren't burned, rather, because there was no reason to rebuild.

I thought about it and tucked it away in my head. Later on, when I got a chance, I would talk to Night about what I had read and see what she had to say. I was looking forward to seeing her. I wasn't sure if I was comfortable with what I was feeling about her. It was a lot easier when you didn't care. Why? Because when they moved on, and they always did, it didn't hurt as much.

Tommy dropped me off in front of the Anchorage. I had half-expected somebody to be waiting for me. Actually, in my head I pictured a crowd of people. Then I would laugh at myself and narrow down who the probable people would be. I figured Night, Max, and the ninjas at a bare minimum. There was nobody waiting. I shrugged off the sting and told myself it was no big deal.

I thanked Tommy; we had an awkward moment, and I got out with my stuff. I heard him pull away and I didn't look back. Life was a bitch, but you just kept going, I told myself. I shouldered my bag and headed off to my room. As I walked I told myself I would get some sleep, then go out and buy some tacos from Taco Man as a celebration. Then maybe see if Max was around. Yeah, I was feeling a little sorry for myself. I unlocked my door and stepped into my room. I wasn't alone. I smiled a real smile, a big smile, maybe the most genuinely happy smile ever. Then I shut the door and said, "Hello, Night." She didn't reply. Instead she patted the bed next to her and crooked a finger at me.

Night left sometime in the early morning. I slept until 10 a.m. I woke up, half-expecting Max to be sitting there.

He wasn't. The room smelled like four hours of great sex. I didn't want to wash my face or hands. I wanted to smell them all day long. I got dressed, rolled out, and headed down to the oak tree. If Max wasn't there, then I would walk the market and see what was up with everyone. The wind was from the east, and the smell of smoke was in the air. Something was burning. From the smoke on the horizon, it looked like trouble at Tyson's Corner. There were a couple of huge malls there, which meant a lot of buildings to burn.

I walked to the vendor stalls. There was one new stall—nice people selling candles and soap. I got two bars of soap and a candle gifted to me. I was wearing my uniform shirt, which had been washed and ironed while I was gone. I stuck my head in the Dollar Store and got gifted ten paper dollars by the old lady. I was in a great mood and really hungry. I walked down to the local restaurant and had an egg sandwich on mystery bread. The family that made them had taken over what had been a Chinese carryout. They slept there and kept the chickens behind the restaurant. Probably not really sanitary, but the eggs were good.

I asked the Ethiopian woman who ran it, "What the hell is in the bread today?"

I would have sworn there was sawdust in it. I never could say her name. She had way too many vowels and letters, same for her husband. I called her ma'am and him sir and left it at that.

She smiled, answering, "Is good?"

"Sure." I went to pay her in U.S. paper and she looked at it with disdain.

"Silver?" She wanted hard currency.

I shook my head and pointed to the misspelled sign that said "Egg Sandwish $4.00." She reached over and ripped down the sign, tossing it on the dirty floor. Then she jumped on it. I shrugged and left four paper one-dollar bills on the counter. I was going to walk the streets, drop by the more mainstream stores, and maybe even get gifted with some more cash. I thought about going by the shelter to see Carol. I decided not to: Why rile up Night, who would know about it before I even got there. I decided I would go check the oak tree one more time. I was starting to feel a bit uneasy. Max should have shown up by now.

The vibe on the street was good, or as good as it got nowadays. I walked our beat. I decided from now on I was going to carry a twelve-gauge. After using one a few months ago, I could see how it would be useful on a foot patrol like this. I would have to go try it out with slugs and double-aught shot to see what worked best, maybe find some abandoned houses or a strip mall to see what it could do to a wall or door. I was headed back when I spotted Max. He was sitting on an overturned five-gallon bucket just inside the doorframe of what had been a title office. I sauntered over, smiling, and he reached behind his back, pulled out another bucket, and said, "Pull up a chair."

"Good to see you, Max."

"Yeah, it's been a while. You got time to talk or you in a hurry to be somewhere?" He grinned.

"Yeah, well, I got some time."

He just stared at me for a couple beats, then shook his head. "You could do a lot worse, but I wouldn't play with her."

"Yeah, I don't intend to."

"Good. Well, I suppose I should catch you up on what happened while you were away."

We spent the next forty minutes or so talking. Mostly it was Max talking and me occasionally interrupting for more details. The colonel had sent men: They had made the rounds, heard the answers, and believed them. I was dead. They had told Max he had a standing offer to come back and see the colonel. All was forgiven as far as Max and the colonel went.

The chief had bugged out last week. He had left Max with some part of the armory, almost all of it the old stuff: shotguns and revolvers, some first-generation body armor—Max called them flak jackets—and ammunition that was at least twenty-five years old. I thought we had got the best part of the armory.

"What did that cost you?"

"Well, you're looking at the new Fairfax City chief of police."

I thought that was funny—as in really, *really* funny. I finally settled down and took a deep breath.

"So does this mean we get paid now?"

"Yep. I think we can even get you some genuine law enforcement training, too, if you want it, that is."

"Let me think about that one. Did he take the patrol officers with him?"

"Yep. They aren't the only people bugging out. I have no idea where they are going, but they sure are gone. Only people moving in around here are Mexicans coming up from the south. A lot of them. I am surprised you hadn't noticed."

I scratched myself and thought about it. I didn't have any problems with Mexicans, so I didn't really care. They were no better or worse than anyone else. It was no big deal.

Max continued, "They aren't all starving victims of a collapsed state either. I think we are headed for a serious gang problem. These pyros aren't helping matters, either. I spread the word that if I hear or suspect anyone of harboring Burner beliefs and the desire to practice them around here, well, they are either gone or dead."

"We don't have much around here to attract them."

"Yeah, well I expect you to do the same thing with them if you run across them."

The look he gave me told me all I needed to know about how successful the Burners had been in recruiting believers. Hell, the smell of smoke in the air was constant now.

"Don't worry. They strike a match around me and I will blow them out."

"You're still an asshole, aren't you, Gardener." It was a statement rather than a question. "But I'm glad you're back."

"Max, you give any thought that maybe we should bug out ourselves? Find someplace better than this?"

He was silent for a while. "Yeah, I have. Even Rome was unlivable for a long period of time."

*Even Rome was unlivable for a time.* This echoed in my head. The idea that current events were comparable to the fall of Rome was a bit overwhelming to comprehend. Then again, why not? It was just unfortunate for me that it happened while I was alive. Well, as my old supervisor used to say: "Shit happens—deal with it."

Max and I walked back to the market and made our circuit. We hung around until the vendors packed up. Then we checked the fancier stores to make sure everything was closed up. Max called it "rattling doorknobs." I never rattled any doorknobs, but I understood what he meant: Check the doors, shine a light if it was dark, and make sure everything was buttoned up tight. Nightfall was coming earlier now and the leaves were starting to change. I loved this time of year. I wished I could find a drink that tasted like the air I was breathing. Chilled, tasteless except for a hint of leaves and smoke—it would pour red with a hint of yellow.

We made plans to meet the next morning at the oak tree. "We need to go by the station tomorrow," Max said. "We are going to need to move a lot of those weapons before someone else does. There are some other items that might come in handy, also. Plus, I need to figure out how we are going to cover the area that the patrol officers were responsible for."

"Sure. Same time?"

"Yep."

I walked back to the motel alone. I walked to my room and Night was waiting for me. She met me at the door. Eventually, I got my gun belt off and tossed it on the bed. She had brought dinner.

"Hey, cool! Chinese carryout!" and I started laughing. Once she figured out what I really meant she smacked me upside the head. Well, I thought it was funny. It was soup with noodles. Spicy, just as I preferred. I liked the spoons she used better than what I had grown up with. No taste of metal, and you could really move some soup quickly into your stomach. We both upended our bowls to drink every bit of it.

During dinner we chatted, just basic stuff: "How was your day?"—that kind of conversation. What Max had said about Rome was still bouncing around in my head. So I asked her what she thought about it.

"You mean that D.C. is Rome and the United States is the empire? That we are in the process of falling apart?"

"Yes, though Rome fell because of repeated invasions." I threw that in just to impress her with my historical knowledge.

"Ah, well, it depends on whether you use Gibbon's model or Ferrill's. There have been other theories, such as the Pirenne Thesis. Of course, you're viewing this through the lens of western civilization, which is understandable. But to answer your question: Yes."

"Okay . . ." Several alternative replies, from witty to sarcastic, went through my head. I discarded them all. The woman was smart—deal with it.

"You ever think we might have to find a better location? Someplace where we can be assured of food and safety?"

She replied, "Sure. I want to hear what you think we would be looking for. Who would come, and how we would do it?"

I sensed a trap. This was one of the reasons I preferred to talk as little as possible. Then again, it was also why I had spent so much time sleeping alone.

"Well, we would need to take your parents." By the way her eyes and her expression changed, I realized I had successfully navigated one possible explosion. "Actually, everyone here would have to go. Max, too, I hope. I don't know if we could do it without him. He might have some people he wants to bring. I think he has a girlfriend."

"Three, actually," Night replied.

"No wonder he has been so tired in the morning," I laughed.

"Don't worry: You will be tired, too."

## CHAPTER TWENTY-SIX

# ALY

The next morning I woke up alone. Night felt it would be disrespectful to her parents not to return to her room before sunup. I wanted her to stay, but she was insistent, so reluctantly, I let her go. I got up, did the usual, and walked down to the oak tree. I had woken early, but I felt good. A little tired, but that was okay. I was going to need some coffee soon. I could smell the coffee vendor making it. What I found at the tree was no Max but two guys in a discussion that was on the verge of becoming heated.

I undid the leather thong that served to keep my gun secured in the holster and stopped about fifteen paces away. I was not in either one's direct line of sight, so they didn't notice me. One guy was Aly, one of the Indians who still lived here. I was surprised to see him. I thought he would have returned to India, as many of his compatriots had. The H-1B program had been shut down completely a while ago and foreigners were no longer encouraged to apply for jobs in America—not that there were any jobs available. Nowadays, the only way you could legally im-migrate to the United States was to pay our government a large ransom. Then, whichever state you planned to live in took the rest of your money. This was for providing you with the wonderful infrastructure that still worked in many places, most of the time.

The other man was unknown to me. He was white and unkempt, but by today's standards he was within the socially acceptable range. "White Man" was armed with a handgun and a knife. Aly had a knife tucked into his belt, but no other weapon that I could see. It was an interesting knife: The blade had a bit of a curve to it—more than was usually seen around here. I would have to ask him about that later. I listened to Aly, who was explaining to the man, very patiently, I thought:

"I never took anyone's job. I have—excuse me, *had*—a small business. I paid my taxes and bothered no one."

"Right! A small business! I know the type: You charged one price for 'your people' and another one for people like me! You and your fucking twelve people in a three-bedroom house, trashing my neighborhood, driving down house prices! That's another thing, goddamn it! Your fucking people!"

He was starting to redline. I put my hand on the butt of my gun and told myself, *One more comment and I move.*

They were standing almost toe-to-toe. Aly held up a hand in a placating gesture. "Yes, sir, I know, I know. Not all of us are like that. Some—"

"Fuck you!" White Man screamed, not giving Aly a chance to finish. "You took my job and my wife!"

With that, his hand dropped to his holstered gun. Aly was fast—faster than the White Man. Aly had his knife out and had cut across White Man's stomach before the guy cleared nylon. A red smile opened across his T-shirt. It was the only smile I had seen so far today.

Aly had a look of calm determination, while White Man's face was so red and contorted that if Aly or I didn't get him, a heart attack probably would. Aly may have been fast, but he had better be thankful I was there. I cleared leather, cocked, and fired at the same time that Aly opened him up. The first round hit White Man in the shoulder; the second, in the head. I walked over to Aly.

"Put the knife away, Aly."

He tried to sheath it, but he was shaking too much.

"It's okay, Aly, just drop it."

He let the knife go, then he turned his head, and vomited. I stepped back a pace, *Whoa, we are going to have a mess here*. Well, someone was—I sure as hell wasn't going to clean it up. Aly wiped his mouth on the fabric of his shirt. Then he stepped back, dropped down to his knees, and placed his hands behind his head and started chanting.

"Aly. Aly!"

I had to say it twice to get his attention.

"Stand up!"

Jeebus. Why did people have to make this stuff so complicated? He stood up at attention, not looking at me.

"Aly, it's okay." I tried to make my voice sound soothing.

"Aly, look at me."

He looked at me, his face pale and shaken. "It's okay. You are not in trouble," I said. He looked at me like he thought I was lying. I shrugged. "You're not." What the hell did he expect me to say? You just won the fucking lottery? The joy spreading across his face, as my words sank in, was interesting to watch.

"You're not going to shoot me?"

"No, at least not today. Why? You forget to tell me something?"

"No! No, I have not done anything!"

"Well, you can do one thing."

He looked at me, his eyes starting to narrow.

"Drag this piece of meat out of the sun. Then go borrow a bucket from someone and splash some water on this mess."

"No problem, Mr. Gardener!"

I started to walk away. I stopped and turned around. "Oh, and I want his weapon and half the cash, if he has any. You can have the rest, plus them boots."

His smile got bigger. He replied, "No problem."

"If you can't find me, leave the stuff at the Dollar Store."

I walked away. I got about a hundred paces from him when I realized I had forgotten to ask about the knife. Oh well, another time. Max was talking to one of the vendors at the market.

"What was that about?"

I told him. "Had you ever seen the guy before?" he asked.

"No. But I have been gone a while."

"Yeah, there's that."

I described the guy to Max; he shook his head, "Nope, doesn't ring any bells. I guess I am going to have to walk over there and take a look at his face."

"Ah, you might as well not bother."

"Oh, okay. Well, let's take a ride over to the police station and see what we can see." We started walking to a small delivery truck. "Sorry I am late. Finding a truck you can haul stuff in has turned into a major pain in the ass around here."

I was surprised to see the two ninjas sitting in the cab. "What?"

"Yeah," Max replied, "They came with the truck. Plus, we need the backs for moving."

As we approached the truck, the door swung open, and the two ninjas dropped to the ground. I said, "Hey, guys." But they just stared at me. "What's the matter? Night cut out your tongues?"

Before they could answer Max told them, "Go around back and climb in. You don't have to close the doors."

We climbed into the cab. Once we settled in, I asked him, "What's their problem?"

Max replied, "They saw you shoot that man."

## CHAPTER TWENTY-SEVEN

# WHY BURN?

We drove to the police station. Nobody was there. City hall looked empty also—when you have no money to pay people, they have a tendency not to want to work. Some states and counties were paying with chits or "state dollars." They were managing to keep some of their people coming in that way. I suppose if it was a safe environment at work and you had someone to watch your house, it made sense. Who knows, maybe you could make something on the side through kickbacks, fraud, or "borrowing."

The Fairfax city hall was empty because it was no longer a safe environment. I did not know for sure but my guess was the commute was a nightmare now, and not just because of the traffic. On the way over Max told me that his duties as chief of police were going to be shortlived.

"Why?"

"Because the mayor decided to shut down the entire city government. No money to pay anybody. He said he is going to tell Fairfax County that the city is now their responsibility."

I laughed. "I bet that is going to go over really well."

"It doesn't matter. He is already gone. He told me he was telling anyone who would listen that if you had somewhere safe to go, you had better go."

"Damn."

"Yeah, that pretty much sums it up."

I backed the truck up to the main door. We pulled the ramp out and were ready to start. Max got us together and outlined what we were going to do. "We are here for weapons and ammunition first. After that, we will walk through the place and see what we can find. I doubt if there will be much. Once we start loading the weapons, I want two people on the truck. You bring a load out, then you wait until the other team shows up with their load. They stay—you go. Any questions?"

There weren't. We worked steadily. The heat was off in the building and was probably going to stay off for the coming winter. It didn't matter. Moving around kept us warm until we stood our turn at the truck. Then I could feel the sweat dry. I was teamed with the taller ninja. He was a good worker, but no conversationalist. We were done by late afternoon, and I was glad because my thigh was starting to throb. Me and the taller ninja went through the offices looking for anything worth taking after all the weapons were loaded. I opened a desk drawer and found a 2005 *Penthouse* that I tossed to him, saying, "Here you go. Just in case the Internet is down or your girlfriend is pissed off at you." He opened it and his eyes got big.

"First time you seen naked women on paper?"

He nodded and kept thumbing through the pages. We went back to the truck not completely empty-handed. I found a Phillips-head screwdriver and Taller Ninja had found a paperweight he liked. The *Penthouse* was rolled up and sticking out of his back pocket. We unloaded everything into the basement of the motel.

When we finished, Max had me stay behind. "Gardener, we need to start planning a bug-out for ourselves."

I can't say I was really surprised.

"Your Dragon Clan is leaving tonight—heading to California, to family from the sound of it—and didn't invite most of the Anchorage Motel part of the clan to go along. Word was, they didn't trust you, what with you being a cop now, and Night wasn't willing to dump you. Only Shorter Ninja is going with them. Apparently, he's got a cousin in the main clan that he came here with originally. That's his closest family here."

"Damn." This was news to me. I started to get pissed, then I thought, *I wonder if it would be better for Night if she left with them*. But I realized I didn't want to be left.

"I think we are going to need to move much faster than I imagined," Max said. "Most of the schedule will be built around accumulating what we need. Every time I think I've got a reasonable list, something else pops into my mind."

"You have any idea where we are going?"

"Right now I am thinking Tommy's farm. It is far from optimal, especially from a defensive viewpoint. We got to be able to eat and trade, though."

"Well, I am open to the idea of being a brigand." I meant it, sort of.

Max grinned. "You ask Mama-san how she feels about that?"

"Oh."

"Yeah—*Oh*. C'mon, let's go eat some soup."

It was Night, Max, and me eating soup with bread that Night had picked up from a vendor at the market. We also had apples that had come in from the Shenandoah Valley that day. I was not happy to see blood on the apple where I had taken a bite. I was going to have to start taking better care of my teeth or take some vitamins. I wasn't sure which. Night went back to her room and reappeared with a school notebook and a couple pens.

"Okay, let's start by each of us making a list of what we think we will need."

"Maybe we should make a list of categories," I replied. "I don't have a clue where to even begin."

We all agreed that my idea made sense. I started writing: guns, ammo, clothes, food, tools, first aid, books, a bed. Then I bogged down. Too many thoughts for my brain to process; one thought led to another.

As in, *we need a truck.*

*Well, how big?*

*How many?*

*How do we estimate the sizes of the loads?*

*Where do we get them?*

*Are we keeping them?*

I was getting so frustrated that I wanted to beat my head on the table. The other two were busy scribbling away. I told them I was going to take a break. I buckled up and went outside. I thought I would walk around the motel, breathe the air, and hopefully quit kicking myself for being so stupid. I walked around to the front of the motel. The Anchorage was on a bit of a rise, enough to let you see some of the surrounding sprawl. There were two major fires and one minor one burning that I could see. Max and I had decided to start running night patrols. The ninjas didn't know it yet, but the oldest one was going to get deputized. We couldn't risk the Burners getting loose in our little neighborhood, at least not until we were ready to go.

I watched as another fire roared into life about four miles away. Someone had invested a lot of fire starter on that one. I imagined the feel of the heat blasting my face . . . watched the dark shadows of the Burners dancing in delight as the flames roared up and out the windows . . . heard the laughing and ecstatic screams as the flames cast their light over the Burner devotees. I didn't know a lot about the Burner cult but I had a good imagination. I could see myself behaving that way. A big fire has a special kind of power, an elemental magic that calls to you. What information I had about Burners came from hanging out at the oak tree and listening to people bullshit or gossip. That and the few times I had checked out their blog. I did enjoy watching the videos. They really attracted some beautiful women. What had made the videos even more interesting was the comment I had overheard about how easy it was to get laid at a Burner event.

As he put it, "They light off a building, start dancing, and once it is really burning they go at it like wild dogs."

I had tucked that little piece of info away in the back of my head, just in case I was in the neighborhood of a Burner light-off. That was what they called them: a light-off.

A helicopter zipped past, flying low and fast and headed for the fires. I could see the lights of another one over the largest fire. Word was Homeland Security had snipers in them and they shot anyone they saw dancing around a fire. It didn't stop the Burners from celebrating. Of course, once the snipers started working, it meant Homeland Security had decided to let the fire burn. Otherwise, if they opened up from the sky prematurely, it made life on the ground hell for the fire response teams.

In California, the Burners reportedly brought in bands to play for the crowds when they did a big light-off. Sometimes the blogger who had started the whole thing would show up and preach a sermon about the rapidly evolving Burner creed. The fire department, if there still was one, would show up to assist in containment. Often firemen and Burners were the same people. The attitude in California was burn and let burn.

It was getting chilly, and faraway fires don't keep you warm.

I headed back to the room. Max and Night were sitting there, talking and planning. Night smiled when I came back in. "Everything okay?" she asked.

By now I knew her well enough to recognize the two levels of concern in that one question. "Sure, the Burners are out tonight. Looks like Arlington is getting fired up." I walked over and kissed her on the cheek.

Max replied, "Arlington never settled down after Homeland Security killed those women in front of that grocery store."

I looked over Night's shoulder at the pages of paper in front of her, covered with lists and notes. "I see you two have been busy."

Max casually replied, "I think your woman here is a logistics genius." She was smiling. I liked that.

"She sure as hell is smarter than me."

Max laughed. "Hell, that makes the both of us."

"Look, I'm not going to be of any help so you guys keep doing what you're doing. I am going to go see if any of the ninjas feel like playing some *Halo*. I'll be back in a bit."

I kissed Night on the top of her head and went out the door. I hadn't played in quite a while. Hopefully, my account was still active. I checked the break room, but only Shorter Ninja was there. He and some kid I had seen around, but whose name I never bothered to learn, were sitting there watching a video.

"Hey."

I got a distracted "Hey" from each in response.

"I thought you would be gone by now," I said to Shorter Ninja. He had his pack by his feet.

"Nah, they aren't picking me up until 9 o'clock."

"So, what's so interesting?"

Shorter Ninja pointed at the screen: "Burner video."

I pointed at the other kid, "Get out of my chair."

He popped up, grabbed a folding chair, and brought it over to sit in.

"Start it from the beginning."

Shorter Ninja restarted it. He told me, "It's pretty cool." Then he added hastily, "Not that I am, like, into it, you know."

"Right."

It was a well-done video. You could tell there was money behind it. As with a movie DVD, you could pick the scenes or play the entire video. I selected "Light-off

Video Metal." It started with a progressive metal track in the background. The screen filled with a spot of fire that gradually grew, bursting in a huge ball of fire as the music crescendoed. The next shot was a burning office building or warehouse. Beautiful young women who bounced in all the right places danced past the flame. Young handsome men screaming and dancing, the girls watching with parted lips. Their moves a combination of Russian cossacks and break dancers. A spoken chant, "Burn! Burn! Burn it all away!" repeated in a loop in the background. Off to the side, half-dressed girls could be glimpsed swaying in the firelight. One of them ran into the scene, grabbed one of the young males, and dragged him back into the darkness. I looked over at Shorter Ninja and his buddy. They were transfixed. The video ended with a close-up of a face. It was tough to tell the gender. The camera went in tight and ended with an eye that filled the screen. A reflection of fire raging in the iris.

I went back to the DVD menu and clicked on the button labeled "Why Burn?"

It was the blog guy in a Jesus robe. He was sitting on a rock watching the wind blow patterns through an endless field of ripe grain. He watched the wind dance while a quiet piano piece played in the background. The camera went to a close-up. He smiled and said, "Hello." It was a good smile—a smile you could trust. The eyes were a different story. They spoke to me, and I liked nothing they said:

"Why do we burn? Why not? What are we burning? We burn money. We burn the machine that has sucked our blood, our lives, and our futures. Devoured them, and then shit the poisoned remains back into our ecosystem.

The same poison that ends up in the food they expect us to eat. We become sick and they take more money from us. They work us, poison us, milk us, and then throw us away. If we protest, we are punished, and then blamed for not giving more!"

The scenes he painted changed with each new movement of music. Each new scene combined with his voice to weave a tapestry of corruption, greed, and selfishness as his hypnotic tone rose and fell with the video stream. All of it seamlessly integrated—it was beautiful: "We must purify our world of the machine, burn it out physically. Hunt down the servants of the beasts and kill them. We must purify ourselves so we will be worthy of it."

Okay, I got the point. I shut it down. "You guys want to watch the naked girl video again?"

I think the other kid was going to say yes, but Shorter Ninja cut him off, "No, we're good."

"So where did you get this?" They both tried to feign innocence.

"Don't even think about pulling that shit on me. You know what Max said about this. Max finds out about it and I may have to shoot both of you."

I watched both of them go into shock. The other kid's eyes actually bugged out. It was kind of cool.

"Just kidding. Come on, guys, breathe. I don't do CPR on males."

They looked at each other. The other kid took a deep breath. "It's mine."

"Go on."

"Some old lady came by the market trying to hand them out. No one wanted to take them. They didn't want Max to find out because then he would send you by to fix them. So she just left them in a stack on the ledge where the dry cleaners used to be."

*Interesting*, I thought, *I am the boogeyman*.

"So you grabbed one?"

"Yes, when nobody was looking."

"Did you see anyone else take one?"

He shook his head: He was back to being scared. He was also lying, but I let it go.

"Okay. Not a problem. Anyone want to play some *Halo*?"

"We can't go online anymore."

"What?" I was genuinely shocked and dismayed.

Shorter Ninja sighed. "Net won't stay up. You get into the game and then you get dropped, like all the time."

This was interesting news.

"Damn. Okay. See you later."

I headed back to the room. I knew that on the East Coast a lot of the Internet went through Reston, which was ten miles down the road. I didn't mind the roads and all falling apart, but I always thought the Internet would be there for me.

*What the hell was the matter with this country?*

Back in the room I found Night alone, sitting at the table studying her lists. I pulled out a chair and sat down.

"You know the Internet is acting up?"

"Yes." She didn't look up from the paperwork.

"Hmmm. So what did you figure out?"

"That this is a lot more complicated than we thought."

She put the piece of paper she was studying on top of a pile in front of her.

"Sorry, I wasn't much help. I guess I am not real good at that kind of stuff."

Seeing all the papers in front of her was kind of depressing. Knowing you may not be the brightest bulb in the chandelier is one thing; seeing it confirmed is another thing entirely. Night heard the sadness in my voice, and she watched my eyes as I took in the piles of notes. She knew what I was thinking. She stood up and extended her hand to me.

"That's okay. You're the best in the world at other things."

I woke up tired the next day—I look back now and remember the next month as the "month of scavenging"— partly for the future move and partly to find food to get us through to the future.

Historians will write that it was this period when we reached the tipping point. The graves from that time will provide the punctuation to the death sentence that the collapse of the American food transportation system passed on to so many of our citizens.

It was beyond ugly.

It was Leningrad.

Except the only enemies that surrounded us were our own greed, hubris, and incompetence.

That, along with the cold, was sufficient to kill us in droves.

## CHAPTER TWENTY-EIGHT
# GRAIN

Constant change was becoming the norm. Max and I would make plans and then have to drop them because the situation changed. Very rarely was it for the better. Our goal was to bug out in the spring. We were going to do a phased transfer of material and people to Tommy's farm. That was still the plan, but right now we had to figure out how to keep ourselves fed and safe. Our first problem was food: Not only were we having to feed ourselves but we were also helping Carol feed the people at the shelter.

She had pleaded with us to help at a meeting at the motel. I didn't mind feeding her; at this point she was spending more time at the shelter than at home. The commute to Leesburg had become too difficult and dangerous to do daily. I figured it would only be a matter of time before she went home and never came back—either because she was with her family, or because she was dead.

When I showed up for the meeting, Max and Night were already there. Carol was looking a lot thinner than the last time I had seen her. She had circles under her eyes and she was wearing a gun, the first time ever that I had seen that. She was brusque. She didn't want to ask for help. She knew that none of us were rich in anything. But she *had* to, so she did.

We were all busy. Night was also starting to look tired, I noticed. Our nighttime activities had abated a bit. I would come in and she would be asleep or vice versa. I thought about waking her sometimes but I knew what time she had to get up, so I would just slip into bed next to her. She had given up on appearances. Papa-san looked at me like he wanted to cut my balls off for a couple weeks but he got over it.

Carol went right to the point. "I need food, and I need enough to feed twelve women, twenty children, and seven men on a daily basis. Can you help?"

We all looked at each other. I didn't want to say anything, at least not first. I knew we could feed ourselves and we had enough to do that for at least a month. Add in the extra mouths and we would be out of food in less than a week. Plus, some of the kids needed kid food. Night was the first to speak. She did the logistics. Her family owned the motel, and she knew more than any of us how many we could feed.

"I won't let babies and children starve while I have food."

She left unspoken whether she was committing us to feed the adults.

Max added, speaking very softly, "Nobody gets left behind. Never."

Carol looked at me.

I shrugged. "Not a problem by me." I wanted to add: *Maybe you should quit taking new people in,* but I didn't.

She started crying. Then Night began. Next thing you know, they are both crying on each other's shoulder. I looked at Max. He looked at me. We both shrugged and left. There was work to do.

The good thing was the manpower it gave us. The women—and it was mostly women—were very good scavengers. We split them into groups. Tito, Carol's security guy, had stayed with the shelter. He and a couple of the men from the shelter escorted groups or helped provide security at the market. We issued the men shotguns and gave them the twenty-round course on how to use one.

We had the twenty-round course for shotguns and the twenty-four-round course for revolvers. That was how many times you fired it as part of the qualification class. That class and one rule were it. The one rule was: If you were seen pointing your weapon at anyone, including yourself, in a nonhostile situation, you lost the right to carry. That usually meant assignment to day-care duty, a powerful motivator for them not to screw up.

Max and I had already taught the remaining ninja how to handle weapons. He got a lot more than the 20/24 courses. We took an entire precious day with him. Plus, I worked with him at night down in the basement of the motel. He didn't realize that when Max would show him something, he was also showing me. We wanted him to be good because We were expecting trouble. After Shorter Ninja left I began calling the older one Ninja. He liked it and soon everyone was calling him that. The ninjas had wanted to teach us—or least me—martial arts, which they were very good at, but I didn't want to learn. Part of it was my pride, and part was that I didn't care. I didn't see any use in it for me at this point. Max had taught me some basic moves, but that seemed like an eternity ago.

I figured that people were either polite or hostile. If you were hostile, then I shot you. It worked for me. If it didn't, well, that would probably mean I was dead.

The ladies from the shelter proved to be excellent scavengers. When I went out with a team of them I always made sure I had Rosa. Rosa was El Salvadoran and beyond extraordinary when it came to finding food or other stuff we needed. We would be driving through an industrial park and she would say, "Stop." She would sit there for a second and then point at a building. I never saw what tipped her off, but she could find the food. If there was a lot, we would call the other groups that were out and tell them to come to our location. We could usually come up with one functioning cell phone for each group. Ninja was usually with me and I let him handle our communications. He liked that.

By midwinter we began to have real problems with communications. The Burners began taking down cell phone towers and relays whenever they could. As food began to be harder to find, we assigned people to do nothing but wait in store lines to purchase whatever was available. Carol opened a stall in the market so we could trade what we found and didn't need for goods or sometimes silver. No one was taking cash on the gray or black market anymore. Silver, gold, jewels, and tradable goods were the only way to purchase anymore.

Rosa brought her friend Maria to see me. Maria was El Salvadoran also. Where you came from was a big deal, even in the shelter. Maria knew we were doing everything we could to find and stockpile food. She had two kids and no man, so she had a stake in our success.

"Hello, ladies, what can I do for you?"

I was sitting at a table in the back of the Dollar Store finishing teaching a class on how to clean a revolver. That was going to be followed by a class on how to use a speed loader. For the speed loader part I was going to have each of my students—there were only three—run out to the oak tree and back, then try doing it, but only after each of them had done it thirty times from a standing position. I had them practicing with wax bullet dummy rounds. I had no desire to end up perforated by a student. One of the scavenger teams had found the rounds in a house, along with a beautiful Colt single-action .45 pistol. Max had looked the Colt over and told me it had been customized for fast-draw shooting. It came with a beautiful holster. I thought about switching from the Ruger to the Colt, but I decided against it. A little Hollywood for me, but I could appreciate the work that had gone into it. I gave it to Night who either traded or sold it for something we needed.

Rosa started the conversation. I noticed that the newer people were very hesitant to talk to me. "Gardener, we are sorry to bother you. We can come back or wait." Her friend was hanging back, standing almost behind her. This being Rosa, I knew it was something important, maybe not to me, but you never know.

I told my students, "Take a break but don't leave the market area."

I gestured for the women to sit down in the folding chairs the students had just vacated. I had to make a point of waving Maria into one or she would have stood behind Rosa. "Not a problem, Rosa. What's up?"

Sometimes I really liked playing *el jefe* or the God-father. I wasn't sure what movie this was yet.

"Maria knows where to find food—a lot of food. Go on, Maria, tell him."

Then Rosa spoke sharply to her in Spanish. Maria began hesitantly, but once she got rolling, she kept going. She would stop only to ask Rosa to translate a word or phrase for her. Pared of all the information I didn't need to know—Maria would go off on tangents about the personal habits of her former employer—what she had was interesting.

Maria had worked for a while as a housekeeper for a wealthy family in Leesburg. They were horse people, which, besides the cultural and status baggage, meant they had horses—a lot of them. The estate was a horse farm. They now also boarded other people's horses, something they had not done previously. Apparently, the last couple years had been less than kind to the family fortune. At any rate, Maria had gone out to the stables a few times; some young man who was in charge of stall cleaning, or something equally prestigious, had caught her eye.

What had surprised her was how well the horses ate, especially the grain. It wasn't corn meal, but it was close enough that it had stuck with her. It was oats, something she was sure would be edible for us. The big deal was how much they had of it—no little five-pound bags. They bought in bulk: big, heavy bags on wooden pallets that her friend said were a bitch to unload and move. I asked how much they might have, where it was, and if they had guards. She didn't think so. The house had a safety room, and she was sure the man had guns. Other than that, she shrugged. I thanked them, told them I would think about it, and called my class back in.

Usually we would meet at the end of the day in the break room back at the motel. There we would eat a communal meal and talk about whatever we thought the others should know. Or we'd just bitch, although that was usually kept to a minimum. Bitch for more than a few minutes and you began to get ridiculed. A more formal planning session was held on Sundays. That group would expand to include Carol, some of the guys like Tito and Ninja, and whoever Night or Max thought had something to bring to the table. Since it was Saturday, I decided to hold off, and bring up Maria's info at the Sunday meeting.

Sunday was in theory a day of rest, not for religious reasons as much as to avoid burnout. What it really meant for everyone was that it was okay to sleep late if you didn't have to stand watch. It also meant that Night and I could stay up late and see how many different positions we could try—three or four were as many as we usually got before I ran out. It was fun. I had not had a lot of experience before Night, especially not with someone who actually enjoyed it instead of seeing it as a way of paying for dinner.

The meeting had already started when I arrived. Max had a thing about punctuality. His idea of being on time was being there fifteen minutes before you were supposed to be there. That never made sense to me. If you meant 0545 hours, well, then say 0545. I figured fifteen minutes late was close enough to being on time that it should count. Plus, I never wore a watch. Why bother? Before, if you needed to find out the time, you would either look at your cell phone or computer, or ask someone. None of those ways worked well anymore. Night kept pressing me to get a watch.

Eventually, I traded four silver dollars and fifty rounds of .38 special ammo for a Rolex at the market.

Tito laughed when I told him what I paid. "You got burned, bro," he said, showing me his. "I paid three silver dollars."

"Nice—too bad it's fake," was my reply.

I didn't know if it was or not, but I loved the expression on his face.

I walked in and sat down next to Night, who had saved me a seat. She rolled her eyes when I walked in— like I had really missed anything that was that important. I did the greeting thing and Max continued with what he was saying.

"We may have a problem with heat soon. The motel is electric, which means if what we have seen lately holds true—and I have no doubt it will—we can expect some cold days and nights this winter."

Everyone nodded their heads, including me. Having a roof over your head meant heat when it was cold. Otherwise we might as well all be camping out in a car, or in the woods with the Tree People.

"We need to find iron stoves, like the old ones they used to use. If we have to, we can use fifty-gallon drums. Regardless, we need wood, a lot of wood, and we don't have the bodies to spare to cut everything we need now. So we need to hit some of the old suburban developments, the ones without gas heat, and see what we can find before everyone decides the same thing."

"Why can't we hire day laborers? It's not like there is a shortage of Juans and Josés around here. We could pay them with lunch and silver."

This got me an elbow from Night. She frowned on my inability to be politically correct at times. We had had a big argument about it once. She had told me, "You only talk that way because you're a white male. If you had grown up inside another color skin, you wouldn't be so cavalier with your comments."

Perhaps she had a point. I can't say I really cared. For her sake, I tried to pretend when I remembered.

They had been going back and forth about the stoves, wood, and hiring help for a while. I really wanted to take Night back to the room for some fun. After that I wanted to clean my guns and go to sleep. I was willing to change the order that I did that in, but that was about it. I interrupted, told them about my conversation with Maria, and was surprised about how excited Carol and Night got about the idea.

They started talking about raiding the nearest southern states and about how we needed hand mills. *Argh* was what I thought about it. Watching them get all excited, talking about how critical this might be—well, I understood it. It was just that, watching them, I knew I would be cleaning my guns and going to sleep, since I could see this meeting going on until midnight.

I looked over at Max. He was just sitting back watching. I caught his eye and he grinned. He may have found it amusing that my sex life was going to suffer, but I knew he was going to be here until they got tired. It passed through my head that Carol wouldn't be going home tonight. I wondered where she was going to be sleeping and if Max already knew.

*Oh well, none of my business.*

I leaned over and told Night, "I'm out of here." She nodded her head. I didn't kiss her—she was not fond of public displays of affection. I am sure it was something cultural. I went back to my room and cleaned my guns.

## CHAPTER TWENTY-NINE

# HELP IS ON THE WAY

The next day I met Ninja under the oak tree. We were scheduled to work the morning shift providing security and discouraging the riffraff. I still wore my Fairfax City police shirt. We had found some patches at city hall for the police department. I had given one to Ninja, and someone had sewn it on a shirt for him. Looking official still counted for something, especially if we bumped into feds. Unlikely, but possible. It was the same reason I hung on to my credentials.

We were walking through the area where not all that long ago there had been real stores.

They were gone. I knew this, but Max and I had agreed to patrol outside our perimeter whenever time allowed. It was always good to know who was lurking out there. Plus, we were looking for gang or Burner signs. I was surprised that a large number of the empty stores were occupied by Mexicans. The men looked thin, tired, and in need of showers. Up ahead, on a corner, stood four of them, just standing, talking, and smoking.

I felt myself become a little more alert. Especially when I heard one of them call me by name. "Hey, Gardener!" he waved. The men he was standing with were a tougher-looking bunch than what I usually saw, and two of them were armed. They were trying to go for the concealed, but I noticed that they touched the bulge they thought they had covered up with their jackets. Max had taught me that. People who don't carry a weapon on a daily basis will touch it every once in a while, especially when they think they are going into a situation. It reassured them that it was still there and was a good "tell" for a cop.

Ninja was still learning. I stopped, but he kept moving a few more paces while watching them. You didn't want to be bunched up, especially if one of them had an automatic weapon. The guy who called out, whoever he was, held up his hands. "We're cool. You're the guy that lives up in that motel and feeds the *niñas* at the shelter."

I said, "Yeah, that's me. Who are you?"

"That's what we need to talk about. C'mon," he used his head to indicate the empty storefront behind him, "Come into my *casa* and let's talk."

I didn't sense anything out of the ordinary. On the surface it didn't look like a great idea, but I wasn't getting any feeling that it was a bad idea. I hesitated for second, long enough to do another scan of the area, including the rooftops. Playing games online had taught me about looking up. I started walking toward him. Out of the corner of my eye I saw that Ninja was pacing me, but keeping his distance.

"So, what's your name?" I asked as I approached him.

"José."

*Of course*, I thought. I stopped about four paces from him. "What can I do for you, José?"

"Please, come inside, it is not good for many people to stand together on the street."

He turned and walked into the store. We didn't bother with the door as there was no need to. There wasn't one. His men stayed close to him, while Ninja stepped away from me and kept his back to the store's wall. It was colder inside the storefront.

"José, you need to get a fire barrel in here."

"Yes, we tried that before. It burned the place down." He shrugged.

"Yep, there always something, isn't there. So . . ."

"We hear that you may need workers—we have workers. We can also help you in other ways."

*Well, someone has been running their mouth too much*, I thought, *and whoever it is has been outside the perimeter. Interesting.*

"So, José, how could you help us?"

"Besides working as laborers? Some of us have skills that you may need. Also, there is that abandoned housing development two blocks from here. We are going to stay there—at least for now. Burners have been through here. We could discourage them. There will be others, also, and we can discourage them, too."

"I see. Of course you will be doing this out of the kindness of your heart. . ."

José and his buddies thought that was funny. I didn't say anything—I just stared at them. José stopped laughing first. He must have seen the look on my face. Somewhere nearby, a baby began crying. It was quickly hushed, as I only heard it for a brief moment.

"No, please, Gardener. We do not laugh at you. It has been a hard trip for us. Some of us didn't make it. Many times we have met those along the way who wanted something for nothing. No, we will work for food and silver. Perhaps you have things to trade us in exchange for our labor? We are not a threat to you and your people. You could end up with far worse neighbors."

Funny, but I was hearing both a plea and a threat in this conversation. "So how many people are you?" For the first time he looked evasive.

"Oh, we are about forty people."

Then one of his men decided to join the conversation: "We are strong. It would be best for you to listen to José carefully, cowboy." His face was pockmarked, and his broken nose and broad shoulders spoke silently of enjoying a brawl. The way he said *cowboy* as he leaned in toward me made it sound like it was lower than a banker. That was not a friendly thing to say. He had just finished and the word *cowboy* hung there between us. His eyes began to sparkle as he enjoyed his macho moment of support for his leader.

I drew, brought the Ruger up, and then whipped the barrel down and across his face. It hit right below the cheekbone and above the jawline, removing any teeth he still had on that side of his mouth. I simultaneously felt and heard the crunch as I stepped back a pace to give myself room to work. I noted the sound of Ninja racking his shotgun slide, and out of the corner of my eye I saw him bring it to bear on José.

The only noise came from whoever the hell it was that I had just whacked. He was beginning to wail in pain from his new place on the floor. José and his men froze in place. José was the first one to speak: "Jesus, you are fast."

I looked down on his man, who was holding his face and cursing between sobs. "You must not have learned manners on your way here. That's for sure. I wouldn't let him sit on the floor too long. It's dirty and he could get a nasty infection."

José sighed. "This is not working out like I planned."

"Yeah, I know the feeling. If I see more than two of your people armed and on my side of the perimeter, I will kill them. Then I will come back here and kill every single one of you. You understand?"

He nodded his head. "Yes, yes. I understand."

"José, lose the asshole and come by and talk with me and Max. All is not lost, yet."

"Gardener . . . ah, okay. Under the oak tree, perhaps?"

"Sure."

I started backing up until I was where the windows had been once. I let Ninja step over the sill and out onto the sidewalk. Then I followed. We both walked like crabs until we had a hundred paces between us and them. "You did real good in there, Ninja," I told him as we put some distance between us and them.

"You know, Gardener, it's like a game in some ways, but a lot more intense."

"Oh yeah, it gets even more intense when you lose, too. So what do you think about them?"

He thought for a couple beats. "He sure knows a lot about us for someone I have never seen before."

"You think they can be trusted?"

He shook his head. "Nobody can be trusted. Not when you have something they want."

We backtracked a bit. I wanted to take a look at the area that faced the Fed Zone. I didn't want to go deep into it—we claimed it, but in name only now. Where I was headed was a huge condo complex that was still close to 40 percent occupied the last time I checked. Next to it was a narrow park, then a concrete plant. Farther down was a large oil and gas storage facility. I had noticed previously that the oil and gas place had excellent private security. I planned on us going as far as the condo complex and then turning back.

Ninja and I paused in a doorway and waited to see if José or any of his friends were following. After about ten minutes we continued on. I preferred being on foot for this kind of work. Bicycles let you cover more ground, but it was awkward to dismount in a hurry, especially if someone was shooting at you. Using one of the patrol cars left over from the city days would have been even faster, but it isolated you from the flow of the neighborhood. Plus, I liked poking through the buildings. I felt you needed to get a feel for the area, which may have been static architecturally, but was anything but that in mood and in the changes people brought to it as they passed through.

We had just walked in the back door of what had been a hot tub store that faced onto Route 50 and were headed out the front when we spotted them: two army Humvees, each one painted in a woodlands pattern. Each had a gunner up on the machine gun. Ninja saw them and said, "Model 1025, I think, with the .50 caliber. We could use a few of those."

"What the hell are they doing out of the Zone?"

I was really talking to myself, but Ninja answered anyway, "Beats me. I only see them going by when they are doing convoy duty."

"Let's head back now," I told him. "There's just been too much excitement for me today."

He laughed, but I had a sense of foreboding. I knew, without knowing how I knew, that those Humvees were not going to keep rolling down Route 50 today. I wanted to get back to the market as quickly as possible. From there I could respond in any direction if we had to. We moved pretty quickly. We could have been faster but I wanted to do it as discreetly as possible. We went in one building and right past a couple who were having sex on the floor on top of an old rug they had dragged in from somewhere. I didn't hesitate. We kept going, and I don't think they even noticed us passing through.

"I know her!" Ninja told me as we crossed the street.

I replied, "That's nice; I think he does too."

We kept moving. We made it back in twenty minutes or so based on the sun. I eased up before we came out into the open before the market, and I was glad I did. The Humvees were just leaving. We waited until they were out of sight before walking over to the market. Everyone was gathered in a knot, clamoring about the poster the soldier boys had put up. They also had left a stack of handouts, one of which was thrust at me by the apple vendor.

"What do you think of it, Gardener?" someone yelled.

"Let me read it first."

I read the poster and then the handout to make sure they matched. They did:

## FELLOW CITIZENS OF AMERICA!

**The government has not forsaken you in these most difficult of times!**

**The president understands that many of you feel abandoned, that no one cares about your needs, your wants, and your dreams!**

**You are wrong! Help is on the way.**

As a country we will return to our position of prominence. As a people, we will once again be able to choose from overwhelming abundance. Work will be made available for those who want to work. Medical care for those who need it will soon be available: not just for the rich, **but for YOU!**—the proud people of this neighborhood and this great country!

Food distribution will begin Thursday, September 17, at 0900 outside the Fairfax City Shelter. Please bring a valid form of U.S. identification.

*Huh, nine days from now*, I thought. I heard all kinds of questions as the people pressed to ask what I thought or to tell me and everyone else what they thought.

I ended up yelling, "All right! All right, goddamn it! I don't know, but I will find out and let you know. Right now, all I can say is if the government is looking for you, then I wouldn't show up to collect food."

I should have kept my mouth shut about that. It just stirred them up again. "Okay! Okay! I'll find out," and I began walking toward the motel.

Once we got away from the crowd, Ninja asked me, "What do you think, Gardener?"

"I think something stinks," was my reply.

## CHAPTER THIRTY

# TIN FOIL HAT

I got back to the motel, and no one was able to find Max. I found Night down in the basement inventorying food with Carol. "Do you know about the poster and the food giveaway next week at the shelter?"

Carol looked stunned.

Night stopped and put her hands on her hips. "What are you talking about?" I handed her the flyer, and she and Carol read it together. Night asked her, "Did you know about this?"

Carol shook her head an emphatic no: "This is news to me. I wonder when they were going to let me know. Sorry, Night, I got to run now. I need to make a few calls and find out what is up." She hugged Night, waved good-bye to me, and was gone.

"So what do you think, Night?"

"It sounds good, but I think the hook is in the identification requirement."

Later that night, when we talked it over with Max, we all agreed that the identification requirement was what was driving this. Max felt it was just a cover for a census.

What he told us made sense: "They want to know how many people are still here. At the same time they will be running a search for warrants when you present your ID. When they get a hit, they can remove some of the more troublesome elements. Based on how many people turn out, they can get an idea of what they are going to need to distribute this winter."

I thought that sounded good, almost too good. I also told them about my meeting with José. I didn't see any reason to mention the pistol-whipping part of it. Max listened to my story all the way to the end. "We are going to see more of this. How many people do you think this area can really support, even if we get the grain?"

I shrugged.

"Not a hell of a lot," Night replied glumly. I guess I looked puzzled. "You want to explain it to him, Max?"

"Think of it this way, Gardener. Once we've eaten all the food from the grocery stores, all the squirrels and deer, all that is edible, including the neighbor's cat, how many acres will you need to feed someone?"

"You won't be able to feed anyone," I replied.

"That's a lot of hungry people isn't it?" Max said. "I wonder if anyone really has a clue about how bad this winter could be."

I thought about it for a minute or so. "Damn, it is going to be like an invasion of the zombies out there by spring. And we've got food . . ." I let my sentence trail off as I realized the implications. "We better hope the government feeds people, or it is going to be totally insane out here."

"Yeah. No shit," Max replied. "We may have to move sooner than we planned."

I looked at his face. For the first time I saw how worried he really was. Night had the same look. I thought about it and decided I was not going to worry about it. If I had to, I would kill every sonofabitch that got in the way of our bugging out of here. When we went to bed later, all Night wanted me to do was hold her. It wasn't what I wanted to do, but I had enough sense to keep my mouth shut and do it. I held her until she quit crying and went to sleep. I lay there for a bit, thinking about our future. Funny thing was—I couldn't see one.

The day of the big food giveaway we went on alert at the motel. This was going to pull in an unknown number of people from the surrounding area. We didn't want anyone, or groups of anyone, raiding us or even being able to scout us. Max had everyone who was staying behind make up a pack with food, ammo, and a set of clothes. From now on we were to keep it handy. He also told everyone where we were to meet if we had to run for it.

"Why?" Ninja asked me.

I explained to him: "Because Max knows that we have no chance in hell against the army. If they want to come in here, we are going to let them."

He got indignant. "We can hold our ground against anyone—"

"Really?" I cut him off. "You think you know more than Max? Because I am sure he has plenty of time for you to tell him how much you know." I changed my tone. "Look, I don't know myself, but we saw those Humvees. With .50 caliber machine guns they can stand off and chew us to pieces. Don't forget, they probably have gunships too. Hell, who knows what they have," I added darkly.

I had a small day pack with me. I opened it up and showed him what Max had given me: a pair of Zeiss binoculars. "If you're good, I'll let you polish them."

"Wow, Gardener, you really are my hero."

"I know. I get that all the time."

The plan was to send a couple of people down to get food only after we had watched for a bit. That was a job for me and Ninja. We set up on the second floor of an empty townhouse that had a great sight line, and there was already a decent-sized line forming. The army was using the parking lot and part of the service road in front of the shelter. They had a semi parked so it made a wall that was anchored to the shelter. Where the cab was, they had pulled in a Humvee with a mounted gun. Two more made up a triangle. Inside the triangle you began the processing next to a vehicle that looked an awful lot like a communications truck. A couple of paddy wagons with no markings had also pulled in.

On the other side of that was a U-Haul truck backed into the screening point. What it looked like was an entrance to a concert. You walked up, showed your ID, had it checked, and then you were scanned at a table labeled Weapons Check. If all that went okay, you walked up the ramp into the trailer and got your food. Then you walked out the other side. It made sense to me—but at the same time it didn't.

I handed the glasses to Ninja and asked him to take a look. "What did you see?" He didn't register what I had seen. "You don't see anything, oh, not quite right?" He shook his head. Well, it was almost show time, so we would find out soon enough.

Word was that this was taking place throughout all of Northern Virginia that fell outside the Zone. The Humvees had been by again the previous Monday, back with more posters and flyers. This time the poster was in color and was very well done, with better grammar. Emblazoned across the top was **Tent Cities Are Not for Tourists!** It extolled the virtues of living in a government "village," where food, shelter, and security were available for all U.S. citizens. As it said, "You will come to visit, but you will never want to leave!"

It was interesting to see all the posters plastered up on the sides of buildings, at the market, just about anywhere they thought people might see them. That, combined with the food distribution, made me feel as if someone in power knew what they were doing. It was reassuring to know that the federal government still had enough resources and skill to pull off something like this. I didn't believe life in a tent city was half as good as they claimed, but at least those who had no resources or brains had a place to go where they wouldn't be underfoot.

When I say *word was*, I mean a combination of gossip and FM radio. The FM band had two stations that began operating in coordination with the food distribution announcements. They broadcast news, specialized programming, and a lot of bad country music. The news content was 100 percent feel good. The specialized programming offered such tidbits as "How long to boil water for drinking," "The dangers of carbon monoxide poisoning," and my favorite, "Squirrel: Is it edible?"

I hadn't listened to a lot of radio lately. I did listen to it more now than when I was on the Internet or watching television, far more. Night and I would turn it on at night in the misguided belief that it would cover the noise we made. I never sat down and surfed the FM or AM band. I took whatever the radio was tuned to and listened to that. Stations had disappeared and reappeared frequently over the months. After hearing about the new government stations, I did turn on our battery-powered radio and scan the dial. The FM band seemed about the same, maybe more religious programming and country music. What was interesting was the AM dial. What had once been almost exclusively ethnic programming, especially Latin American, was now silence or static.

Looking back, it should have been glaringly obvious that the government was planning something. It was just that most Americans had resigned themselves to the fact that federal government incompetency and greed on a huge scale was what we were stuck with. The idea that the government might turn on part of the populace was too bizarre to believe. That was something only your drunken Uncle Dave—whom your Mom called "a tin foil hat–wearing asshole"—believed and talked about endlessly.

## CHAPTER THIRTY-ONE

# W.T.S.H.T.F.

I took turns with Ninja watching the distribution center. A crowd had begun forming as soon as the sun was up. They were in place earlier than we were, which was fine with me. I wasn't really good at sitting and waiting. I amused myself for a while, scanning the people and looking for good-looking women. Not a lot of that was happening. My guess was that good-looking women did not have to wait in line for food on a cold morning. They were still in bed with someone who took care of things like that for them. I was surprised at the number of people that showed up. Many of them I had seen before. More than a few had brought the entire family. If the army had been smart, they would have brought balloons to give away to the kids. Even from here I could feel the festive vibe that the free food was generating. People were relieved and happy that the government was doing something constructive for a change.

What I know about what happened next is based in part on what I saw from afar and in part from when I was down there later. Some is what people who were there told me, and some I am just guessing at. The army began the distribution on time. The two men and one woman who manned the machine guns didn't even get on their guns until minutes before the giveaway began.

I watched as one of them handed out a couple of cigarettes to people in line. How it worked was you, or you and whomever you were with, would go forward and present your identification to an officer sitting at a table. He handed it to an enlisted man, who did something with it involving a computer. At the next station they asked for any weapons you were carrying and handed you a claim ticket for them. Here was where the friction began to develop:

*No one wants to hand over their weapons, and yet here you are.* You're no longer in line where you can just walk away. You have already been moved down the chute. It's still possible, but you have invested your time, shown your identification, and are now just steps away from picking up your food. The nice army man is reassuring, so you reluctantly hand over your weapons and take the claim check.

You walk up the ramp into the semitrailer, and the nice army woman reads you the three entrées they have and asks if you have a preference? You start to get that loving feeling back: This is actually working out. Based on how many of you there are, they give you your case or two of MREs and then out the other side of the trailer you go. You walk down the ramp, and there are a couple of soldiers in real television-style battle suits with armor to meet you. You look around. The Humvee gunners are no longer recognizable; they now wear helmet and sunglasses for some strange reason. You realize that the machine gun is pointing at you, and you realize what a vicious looking weapon it is from this perspective. Nobody smiles at you. No more loving feeling. In fact, a little alarm bell goes off in your head.

You ask the soldier, "Where do I get my guns?" You already have a feeling you know what the answer is going to be. You are right.

"Sorry, sir. Your guns will be made available to you at a later date. Please move along."

The people standing in line behind you listen to this.

"Sir, I need you to move along."

Out of the corner of your eye you see more soldiers drift over.

Your woman tugs at you, saying, "C'mon, honey, we will get them later." You look down; your daughter looks up at you, and her eyes are wide. You want to give in and go, but you know that if you do, you will be lucky to make it back with the food to wherever it is you are sleeping tonight, or this week. You do not even want to think about what will happen to your wife and your daughter if word gets out that you have nothing to protect them with other than a Chinese stainless steel steak knife that stopped being sharp the second time you used it.

"No, I am not leaving without my guns!" You start walking. You plan to go around to the front and cut through to where they took your guns. A soldier stands in front of you. He isn't alone. You can't see his eyes because he is wearing sunglasses; they all are, you realize.

"Sir, I need you to leave the area."

"No! Goddamn it! I am not leaving the area! Give me back my guns!"

Meanwhile, the people who were processed behind you, who turned in their weapons, get the same answer. They are becoming very unhappy.

A couple who have either come unarmed or are willing to give up their weapons walks past. They look at you. You recognize the look. It says, *You are a dumbass for trusting them*. You flash back to how you had trusted the mortgage broker, the attorney, your boss. . . And now you realize that once again you and your family are going to get fucked. You hear someone yell to the people waiting to be processed, "They are taking our guns!" The people behind you are now enraged. The soldiers pull out plastic restraint cuffs and they take down the guy behind you.

You hear your daughter's voice, as clear as if it were being beamed directly into your ear through the crowd noise, "Daddy!" A soldier reaches for her. You see the plastic cuffs. You snap. You punch the soldier in his gut. You think to yourself, *Shit, fucking body armor*, and then your world explodes . . .

I couldn't believe it either. I was watching you the entire time. I saw you fall, your woman and child screaming and reaching out for you as you went down. Then I dialed back so I could see more of the entire scene. I could hear some army guy on a bullhorn, probably the officer in charge, telling everyone to remain calm. Then someone shot him and the situation spun out of control.

It didn't matter to me; I had passed the glasses to Ninja. When I saw you fall, when I saw your daughter grabbing for you, I was already on my way. I went out the window, hit the ground, and rolled like I had finally learned to do. Ninja stuck his head out, and I could see the balloon form above his head, like in a comic book, *What the fuck?* floating inside it.

"Shotgun!" I yelled.

His head disappeared and quickly reappeared. He tossed me the shotgun and then he jumped. His landing was awkward—bad awkward. He tried to stand but crumpled as his leg gave way underneath him.

"Goddamn it. Help me up, Gardener."

"Sorry. If I can, I will be back for you."

I began running toward the distribution center, long strides and deep breaths. I heard Ninja scream, "Gardener!" but I didn't look back. I was focused. More focused than I had ever been in my life. I ran but I felt like I was floating. My vision had sharpened. I felt like a machine.

The machine gunner on the Humvee nearest the crowd had cut loose and was scything the crowd in long controlled bursts. The gunner on one of the other Humvees opened up, but took a hit immediately from behind and slumped over. I ran directly toward the gun that was firing. People lay dead in clumps on the parking lot. Their blood formed little pools on the asphalt. I could hear automatic weapons fire from behind the trailer, mixed with the sound of big-bore handguns. I kept going, leaping over a couple bodies that lay in a twisted mess on the ground.

I wanted whoever was on the machine gun. I was going to pull him down and beat him to death. He hadn't focused on me—one person was not as good a target as what was left of the crowd. A soldier popped up next to the desk, M-16 shouldered and pointed at me. I fired the shotgun without stopping. I missed him. Another soldier appeared next to him. *Yep, I am dead*, I flashed, but I didn't stop running. That's when the machine gunner on the final Humvee opened up.

The gunner hosed the soldier who was scything the crowd, making him dance in place, and then fall out and over the side of the vehicle, disappearing from sight. The Humvee gunner then shot the two soldiers who were taking aim at me, making their bodies jerk as if someone had taken a sledgehammer to them, and finally began taking out anyone who wore an army uniform, not to mention ripping a line down the side of the trailer. One of the paddy wagons started up suddenly—apparently someone had decided they had a meeting to attend elsewhere. The .50 caliber took the vehicle apart. I jumped inside the Humvee in front of me and clambered up to where the machine gunner had been. I stood up and looked around.

It was over. The quiet was deafening. A crow cawed from a tree nearby. My ears were ringing. People were moaning. I heard boots pounding as people came at a run. I grabbed the .50 and swiveled it toward the sound. It was Max running hard in front, followed Night and Tito.

Max stopped, took in the scene, and yelled, "Hide if you hear a helicopter coming. Strip them for weapons, magazines, and body armor, and pile it under that pine tree. Go!" He pointed at me. "You help them!" I went over the side of the Humvee, coming down next to him. "I know how to use a .50," he said. "You don't. Make sure no one gets caught in the open if we get visitors."

We weren't the only ones stripping bodies. Some other folks had the presence of mind to do the same thing. I came up on an old guy and his wife. He looked to be in his early fifties, with a weathered face; she was skinny. They were working together on rolling a black soldier out of his vest. The soldier wasn't cooperating; he was missing the side of his head. Before I could say anything, the old guy growled, "My kill. My stuff."

I nodded and kept going. I ended up helping Night get the armor off a petite, young Hispanic girl. "You okay?" Night asked me.

"Yeah, I am fine. You?"

She was breathing hard. "No. I am not fine. I want to kill some motherfuckers."

I just said, "Yeah." It was how I still felt. Right behind Night was a mother and her two sons. At least I think they were boys. In between the gunshot wounds and the fact that the woman had either fallen or flung herself over their small bodies, it was difficult to tell. We finally got the vest off. I grabbed the dead Hispanic's M-16 and searched her for anything else worthwhile. We moved on to the next soldier. I thought he was another dead one. Sloppy thinking on my part.

I was trying to unfasten the harness he was wearing when he scared the crap out of me by whispering, "Medic."

"Did this asshole just say something?" Night asked. Looking at the guy she said, "Hey! Hey, baby killer. You say something?"

He opened his eyes but was unable to focus. Once again he whispered, "Medic." And he shut his eyes again.

"Medic? You need a medic!" Night screamed. "How's this?" She kicked him in the head. "Huh, how's this feel?" and she reared back and drove the toe of her boot into his temple. I grabbed her and pulled her tight against my chest. She was struggling, screaming at me, "Let me go! Let me go!" Then she broke down and began sobbing into my chest. I could hear her whispering, "Poor boys. Poor little men." She was hacking deep sobs. What had happened here had gone off inside of her like a bomb.

"Hey, baby. I know. I know." I was racking my brain. We needed to move, not do a total meltdown, but I had to figure out a sweet caring way to tell her to get her shit together. I couldn't think of anything. "Night, baby, listen to me—"

That's when the .50 that Max was sitting on opened up. Quickly followed by the gunner who was still on the third Humvee. I could hear it now—a helicopter. It was trying to come in low and fast. Max and the other gunner chewed it up with those .50s and it exploded about a hundred yards short of the market.

*Thank God, it missed the tree.* "C'mon, Night. We got to move."

She pulled away from me, snot dripping from her nose and all over my jacket. She nodded and sniffled. Then she bent down and grabbed her share of plunder, and we both headed to where we were supposed to drop it. The others were already there. There was a lot of black plastic weaponry and green metal boxes. Ninja was there, sitting with his back to the tree, his leg stretched out in front of him and a shotgun cradled in his lap. "You okay?"

He nodded his head. "I'm cool—and so is this stuff." He looked at Night: "Gross." He fished around in his cargo pants pocket until he found his bandanna. Handing it to her he said, "Jeebus, clean yourself up, girl." She wiped her face and handed it back to him. He threw up his hands, "Ah . . . that's okay. You can keep it until you wash it."

"Let's make one more circle."

We ended up back at the Humvee that Max was sitting in. He was watching a couple guys strip the second
Humvee of its machine gun. At the last one, the gunner
just sat motionless.

"What's up, Max?"

"Night, go get Tito. Tell him I need help pulling this
weapon. Get some of them ladies from the shelter shut-
tling what we found up to the motel. Then I need you to
look at Ninja's leg."

"Got it." And she was gone.

He was silent for a couple beats. "I forget sometimes
that you and me are about all we got for combat vets. It
was hard on her seeing this?" I nodded. "Well, she is going to see a lot more." He sighed and began working on
pulling the gun off its mount. "Do me a favor."

"Sure."

"Go ask the young lady over there"—he indicated
the lone machine gunner—"if she wants a place to stay
tonight."

"Damn, Max, I thought that was a short guy with a
fat ass."

"Well, don't tell her that, at least not while she is sitting up there."

I shrugged and walked over to where she could see
me. "Hello. Ma'am?"

She was alive. She moved her head a fraction of an
inch to look at me better. Her face below the sunglasses
was expressionless. "You want to come with us? Maybe
get something to eat and a place to sleep?"

I waited for what seemed like a small eternity before
she decided to reply: "What's for dinner? And you better
not tell me it is MREs."

"Actually, I am not sure. Maybe soup. If it isn't soup, then it won't be much better than MREs."

"Ha! Spoken by someone who hasn't been living on them. Anything is better than MREs. Well, get your ass up here and help me pull this weapon. It can be part of my dowry."

She knew what she was doing. I didn't. "Okay grab it from underneath and lift," she said. I did. This was one heavy piece of metal. "Okay, you got it?" I nodded. "Then toss it over the side." It was more like *lean over a bit and let it go.* She dropped back down into the vehicle and began tossing out ammo boxes. The sound they made as they hit the ground told me they weren't going to be light either. "Check up front." I started looking around. I didn't find anything worthwhile except a couple of empty plastic water bottles. We used them as canteens. "What did you plan on doing with this stuff?" she asked.

"We are stacking it under the pine tree on the other side of the building."

"Okay, let's go! They aren't going to leave us alone forever." She took the barrel and I took the other end. Max had sent someone up to the motel to bring down our two functioning vehicles. We loaded them with everything that was under the pine tree and sent them back with Ninja riding in the only empty passenger seat.

We stood there—Max, me, and the army gunner—looking at each other. Max asked her, "You have a full name Corporal Singer?" He had read her name tag.

She took off her sunglasses and helmet. She just let the helmet drop to the ground while she shook out her hair. She had green eyes and dark brown hair, longer than

I expected. She was, I guessed, in her midtwenties. She stuck out her hand. "Singer. Jane Singer."

"I am Max and this is Gardener. We can walk and talk."

"Max, you seen Carol?"

"Last I saw of her she was inside the shelter. I'll go check on her. You go ahead and walk Miss Singer up." Max didn't look at me directly. He just left.

I nodded my head and thought to myself, *I should have known*. I caught her looking at me quizzically. She didn't say anything, though. I started walking and she fell in beside me.

"So, why did you do it?"

"Because they were assholes. Because this isn't some little mud-brick village in some freaking raggedy-ass country. This is America. Because I didn't sign on to kill kids." She shrugged. "It's also that time of month."

I laughed. After a minute she did too.

"So where we going? The motel?"

I stopped dead.

"How do you know about the motel?"

"Because in the army they brief you about stuff like that. What? You think we have spies?"

"What would you think?" I replied.

"We do. They just aren't human."

*Oh, crap.* The realization of what she meant flooded through me. "You think one was overhead?"

She laughed.

It was a dry laugh, more of a snort actually. "There is always at least one overhead around here, plus satellite coverage." She was talking about surveillance drones.

"So what are the odds we were seen?"

It was dusk. I could feel the chill in the air deepening. It wouldn't be long before the first hard frost. She thought about my question as we walked. We had almost reached the motel, which gave us a view of the suburbs and city around us.

"Look out there," she said.

I had been, but I was interested in what she saw. There were more than the normal amount of fires burning. There were also a lot more helicopters in the air. Small-arms fire was audible, so much so that I wasn't hearing it. Far off in the distance I thought I saw tracers being used.

"I can tell you what the army is seeing: large-scale civil insurrection. Possible terrorist groups engaged in attacking the homeland. From what I was hearing on the radio before everyone freaked out, this wasn't the only distribution center they were having problems at. After all, how freaking stupid was the idea of taking guns from people. I swear that everyone in the army with the rank of colonel or above has their head up their ass."

"So I guess that means they won't be back with anymore free MREs?"

Again the snorted laugh. "Oh, they will be back . . . yes, indeed."

We didn't talk after that. I took her to the break room and gave her some soup. Ninja's girlfriend was sitting there watching television. I asked if there was anything on about what had happened earlier. She shook her head. Somehow I doubted if she had even checked. I asked if she had seen Night. She hadn't seen her either.

"So what are you doing, then?"

She looked taken aback. "Why, I am watching television."

I went over and turned it off. "Now you're not. So why don't you get off your ass and do something other than using up oxygen. I suggest you go down into the basement and find something to do. If you can't find anything, then you can clean off the body armor we brought in today."

She looked as if she really wanted to say something. She even made it as far as opening her mouth before she decided not to. She did slam the door on the way out. I shook my head. I also caught the faint smile that appeared—and then just as quickly disappeared—on Jane's face.

"Look, I'm sorry, but I am going to have to leave you here for now. I need to go find some people. Either I will be back or I will send someone to help you get settled in."

"Not a problem. I come from the land of hurry up and wait."

I felt uneasy about leaving her alone but I didn't want her tagging along with me. I checked our room, the basement, and the lobby—no Max or Night. I went out front and checked the hill where I knew Max liked to sit sometimes and smoke the cigarette that he denied ever smoking.

He was there.

I eased in next to him and sat there silent. We both sat and watched the fires burn. Off in the distance a building exploded in a fireball.

"Propane?" I asked.

"Maybe. Or it could have been a Predator strike. As crazy as this shit is getting, it wouldn't surprise me."

I told Max about Jane's belief that there were drones watching us now, and probably had been for a while.

"Yeah, I figured as much. My hope was that we would be too small and so obviously nonthreatening that we would never show up as the subject of anyone's briefing."

"I guess that changed today? No, don't bother replying; I know it changed today. So, how badly are we screwed, Max?" He didn't say anything. The roar of military jets flying overhead blocked all the other night sounds for a minute or so.

"Between me and you?"

I nodded.

"I can't make you not tell Night, but I wouldn't if I were you. She will know soon enough anyway. Let her be as close to happy as she can be for another day or so."

"We're going to die?"

"More than likely. I am surprised we aren't already dead. It must be because we are American citizens on U.S. soil that they haven't taken action. That won't last long. They just need to go a little higher up the chain of command for approval, and then figure out an operation plan that will give them plausible deniability."

I said, "As if anyone will ever know or care." I wasn't even bitter. I understood. There was a moment of silence and then I asked Max, "So what are we going to do?"

"Right now I am going to sit out here and think about it for a bit. I'll let you know."

I was walking back to the house when I heard them: two helicopters headed our way. No lights. I saw them only because of the black holes they created in the backdrop of city lights. Black holes that became illuminated as the pilot of the one on my right released the missiles. My world disappeared in flames and then darkness.

# OTHER BOOKS FROM ULYSSES PRESS

**Patriots: A Novel of Survival in the Coming Collapse**
*James Wesley, Rawles, $14.95*

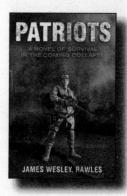

A thrilling narrative depicting fictional characters using authentic survivalist techniques to endure the collapse of the American civilization. Reading this compelling, fast-paced novel could one day mean the difference between survival and perish.

**Bug Out: The Complete Plan for Escaping a Catastrophic Disaster Before It's Too Late**
*Scott B. Williams, $14.95*

Escaping a doomed city during the first 72 hours of a crisis can make the difference between life and death. From preparing supplies for three days of wilderness living to mapping out an escape route to a remote location, this book turns the ordinary urban-dwelling American into a savvy survivalist.

### Getting Out Alive: 13 Deadly Scenarios and How Others Survived
*Scott B. Williams, $14.95*

A unique combination of fictional scenarios, true accounts, and instructive information, *Getting Out Alive* presents captivating stories of people stranded and fighting for their lives against harsh, unmerciful conditions.

### Save Your Ass: An Illustrated Handbook for Surviving a Natural Disaster, Terrorist Attack, Pandemic or Catastrophic Collapse
*Alexander Stilwell, $15.95*

Packed with expert tips and techniques, *Save Your Ass* explains the logistical preparation, survival skills, and mental focus needed to navigate any emergency. Breaking down various crisis scenarios, the author guides readers step-by-step through the counter-disaster process.

### Special Forces Survival Guide: Wilderness Survival Skills from the World's Most Elite Military Units
*Chris McNab, $15.95*

With detailed instructions, helpful photographs and step-by-step illustrations, this book arms readers with the same battle-tested techniques used by the military's bravest, most elite soldiers. Learn everything from constructing shelters, finding water, and starting fires to making arrows, tracking animals, and navigating by the stars.

**The U.S. Army Survival Manual:
Department of the Army
Field Manual 21-76**
*Headquarters, Department of the Army, $14.95*

Drawing on centuries of rigorous training and treacherous field testing, this field guide covers every imaginable scenario from finding drinking water in the desert, stalking game in the arctic, and building a fire in the jungle to recognizing signs of land when lost at sea.

To order these books call 800-377-2542 or 510-601-8301, fax 510-601-8307, e-mail ulysses@ulyssespress.com, or write to Ulysses Press, P.O. Box 3440, Berkeley, CA 94703. All retail orders are shipped free of charge. California residents must include sales tax. Allow two to three weeks for delivery.